POMONA AFTON
Can So Solve a Murder

POMONA AFTON

Can So Solve a Murder

A Novel

Bellamy Rose

EMILY BESTLER BOOKS

ATRIA

New York Amsterdam/Antwerp London Toronto Sydney New Delhi

EMILY
BESTLER
BOOKS

ATRIA

An Imprint of Simon & Schuster, LLC
1230 Avenue of the Americas
New York, NY 10020

First Emily Bestler Books/Atria Books hardcover edition March 2025

EMILY BESTLER BOOKS/ATRIA BOOKS and colophon are
trademarks of Simon & Schuster, LLC

For information about special discounts for bulk purchases,
please contact Simon & Schuster Special Sales at 1-866-506-1949
or business@simonandschuster.com.

The Simon & Schuster Speakers Bureau can bring authors to
your live event. For more information or to book an event, contact
the Simon & Schuster Speakers Bureau at 1-866-248-3049 or
visit our website at www.simonspeakers.com.

Interior design by Davina Mock-Maniscalco

Manufactured in the United States of America

1   3   5   7   9   10   8   6   4   2

Library of Congress Cataloging-in-Publication Data has been applied for.

ISBN 978-1-6680-7565-4
ISBN 978-1-6680-7567-8 (ebook)

This book is for Ella Mae,
who can so do anything she puts her mind to.

CHAPTER

One

The first time Grandma called, I ignored her. That probably sounds heartless to you, but only because you're picturing a stereotypical grandmother. You know, one who bakes cookies. Gives lots of hugs. Loves her grandchildren unconditionally.

Marion Elizabeth Hunter Afton hugged you as if your clothes, no matter how clean, would dirty her impeccable tea dress. Any cookies she'd bake would probably have arsenic in them.

So when my phone lit up with GMA MARION as it buzzed against my breakfast table, I pushed it to the side so I couldn't see it. It was early still, or at least early for a Saturday. For all she knew, I was sleeping.

I probably should still have been sleeping, considering how late I was out last night. And, okay, how much I'd drunk. My stomach was sloshing around at the mere sight of my usual egg whites with spinach and mushrooms. I couldn't even think about eating them yet. It was enough, surely, that I was awake, sitting upright, staring at Central Park spreading out very green and way too bright through my picture window.

Her second call was harder to ignore, considering I'd pushed my phone so far to the side that it buzzed itself off the table. It landed with a clatter on the elaborately detailed porcelain tiles I'd picked out last time I was in Italy. They were hand-fired and hand-painted and hand-glazed and had nearly earned me Grandma's hand slapping against my cheek when she learned how expensive they'd been. "I did not give permission for you to change the tile in your kitchen. Is this *your* hotel, Pomona?"

It wasn't. None of the Afton hotels were, no matter that I'd grown up playing hide-and-seek in their fancy lobbies and ordering room service to their various feather beds, and they never would be. For many reasons. My older brother, Nicholas, the heir apparent, had gone to Princeton and majored in business and immediately come home to work for the family. I had done . . . well, pretty much the opposite of that.

"Pom."

I jumped in my seat. My phone had stopped its buzzing on the floor, but my stomach hadn't stopped flip-flopping all over the place like a dying fish. "Yes?"

Lori popped her head out of the kitchen doorway, where she'd been cleaning up after making my breakfast. "Do you need anything else before I head out?"

I shook my head slowly, the motion making the room swirl around me. Eyes closed. "I'm okay."

"There's a chicken Caesar salad in the fridge for lunch. I figured you'd want to eat light before the gala tonight," Lori said. The smell of lemon drifted into my nostrils as she passed by, fresh and bright. Ugh. "See you Monday."

I didn't open my eyes again until the lock on the front door had clicked shut behind her. I'd totally forgotten about the gala. What was it even for? I vaguely remembered my mom talking about the latest charity she'd adopted, something about feeding starving orphans to endangered rhinos. No, that couldn't be right.

At least I knew Grandma wouldn't be calling about that. She and my mom hadn't been at the same gala for at least two years now. If anything, Grandma would be hosting a competing gala raising money to feed endangered rhinos to starving orphans.

The third call rattled against my beautiful tiles, which had taken me weeks to choose. I could only put this call off for so long. I grabbed it and, for some reason, sang into the receiver. "Goooood morning!"

I regretted my attempt to sound cheerful and fully awake as soon as the words left my mouth, and braced myself to hear Grandma tell me she could see why my singing career hadn't worked out. (In my defense, you couldn't really call it a singing career when it was only one album I'd put out as a teenager, and the YouTube parodies of it had reached more ears than my actual songs.)

But the caller wasn't my grandma. Not this time. "You sound like death," said my older brother, Nicholas. "No, you sound like a rattling skull who spent its time on earth chain-smoking and chewing on rubble."

"How poetic," I said.

I could practically hear him preening through the phone. He'd had a few poems published in literary magazines and chapbooks before dear departed Grandpa declared it was time for Nicholas to stop toying with his silly poems and focus fully on the business. He'd started working fourteen hours a day after that, leaving no time for poetry. His work, plus his girlfriend of a year and a half, Jessica, left no time for his sister either. Mostly I saw him at formal family events he had to go to or in the elevator going to or from the floor we both lived on.

"Anyway, enough about how talented I am," said Nicholas. "Grandma says to call her."

I groaned on the inside. Then on the outside. I should have figured as soon as I heard his voice. Normally Nicholas would have been far too busy to spend even the slightest amount of energy speaking to his one and only sister on a workday, also known as every day. But when Grandma beckoned, he jumped.

Which made sense, I guess. She had become the sole head of Afton Hotels after my grandpa passed four years ago. And Nicholas might be the heir apparent after our dad, her son, but she'd make all of the company decisions until the day she died, or until she became incapacitated enough that Dad could make a convincing-enough case for power of attorney.

I asked, "Did she say why?"

"I'm not an answering service, Pom. Call her."

"Do you think it has anything to do with last night? The Vienna thing?"

"I doubt it." Just the fact that he knew what "the Vienna thing" was without me having to spell it out didn't bode well. It was only last night that someone had recorded that video of me in the club. Apparently news traveled fast. I grimaced, twisting the tie of my Afton bathrobe around my finger. The fabric, some optimally formulated cashmere-silk blend, was almost softer than baby skin. "You know Grandma doesn't use her phone for anything but calling people and taking the occasional blurry photo with a finger blob in it."

"Someone could have told her." Her housekeeper. Another employee, feigning concern about my drinking habits. One of the "old hags" (her words) in her Pilates class.

"So what? It's not like this was your first time dancing on a table at a club."

Which was true, but it *was* my first time dancing on a table at a club while shotgunning champagne to the *Wizard of Oz* classic "Ding, Dong, the Witch Is Dead." Vienna wasn't *really* dead, of course. Just metaphorically dead, cast out of the social scene. And yes, people in the comments, I knew the difference.

I sighed. "I'm busy. I have to get ready for the gala tonight."

"I'm not telling Grandma that you can't call her back because you need to spend the next six hours getting dressed, Pom," he said. "Just get it over with before she disinherits you or something."

The thought sent a cold shudder through me. What would I do without the family? Grandma had asked me to curate the corporate art collection right around when I graduated from college, telling me that maybe I could put that ill-advised art history major to good use. I'd thrown myself into it, excited to be given a chance, declining party invitations and letting my social media go dark, even leaving my front-row seat at The Avenue's inaugural Fashion Week show empty. Finally I'd presented my decisions to Grandpa, Grandma, and my dad in a Power-

Point, pearl studs in my ears, my straight brown hair tied back into a professional chignon.

I kept my eyes on the presentation, hoping my passion for the work would shine through them onto the screen. My recommendations were to mix up our collection a little: sell some of the old, stagnant paintings by dead white men and invest in more art by women and people of color, younger people, queer people, pieces that incorporated physical space and music and motion. It wouldn't just be good for the artists and the art world; it would be good for our public image. We could even donate a few of our older pieces as tax write-offs, making sure the world knew how charitable we were while keeping our portfolio in the black.

I finished my talk to a photo of me smiling toothily from the screen (my teeth were very white, I admired) and resounding silence from the room. My real-life toothy smile faltered a little when I turned to my family members only to find them staring stone-faced back at me. "Was this a serious presentation?" my grandma finally said.

"Yes?" I squeezed out meekly.

Grandpa chuckled and shook his head. "Dear, I wanted to know which pieces we should be rotating in and out for corporate events."

Oh. My stomach crumpled up like a discarded piece of paper.

"Even if we were looking to make a full overhaul," Grandma said, "none of this fits the goals or public perception of the business. What were you thinking?"

I'd had so many thoughts while I was making this presentation. And yet somehow, at this moment, I couldn't pull up a single one of them.

My dad jumped to my defense. Well, kind of. "It's okay if Pom doesn't have a head for the business. She's good at so many other things." I waited for him to elaborate upon exactly what those other things were, but he just patted me on the head like a prized show dog as Grandpa nodded in agreement, his eyes almost apologetic. Not too apologetic, though. He didn't apologize or change his mind before his death a year later.

And maybe they'd been right. Maybe I didn't have a head for business, or money, or helping the world, or whatever. There were plenty of other things to keep me busy.

As long as I wasn't being cut loose. "Grandma wouldn't disinherit me over the phone, would she?"

"Probably not. She'd want to see the look on your face."

My breathing was coming a little bit faster, my heart pumping hard like I was running away from something. Grandma never called about nice things, like to say she loved your latest post and was impressed by how many likes it got, or that the "simply enormous" nose you'd inherited from your mother was beautiful and perfect and didn't need any sculpting or shaving down.

Deep breath, Pom. Deep breath.

"By the way," Nicholas continued, and just the fact that this meant we were moving on from Grandma made the deep breaths come a little easier. "Speaking of people who have been disinherited, did you hear that Farrah and Jordan are in town?"

"No, nobody told me!" Maybe that was what Grandma had been calling me about. Then again, ever since she'd cut my cousins off along with their parents, my uncle and aunt, she'd done a bang-up job pretending not only that they didn't exist but that they'd never existed at all. Which also made me breathe a little easier. Because it wasn't like she had an unlimited supply of grandchildren. She couldn't disinherit *all* of us, surely. I continued, "What are they doing here?" with a pang in my stomach. Farrah and I were the same age, had grown up side by side, giggling our way through Broadway shows and going on shopping sprees at the American Girl store and running wild in our family's private box at Yankee Stadium. And now I hadn't spoken to her in over a year.

"Not sure," Nicholas said. Being older and also a boy, he hadn't been as close to them as I'd been. "They didn't tell me they were here. I found out from a friend who'd seen them downtown at some party."

"Weird," I said.

A muffled voice came through on Nicholas's side. If he was working at the office, it was probably his secretary; if he was working at home, it was probably his girlfriend, Jessica. Either way, it probably meant he had to go. "Well, thanks for letting me know about Grandma," I said. "See you later?"

"I'm coming," he said to whoever'd spoken, and then back to me, "I have to go. See you later?"

He wouldn't. Still, I let myself pretend for a little bit. "Sure. See you later."

I took a deep breath as he hung up, though it didn't dislodge the swell of anxiety in my chest. My fingers twitched on the table next to my now-cold eggs and congealing spinach. The urge to call for reassurance seized me. To call for the most maternal, motherly person I know, the one who always used to soothe me when I felt overwhelmed like this, who would envelop me in a big, soft hug and tell me everything would be okay.

My former nanny, Andrea.

My fist clenched before my fingers could reach for my phone. I couldn't call my former *nanny*. I was twenty-eight years old. I hadn't had a nanny since I was twelve and Nicholas was fourteen and our parents deemed us old enough not to need nurturing anymore. "You're almost an adult," my dad had said. "Do what the rest of us do and stuff your feelings deep inside, where no one can see them."

Maybe those weren't the exact words that had come out of his mouth. But the meaning had been clear.

"You're losing it, Pom," I told myself. "Just call Grandma back. Whatever it is, it can't be that bad."

So, of course, I started suiting up to go for a run. What better way to make yourself less miserable emotionally than to make yourself miserable physically? A quick outfit change later—out of the oversize T-shirt and boxers left behind from some random hookup into sleek, formfitting all-black with the exception of a hot pink sweatband—I was ready to go. I would run around the Central Park Reservoir a few times, I decided. Get out some of this stress while gazing across the water and listening to a podcast, absorbing enough to distract me from the burn in my calves. Once my body was nice and high with endorphins, I'd give Grandma a call back and weather whatever it was she wanted to throw at me.

Out into the hallway, where at least I didn't have to worry about running into my parents—they'd relocated into a smaller but better-situated apartment a floor higher in the hotel when my brother and I had moved out. My family had apartments in our big hotels, plus use of rooms in other ones whenever we were there, obviously. Grandma had the penthouses here, in the Afton Palm Beach, and the Afton Los Angeles. My dad, as her son, had claimed the one in Jackson Hole, though I knew my mom coveted the LA penthouse, already scheming to inherit it whenever Grandma died.

The mirrored elevator was empty when I stepped inside. I turned away before I could catch more than a glimpse of myself—I was due for work on my tan, and the tightness of my brown ponytail meant that my eyes, already wide-set, made me look a little like an alien. The elevator stopped at a few floors, letting some more people on. A businessman in a tailored suit and Hermès tie who didn't glance away from his phone at me. An older couple holding hands and giving each other such smoldering glances and sneaky smiles that they had to be here having an affair. A few teenage girls with an older woman who was surely their chaperone.

I stiffened as I felt their eyes land on me, crawling like flies. One whispered in another's ear. The other giggled. That club video really must have been making the rounds. I stuck my headphones in, bowing my head as I scrolled through my phone in search of my podcast. If only I had a private elevator like my grandma and my parents, one where you needed a special key to get to their floor.

Podcast found. I turned it up so that I couldn't hear the giggling anymore, then winced a little bit as the host's sharp voice cut into my ear. *You're on Episode 3 of* Here to Slay. *I'm your host, Doe. Today we'll be looking at the seething pit of vipers that surrounded our victim, Danica Moore, before her fateful final day.*

If you looked at it through a judgy side-eye, I probably counted as one of those vipers. I wasn't a true crime junkie, but I'd known Danica—we'd modeled together a few years back before I decided modeling wasn't for me (too many reviews on how I didn't glide down runways, I clomped). We hadn't particularly liked each other, but there hadn't been anything personal about it; we were just both hangry all the time. I hadn't even heard she'd disappeared before the podcast hit the charts. Now I had to know what had happened to her.

I strode out as soon as the elevator doors opened to the lobby. Crystal light fixtures twinkled above me; I caught the smiles of the front desk clerks in the corners of my eyes.

"Pom! Pom?"

There was no ignoring that voice, even through my headphones. I stifled a sigh, pulling them out and pasting a smile on my face. It hurt my cheeks. "Fred. Good morning."

Fred chuckled in what he probably thought was a fatherly way but came off more like a robot's first attempt at mirth. "I think you mean good afternoon."

Though it was the weekend, he was still decked out in a suit, one not nearly as well fitted as the businessman's on the elevator. You'd think he'd be able to afford a good tailor, considering he was the CFO of Afton Hotels, ranking only beneath my grandma, my dad, and Nicholas. I'd known him my whole life, watching his blond hair fade to gray and fall out and placing secret bets with Farrah on how long his nose hair was in centimeters.

I couldn't imagine feeling so free to look that old and weird. My mom had already started talking about how I should be working on my preventative Botox.

"Good afternoon," I said impatiently, glancing behind him toward the front doors. So close!

"Pom." He leaned in closer, so that my nostrils filled with his coffee breath. I tried to shift backward without making it too obvious what I was doing. He might be old and weird, but I still didn't want to hurt his feelings. "Has your family mentioned anything about a . . . ."

He trailed off, and backed away much more quickly than I had. "Never mind," he said. "I shouldn't be asking you about it. You wouldn't know. Anyway, it was nice to see you."

Well, now my interest was piqued. "What are you talking about?"

He laughed shakily, wiping the sweat off his forehead with the sleeve of his jacket. "It's not important. I just had to come see your grandmother right away. Do you know if she's home?"

I blinked. "You didn't call her first? You know she really doesn't like surprises."

He chuckled again, just as shakily. "See you later, Pom." He stuck his hands in his pockets so that his suit jacket tented even more before walking briskly past me toward the private elevator in the back that would take him up to my grandma's apartment. He had a key to get up there, of course—my grandma often worked from her home office, which was pretty much a separate wing from the penthouse's living quarters. I had a key, too, as did all the rest of the family members. I couldn't remember the last time I used it, though.

Well, good luck to him. I'd made it out through the whisked-open doors into the chilly early spring air before the thought occurred to me: Grandma would be busy in a few minutes. I could call her back now, put up with whatever she had to say to me, and then get cut off before I had to deal with it for too long. The perfect crime.

"Call Grandma," I said into my phone. It began to ring. For someone who was apparently so eager to speak with me, it took her a lot of rings to pick up.

"Pomona," she said without preamble. She was one of the few people allowed to call me by my full name, mostly because I was too afraid of what would happen if I asked her to call me Pom like everybody else. "Please tell me you didn't wake up only now."

I wanted to take a deep breath to soothe myself the way Andrea had taught me, but considering I was walking beside a giant pile of garbage bags, that was not particularly advisable. "Of course not. I've already eaten, done some preparation for the gala tonight, and I'm going for a run now."

"You're running right now? Amazing. Usually you gasp and wheeze and grunt like a stuck pig when you exercise," she said. I pressed my lips together. I guess that now I had the answer to why I'd never been invited back to her Pilates class. At least she hadn't asked what preparation I'd done for the gala tonight, since that preparation consisted entirely of learning that there *was* a gala tonight. "Anyway. Pomona. I must speak with you."

"You're speaking with me now." I tried to keep my voice light as a bicyclist nearly swerved into me while I crossed Fifth Avenue. So what if I was walking against the light? I was a pedestrian, and pedestrians always have the right of way. I stopped at the entrance to the park, leaning against the mossy stone wall that encircled it as I waited for this conversation to be over.

"No, not on the *phone*." She sounded like I'd asked her to meet at the Times Square Olive Garden. "In person. It's important." Her voice softened the tiniest bit. "Pomona."

Okay, I was intrigued. She certainly didn't sound like she was gearing up to tear me to pieces with her sharp tongue. Not with her voice going soft like that. "Should I come up?"

"All sweaty and smelly from your run? Certainly not."

It couldn't be that important, then. I rolled my eyes.

"Afterward," she continued. "You need to—" Her voice cut off as the chime of her doorbell sounded, which got louder each year in the same increment that her hearing diminished with age.

That had to be Fred. I listened to her shuffle across the floor and pause, probably her peering through the peephole. "Oh. It's you." She sounded vaguely annoyed. "Well, you might as well come in." Then back to me. "Pomona, I have to go. Can you come by later tonight?"

"I've got the gala," I told her. I didn't know what time or where it was, but these things were always at the same time, at the same few places, with the same mediocre food and free-flowing drinks. The only things that changed were the names of the charity and the guests' outfits. "Tomorrow?"

She paused again, but this one felt heavier. Like she was weighing her words before she said them. "I suppose that will have to do."

She hung up without saying goodbye. Which was fine. Let her have her secret meeting with Fred about something he assumed I was too stupid to know about. Whatever. I didn't care. I just let my feet pound the dirt track around the reservoir as fast as they could, which, to be entirely honest, was not all that fast. In my high school days of running laps around the court before tennis practice, I was a fixture at the back of the pack. Still, I finished my run feeling vaguely queasy, and not just because I'd seen not one but two dead pigeons being eaten by rats and listened to one of my and Danica's former model friends dish about how she'd hated everyone she worked with, including me.

Who cared what people thought of me? I threw myself into getting ready for the gala. I had to exfoliate in the shower and wash my hair, barely finishing before Kelly showed up to blow it out. Then I had to pick out a dress before Kai came to do my makeup. The Avenue and Poquette had sent over new gowns since the last time I'd been in that section of my closet, as had several up-and-coming designers I'd asked the family assistant to look into. I decided on a black and green silk dress with geometric, origami-like folds created by a local FIT graduate— she'd appreciate the boost my patronage gave her label more than The Avenue or Poquette would.

You know what would go perfectly with an avant-garde dress like this? My mom's chunky emerald and diamond earrings. I grabbed my parents' key from where it hung on its hook beside the front door, stuck my feet in the fluffy hotel slippers, and ran up the back stairs.

My dad was out golfing, but my mom was in the same headspace as me. Her hair had been done in an elegant updo, her makeup understated and soft on her long, oval face. She turned to me as I entered her closet, where she sat perched on a blush velvet pouf, surveying her racks upon racks of clothes and shoes and accessories. "I've simply been so busy today trying to decide what to wear tonight. What do you think?"

I counseled a navy blue sheath that showed off her toned calves and arms with a classic yet modern silhouette. She pursed her lips and chose a glowing magenta floor-length gown with full-length lace sleeves and a high collar. Par for the course.

"Anyway, I wanted to borrow your emerald and diamond earrings," I said. "Is that okay?"

She pursed her lips even harder. "The emeralds? Pom, dear, you know that emeralds make your skin look sallow."

I hadn't known that, but okay. "What about the plain diamonds?" She looked at me blankly. "The cluster?" She still looked at me blankly. "The five-cluster?"

Those she deemed more acceptable. As she dug them out of her jewelry safe for me, I went and grabbed her shoes for her. I didn't have to ask about those: she always wore her signature custom-made stilettos, so high and so sharp that other women fell over or got stuck in the ground when they tried to walk in them. It was a point of pride to her that one of her friends had broken a bone after she'd borrowed them without her permission. I had never even bothered asking. Just looking at their tall, black, narrow silhouette scared me. Probably from the time when I was a kid and ran up to her for a hug, and she'd accidentally stepped on my foot. I'd almost lost a toe.

"Thank you," she said, glancing at them, then immediately down at her phone, frowning hard. Which was unusual for her. Not just because it was difficult for her to make expressions through all the Botox, but because she liked to advise against both frowning and smiling because of wrinkles. Botox couldn't catch all of them without making you look like you're wearing a mask, she liked to say.

It made me curious enough to risk asking her a question. "Are you okay?"

She scrolled viciously through what appeared over her shoulder to be someone's feed. "It's just that bitch at it again."

Well, that could apply to pretty much anyone she knew, friend or enemy or random stranger. "Which bitch?"

"That anonymous bitch." She stabbed at something with her finger. "RibbetRabbit."

The name sounded vaguely familiar. "Some anonymous celebrity gossiper? Is it another DeuxMoi?"

"No. This one—it's easier if you just look." And she thrust her phone at me. I took it, scrolling through the feed, which consisted of pictures of . . . herself? I took a closer look, swiping through them. They were all pictures of my mom dressed up for various galas and events, looking stunning as always, each dress or power suit selected to accentuate the features she liked (the large, wide eyes we shared, the straight nose a very talented surgeon had given her, the definition of her calves) and downplay the ones she didn't (her narrow lips, the small bust she refused to augment because "that would be tacky" in a way the nose job apparently wasn't). But the captions mocked her and her outfits, one calling her in a green lace dress "a frog coated in pond scum," another saying that a formfitting white dress "emphasizes every bulge and lump in her figure like she's the Michelin Man."

I wanted to snicker, but I knew better. Handing the phone back, I said, "It's just some jealous wannabe." That may or may not have been true. It could also have been one of the many ex-friends or frenemies she'd betrayed or talked shit about behind their back for years. If I had to write up a list, it would have overflowed pretty much any standard-size sheet of paper no matter how small I wrote. "So what? Just ignore them."

Advice that was always easier said than done, as I knew well from my hours in the middle of the night scrolling through comments on pieces about me. And Mom didn't give it any more credence than I would have, huffing and rolling her eyes.

"Seriously," I said. "You look gorgeous in all those pictures. None of what this person is saying is true."

In other mother-daughter relationships, this might have led to a moment of bonding. She might have told me that I was always gorgeous, too, and then she might have leaned in for a hug, and we might have gotten ready for the gala together, zipping each other up and finishing each other's makeup.

But this was the Afton family, and so she only frowned harder (but not too hard, per her credo). "No, I'm hideous." This might have led to a cycle of reassurance, where I tried to tell her she was beautiful and she kept denying it and so on, but instead she continued with "By the way, have you talked to your grandma yet? Apparently she was looking for you."

A change of subject would usually have been welcome in this situation, but the last thing I wanted to talk about with any of my relatives was any of my other relatives. "I'd better go get dressed," I said, already moving toward the exit, earrings clutched tight in my sweaty palm. "See you soon!"

By the time to leave for the gala, I was exhausted from shimmying into shapewear and then twisting all the way around myself like a pretzel to zip up the back. Since the spring day had cooled down considerably by now, the heated seats in the back of our black car were so welcome. I leaned my head back against the leather and almost let myself drift off to sleep.

Mom shook me awake as the car slid to a stop. "We're here." The gala was being held at the American Museum of Natural History, right across the park and a thematic setting for this charity event meant to raise money to protect endangered rhinos (I'd been half-right). Our car pulled up and deposited us neatly in front of the building, where a small crowd was clustered around a safari-themed backdrop. I sashayed through the crowd—sashaying over cobblestones in heels as high as these was tricky, but I was a pro by now—and posed in front of the backdrop, tucking my chin, smiling without teeth, turning from side to side with my hand on my hip as cameras and phones flashed before me.

"Who are you wearing?" somebody called.

I spun so that they could get a good view of the back of the dress, where the most ingenious folds were. "Rita Ngo. She's new."

Though she wouldn't be new for long, not now that I'd shouted her out. I grinned at the lenses again before heading into the venue, where the famous model of a blue whale swam overhead, suspended from the ceiling.

I was picking a goblet of champagne off one of the circulating trays, a little mesmerized by the way the golden bubbles shimmered under the lights, when I heard a telltale cooing and swishing behind me. I spun just in time to embrace my best friend, Opal, and give her some air kisses on her perfectly contoured cheeks. My other best friends, Millicent and Coriander, were next.

"Oh my God, Pom," gasped Opal, green eyes wide and round in her heart-shaped face. Her auburn hair, the shade carefully calibrated by the pros to bring out the rose tones in her cheeks, brushed my face as she pulled away. "That dress is the best thing I've ever seen."

Millicent and Coriander murmured in agreement as I struck a pose. Then unposed and leaned in a little more modestly. "No way. *Your* dress is the best thing I've ever seen."

It wasn't; it was just your standard LBD. She really should have gone with a more understated necklace than that chunky pink thing, which made the neckline look busy, and put all the flashiness into her shoes and earrings instead. But Opal beamed when I said that, which made the little white lie worth it. She leaned in, snickering a little. "What do you think Vienna's wearing tonight? Yoga pants? *Sweat-*pants?"

Millicent and Coriander snickered along with her. To be fair, they'd gone more adventurous than Opal, Millicent in a pure white tulip gown that made her olive skin glow bronze and Coriander in a shimmering gold Grecian one that made her tiny frame a bit more imposing.

I'd almost managed to forget that, typically, Vienna would have been at the front of the crowd, leaning in for the first air kisses, smelling like roses. Opal smelled like roses now, actually. Had she claimed Vienna's perfume now that Vienna was out? The thought kind of made me want to stab myself with one of the sharp-looking commemorative brass rhino horns that served as gifts to everyone who'd donated over a certain amount.

I drew in a deep breath, then regretted it, because Opal's perfume just made me think harder about Vienna. About the things she'd said to me. About the knife she'd twisted in my back. She was *lucky* all I'd done was push her out of the social scene. She was *lucky*—

Stop it, Pom. Or you're going to start crying and ruin your makeup.

I took a big gulp of champagne to push the tears down. It was not nearly as crisp or dry as the Moët my parents liked to break out for special occasions. The people throwing the gala had probably sunk the beverage budget into bathing the rhinos, or whatever. "I don't even want to think about Vienna," I said. "Can we just pretend she doesn't exist?"

"She may as well not exist," said Opal, but, loyal friend that she was, she changed the subject. "So, real drinks sometime soon? I think there's an actual bar up near the dinosaurs."

I slipped my arm through hers as I tossed down the rest of my cheap champagne. It glittered down my throat, then rested, sour, in my stomach. "Why wait for soon?"

Well. The night got a little blurry from there. With all due respect to the rhinos, we didn't stick around the gala very long.

I blinked and we were on the street, weaving on our heels as we waved down one of the other girls' cars, and then we were bypassing the line at some exclusive new club, and then I blinked again and I was on top of a table, some liquid spilled down the front of my beautiful, beautiful dress, and people were cheering at my frozen smile. Opal and I were dancing, shouting along to some new song I hated, but she was holding me up so that I wouldn't slip and embarrass myself, and that shot of love and appreciation I felt for her was the last thing I remembered.

CHAPTER

Two

I was relieved to wake up on my couch. It wasn't quite as good as waking up in my bed—my back would groan about it later—but it was better than waking up next to some strange guy or on Opal's floor. I sat up, blinking hard to get the crust out of my eyes, stretching and feeling all my joints pop. My mouth tasted like dirty socks.

Sunlight streamed through my open window, which meant it could have been anywhere from 7 a.m. to noon. I rubbed my forehead, feeling makeup crumble like powder. Ugh. I hoped I hadn't done anything last night to embarrass myself. Or at least not embarrass myself too much.

Someone yawned loudly from my bedroom, which cleared some of the fog from my head. I popped to my feet, only to sag down again when Opal padded out of my bedroom wrapped in one of the hotel's robes that always showed up hanging on my bathroom door like magic. "What a night," she said, yawning again. Mascara was smudged around her eyes. "Sorry again about when we got back."

"When we got back?"

"When I puked on your pillow," Opal clarified. "That's why you slept on the couch."

Oh. I cringed. Great.

"I also borrowed one of your tracksuits. Because of the puke. I'll get it back to you eventually. Anyway," Opal said, padding toward the kitchen, "I desperately need coffee."

I let her go, sitting back down on the couch and sliding my fingers through the cushions in search of my phone, which usually fell—there it was. My eyes widened. Over the background of my cat Squeaky, whom I'd gotten when I was fourteen and who had run away and disappeared right after I went off to college (I'd cried for weeks, even though my parents tried to convince me that he was probably living happily in Central Park gorging himself on a buffet of rats), notification after notification appeared. Like, I was someone who usually got a lot of notifications, and this was a lot even for me.

Opal poked her head out of the kitchen doorway. "So, I have no interest in consuming coffee beans that have been excreted by an animal, I don't care how rare they are. What's the number for room service again?"

I also had no interest in the coffee beans. Nicholas had gotten them for me for one birthday or another. Apparently they tasted like cherries and almonds. I waved my hand vaguely in the direction of the bedroom, where the shiny black hotel receiver sat on the bedside table. "Dial 49."

Opal disappeared again as I scrolled through my list. The social media ones I disregarded—they were mostly just tags or comments or harassing messages, which I could read and obsess over later. But I had a bunch of missed calls and texts. A few from my mom (Where did you go?). A few from Nicholas (Mom says you disappeared from the gala and she's mad. Where did you go?).

Those I ignored too. What was with everyone using Nicholas as the Pom-whisperer lately? Thank goodness they didn't know the miracle that was location-sharing. My best friends and I always made a point of sharing our locations with each other in case we got separated during a drunken night out, but that was a privilege I did not want extended to my family.

What I couldn't ignore were the missed calls from Grandma. There had to be—I kept scrolling—at least ten of them, from soon after we left the gala and continuing for a few hours afterward, while I was at the club. How had I not felt my phone vibrating through my jeweled clutch?

I hit the return-call button and held the phone to my ear. It rang and rang. No answer. I pulled it away with a frown, noting the time. It was on the later side of the window I'd given myself earlier, after 11 a.m. Grandma never slept later than eight. Maybe she was in a Pilates class, or out for an early lunch.

Still, ten phone calls. That wasn't just someone who wanted to talk to me. That was someone who *needed* to talk to me.

I had to go up there. After a quick stop in my bathroom to scrub the makeup off my face and brush my teeth so that I wouldn't hear anything about my breath and an even quicker change into a velour tracksuit the exact shade of green that made my brown eyes pop, I grabbed the key to Grandma's penthouse from its hook. "I'm just running upstairs for a bit, I'll be back in a few," I called to Opal.

"Okay."

I opened the door and nearly stepped right into the hotel employee who'd been sent up with our coffees on a tray. He really should be more careful, or he'd hurt himself. I shook my head at him and swept over to the stairwell.

My pounding head and dry-as-sandpaper throat regretted climbing even those two sets of stairs by the time I made it to the top and into the penthouse. I stood an extra minute in the foyer to catch my breath so that I wouldn't catch some snide comment about my gasping and wheezing and grunting again. "Grandma?"

Grandma's apartment was in another stratosphere from mine or even my parents'. It took up the entire top floor of the hotel with sprawling, luxuriously decorated rooms that had incredible city views. I bypassed the work hallway and headed down the home hallway, passing by portraits of various Aftons dressed up, some candid at galas and some official photo shoots (she especially loved the one that she and I had done with *Vogue* some years ago). My past self smiled down on me as I moved through them, noting that the photos of Farrah and Jordan and their parents had disappeared. Grandma probably got a certain satisfaction from that—she'd always been a little old-fashioned, and by "old-fashioned" I meant quietly racist, the kind that would never say it outright to anyone's face but who would have preferred that her younger son, Farrah and Jordan's father, hadn't married a Black woman.

Into the living room, where the nineteenth-century fireplace, transplanted here from one of those old Fifth Avenue mansions they'd "remodeled," was crowned by Grandma and Grandpa's wedding portrait. Neither of them was smiling, even though Grandma's formfitting lace dress was still brought up in fashion magazines and top-fifty countdowns as one of the most iconic looks of all time.

Her dirty secret? This wasn't her original wedding portrait. She and Grandpa had begun with a smaller wedding, a cheaper wedding, in their early twenties, right before he bought his first hotel. They held this big one with the iconic dress almost ten years later, when the first hotel had turned into a fleet of them. Once I'd asked her what dress she'd worn for that first wedding. She wouldn't even tell me.

"Grandma?" I called. The air hung around me like a blanket, thick and warm. Was the AC off? That was odd. Grandma preferred her rooms chilly enough to make visitors wish for a sweater.

A quick peek into the informal living room, the kitchen, and the dining room with its floor-to-ceiling windows overlooking Central Park: empty, though two wineglasses still sat on the antique table. "Grandma?" I called down the hallway that led to the bedrooms. Silence echoed in response.

I stood there for a moment in the dining room, shifting from foot to foot, debating what to do next. Nobody was supposed to go into her bedroom, or even into the bedroom hallway, without permission. But what if she'd fallen or something and couldn't get up? She was getting older, after all. She'd protested to physical therapist after physical therapist, but her hips had finally forced her to downgrade her heels from four inches to two.

I took a step toward the hallway, then chickened out. Pulled out my phone, and dialed again. It rang in my ear . . . but it also rang down the hallway, where I could just hear the tinny tune reverberate.

My stomach soured as I hung up. "Grandma? I'm coming in."

No response, yet again. I marched down the hallway, my slippers shushing against the runner, and pushed open her bedroom door.

I'd only been in here a handful of times, and each time I'd spent that first step marveling at the massive canopy bed, the original Chagall hanging on the far wall for only her and my grandpa (well, before he died) to enjoy, the big windows looking out on Central Park. Not this time.

This time, I zeroed in immediately on the blood.

I stumbled back, my heart stuttering. Blood soaked the bed, dripped down onto the floor, formed abstract splotches on the Oriental rug. So much of it. So much of it that it took my brain a second to catch up to the fact that the blood had come from a person. A person slumped onto the bed.

I kept my hand on my phone in case I had to call for help. I took a deep breath, then held it, the tang of metal making me want to gag. One step forward. Another step. The slipper squelched into blood as I stared down onto the bed, at my grandma's bloody face, her lips frozen into a silent scream.

My own scream wasn't anywhere close to silent.

CHAPTER

Three

I didn't remember calling for help, but I must have, because only a few minutes after I found my grandma's body, the penthouse was swarming with a succession of people in uniforms. Hotel security. Real cops. More important real cops when they realized who the dead person was. Somebody led me into the dining room out of the way and put a mug of tea in my hands. It was cold. I couldn't bring myself to drink it.

My parents showed up soon after, a lawyer trailing behind them. "Don't say anything," my mom warned, pulling me against her bony shoulders in what might have been intended as a hug.

I broke away and stared at her, my vision still wavery with tears. "Do you think *I* did this?"

"Of course not!" She sounded offended at the very thought, which appeased me somewhat. "But still, you never know what the vultures will seize on. Just don't say anything."

My fingers curled around my phone. I wanted badly, so badly, to call my old nanny—to hear her voice tell me everything would be okay, like after my first and second ponies had died. But I couldn't. My parents would think I was either losing it or that I was a child. And besides, what if she didn't pick up?

I did talk to the police, no matter what they said. I was the person who'd found the . . . the body. There was no getting around it. But it wasn't like anything I said was helpful. They seemed interested in the missed calls she'd left for me, but there was no indication of what they'd been about. No voicemails. No all-caps texts, which were the only kinds of texts she sent. They duly noted the time stamps as being toward the end of the gala, meaning that she had to have died after it, but that only narrowed it down so much. It wasn't like she'd left a voicemail that cut off in the middle with her screaming, "I'm being stabbed!" (Unlike Danica in *Here to Slay*, who had been livestreaming a run when her phone all of a sudden went dark. It all seemed so much . . . neater and cleaner in my headphones.)

The police did as much talking to me as I did talking to them. And said just as little. I'd asked them, tearfully, "What if the murderer comes after me next? What if someone's hunting down Aftons?" After all, who would kill a defenseless old lady in her bed? No matter how rotten and nasty she'd been to people, no matter how many businesses she'd screwed over, no matter how many . . .

. . . okay, maybe there were a number of people who would've wanted to kill her who would have nothing against me. That only calmed me slightly until my parents said they would hire security to stand outside our doors, and extra for the hotel.

I was still making plans to go to the South of France—maybe Greece—for a while. As soon as my parents said it wouldn't look suspicious for me to hightail it out of the country. I'd lie on some white sand, wear big sunglasses, fill my mind only with the lapping of the waves and hunting down the perfect beach outfit (something pastel and gauzy that hit my ankles). Then I'd come back refreshed once the murderer was caught, ready to resume my life.

The reading of the will happened about a week after the murder, when the autopsy results came back (to no one's surprise, Grandma had been defiantly healthy aside from the seven stab wounds in her chest and torso made by an unknown small, sharp instrument). My parents and Nicholas had asked if I wanted to go with them, the other more distant relatives in town who hadn't been disinherited, and the top business associates at Afton Hotels, but I'd declined. I already knew I wasn't getting any of the business, and I could wait to see what else she left me without having to spend all morning in a stuffy conference room breathing in old men's body odor and nervous sweat.

The afternoon of, right before lunch, I was slumped on the couch scrolling through my phone when somebody pounded on my door. Lori was cooking up something that smelled good—had I remembered to tell her I'd decided to go gluten-free for the week?—but when I didn't stir, she went to get it.

I cocked my head, waiting to hear if it was Nicholas with a list of all I'd been left, but all I heard was a deep voice asking, "Are you Pomona Abigail Afton?"

I popped to my feet, at first just feeling insulted. Lori was in her forties and was wearing a rayon top with jeans from ten years ago, out of style but not yet vintage, for God's sake. But as I got close enough to see the people standing there in the open door, my steps faltered. The pair of people waiting there weren't paparazzi. They were hotel security. I stopped, just in case they were assassins wearing hotel security uniforms, but then I realized I knew them. Had known them most of my life.

Then why were they asking Lori if she was me?

The questions were answered when Lori stepped to the side, revealing a third person standing there. This one was a man in a midrange suit, probably off-the-rack but tailored, and a wonky nose that looked like it had been punched a few times and set crookedly. He held a big envelope in front of him, one with the crest of the family law firm on it.

So this had to do with the will reading. My heart fluttered. I'd seen movies like this. Where the underestimated family member, the one who toiled away thanklessly in the background, was finally seen for their efforts and rewarded appropriately. Sure, I couldn't say I'd really toiled away, or toiled at all, but I was certainly in the background. I pictured the eyes of all my family members and the family business associates popping out of their head as the lawyer proclaimed, "And the business has been given to—"

"Pomona Abigail Afton?" said the man with the wonky nose, now looking at me.

I nodded.

"I need to hear you verbally confirm it," he said.

I cleared my throat, already picturing how I'd recount the moment to the press. *Something inside me knew that, as soon as I said yes, my entire life was about to change, and I savored that moment right before, the way the motor thrums beneath you just before your yacht takes off into the sunset over the Mediterranean Sea.* "Yes, I am Pomona Abigail Afton."

The man handed me the envelope. It was surprisingly light. "Pomona Abigail Afton, you have thirty minutes to vacate the premises."

I blinked. "Excuse me?"

The man repeated himself, then added, "If you do not exit the premises voluntarily within thirty minutes, hotel security will remove you."

I looked over his shoulders at the pair of security. Their eyes skated off mine no matter how hard I sought them. I opened my mouth, ready to appeal to these men I'd known for years, then stilled as I realized I didn't know their names.

My phone buzzed in my hand, rescuing me. Nicholas. I took a deep breath, calming myself. This was clearly some kind of mistake, and Nicholas was here to clear it up. I answered, injecting a bit of humor into my voice as I said, "Nicholas, you would not believe what some guy just said I have to—"

"It's not a joke, Pom." All the calm slipped away, because I'd never heard Nicholas sound like this before: both defeated and crushed at once. "It was in Grandma's will."

A squeak escaped my throat. "She disinherited me?"

"No." A horn blared behind him, and someone shouted something indistinguishable. Where was he? "As it turned out, she had a clause in her will that activated in the event she 'died an unnatural death.' She had it put in a few months ago when she changed the will after disinheriting Farrah and Jordan and them." He paused, and I could picture him gathering himself, licking his lips. "It seemed she had a suspicion she might be murdered."

"Why did nobody tell us about this?" Lori and the men at the door were all watching me with caution, like I might explode at any moment. I turned to the side as hot tears pricked my eyes so that they wouldn't see me cry.

"I don't know," Nicholas replied. "But the clause said that, in the event of an unnatural death, everything gets frozen. The trusts. Our living quarters. The houses in the Hamptons and the Berkshires. And the business, and everything associated with the business, get placed in the hands of a caretaker council who will do the bare minimum necessary to run it day by day. For a year."

I turned further, hunching into myself. "What do you mean, frozen?"

"It means that your trust fund won't give you money anymore," Nicholas snapped. I winced at the force in his voice. "It means that you don't get to use the Afton hotels anymore. It means that your credit cards stop working and that it's the same for all of us. For a year. Apparently she was paranoid someone close to her hated her enough to off her, and she didn't want any potential murderers benefiting from her death."

A little bit of calm trickled in. I could survive for a year. I could bum around my friends' apartments and summer houses in the Hamptons and the Berkshires and Jackson Hole. I could call a driver and . . . wait, I couldn't call a driver if all that was frozen. Or use the family jet. How was I supposed to get anywhere?

I took a deep breath and held it. "And after a year it all comes back?"

"Only if the murderer is caught," Nicholas said. "If nobody is caught, then . . ."

My throat was suddenly very dry.

"Then it doesn't come back. Ever."

I couldn't even process the thought. I blinked into the corner of the room, at the dust in the corner. There shouldn't be dust there. Lori would have to clean that up.

"Not to say I told you so," Nicholas said, "but I told you so. You should have gotten a job or gone back to school to obtain some kind of skill. Because without the hotels and your trust fund, you're—"

"Says the guy who's spent his entire life working for the family business," I snapped, not to hurt him, but to stop him from continuing. I knew what he was going to say, anyway. I'd heard it from him several times over the past five years or so, all variations on the same theme. *What are you doing with your life, Pom? Don't you want to do something meaningful? You just fritter away your days with the money somebody else earned for you.*

I thought I had a pretty good life, actually. I got to do whatever I wanted, whenever I wanted.

Except now, I guess. All of my freedom was frozen now. As was his. "You know, Nicholas?" And okay, maybe this time I wanted to hurt him a little. "You're just as screwed as I am right now. So shut up."

"I have work experience and connections that will help me find another job if I need one," he said evenly. Unlike me, which went unspoken. "And I'm going to stay with Jessica at her apartment. It's tight, but we're lucky that she wanted to keep it for a bit just in case when she started spending most of her time at my place."

"Well, excuse me for not being in love."

He sighed. "Obviously that's not what I meant," he said. "Pom, you should pack a bag and get out of there. Don't let anyone take a photo or video of you being escorted out. People will have a field day. Walk out with your head held high, okay? Come meet me at Jessica's. I'll text you the address."

This couldn't be happening.

"Okay?" he prompted.

I whispered, "Okay."

He hung up. Silence rang in my ear. I lowered the phone and turned around, trying to sniff the snot back up my nose.

"You have twenty-five minutes to vacate the premises," said the man in the doorway.

Pack a bag and get out of there. Walk out with your head held high. Meet Nicholas. Those were three things I could make my body do, even if my mind couldn't process them yet.

So, with Lori's help, I unearthed one of my leather suitcases from my closet—it seemed that they were kind enough to let me take that, at least. And then proceeded to pack my bag with not even close to everything I needed. Like, how could I pack my entire life into a bag? I didn't know what clothes I would need—how many galas would I be going to in the next few weeks until this was all surely resolved, and could I pair these darling gold heels with multiple dresses? What about all of my skin creams and my hair stuff and the pure silk pillowcase I'd gotten to replace the one Opal puked on—how could I sleep without it?

I was paralyzed with indecision, which meant Lori did most of the packing. And by "most of the packing," I mean she did all of the packing while I sniffled and tried to compose myself so that I wouldn't be crying when I went back out into the foyer.

Just as the man who'd served me yelled, "You have five minutes left to vacate the premises!" Lori thumped the bag in front of me. Its contents strained against the zipper, threatening to explode.

I sucked in a deep breath. "You think that's everything I'll need for a week or two?"

"I think it'll give you a good start," Lori said. "And you can buy more. I know your trust fund is frozen, but don't forget, you have the checking account where you deposited your fee for that sunglasses campaign, remember? Do you have that information? It should hopefully help you get on your feet."

I squinted at the professional sunset photograph on my wall. I remembered doing the sunglasses campaign on social media, and they'd paid me, but it hadn't been very much, not even $25,000. It hadn't been enough to bother the lawyers about, so I'd had Lori put it away somewhere so that the campaign would stop bugging me about not cashing the check. "It's probably in my nightstand."

She did indeed find it in my nightstand drawer, and handed it to me just as the man was trumpeting from the doorway that I had three minutes left. "Jesus Christ, this guy," I said under my breath, and turned to get out of here before he made security drag me out—he seemed like the type who'd enjoy giving that order. "Wait. My outfit. I should change." I was wearing an oversize white T-shirt and mom jeans with platform sneakers—not a terrible look, but if there were going to be people out there waiting gleefully to see me fall, I'd want to be wearing something badass. A power suit? Something metallic?

But Lori stopped me with a touch to my shoulder. "I know you just heard about this, but could you please let me know ASAP when I'm going to get paid? Or if I still have a job?" she asked. "I already didn't get my usual paycheck after your grandmother passed, and . . . well, I really need it."

I felt a little bit like I'd swallowed the Fabergé egg Grandpa had used as a paperweight on his desk. Somehow I'd assumed Lori would be coming with me. She was just always there: cooking my meals, running my errands, taking care of my apartment. Who would take care of me now?

Despite all my efforts, my eyes brimmed with tears. Lori blurred before me as I leaned in for a hug. "So we're in the same position right now, then," I choked out. "Both penniless."

She pulled away in time for me to look toward the ceiling and blink very hard so the tears couldn't actually drip down my cheeks. "Pom, we are not in the same—"

"YOU HAVE TWO MINUTES LEFT TO—"

"All right! I'm coming!" I shouted at the door. So much for changing my outfit. I turned back toward Lori with a sympathetic frown. "We can make it through this. I believe in us."

"But Pom, we're not in the—"

I shushed her. "No negativity. We are *strong*."

And just like that, I was out on the sidewalk, my bag in front of me, still reeling from the shock.

CHAPTER

Four

Somehow the sun had the nerve to be shining right now. I stood there on the sidewalk, blinking into the bright light, as people swerved around me. Had I remembered to bring any of my sunglasses? Surely they'd let me back in to get something I forgot, if Lori hadn't packed any in my suitcase? But then I pictured the very smug face of the guy with the wonky nose. That door was barred to me.

Belatedly, I thought about my parents, who might not even be back yet from the will reading. What would they do? Where would they go?

As if my mom had read my mind—*shudder*—my phone began to buzz, MOM flashing across the screen. I picked up. "Hello?"

"Oh, my dear," said my mom. "I assume Nicholas has told you the news?"

"He has." I glanced over my shoulder to see not just that the hotel security had followed me out, but so had a few people from the lobby to gawk. I scowled at them before remembering that the picture I wanted going around in regard to this whole situation wasn't one where you could see the lines on my forehead. I relaxed my face, picking up my bag and speed-walking around the corner to where hopefully they wouldn't follow me.

There, on a quieter block currently inhabited only by a few doormen too professional to stare and some plump pigeons, I let myself continue. "What's the plan? We've got to be able to stop this."

Mom sighed deeply into my ear. "We've got the lawyers on it, but their first impression is that it's ironclad. She was in her sound mind and everything. Unfortunately." She muttered something I was kind of glad I couldn't hear. "Since the Hamptons and Berkshires houses technically belonged to your grandmother, your father and I are going to go hide out in Bailey and Teddy's place in the Hamptons to recoup." Two of their close friends. "It's the off-season, but I suppose there's nothing we can do about that for now. Better there than here, with the paparazzi lurking around every corner. You can come if you'd like. They have five bedrooms, and only two belong to their dogs."

My first reaction was to do a full-body cringe. My second reaction was to do another full-body cringe. I could just imagine what my friends would say. How they'd snicker behind my back not just about me losing my money, but about me having to move in with my parents and my parents' friends and my parents' friends' spoiled dogs.

I'd been so excited when I graduated college and had been given my own apartment. No more waking up and padding into the kitchen to my mom's critical "Oh, you're eating breakfast today?" No more trying to control when I went to bed. No more criticizing how late I came home or arguing about how loud my music was or who I wanted to date. No more watching over every single little thing I did. Sure, maybe I'd wanted to move downtown with some of my friends, who were living in Chelsea or SoHo or even the fun parts of Brooklyn, but we all had to play the cards we'd been dealt.

But anyway. "Nicholas said I can stay with him and Jessica for a bit until I figure myself out," I said.

Silence on the other end. "Good luck with that, Pom," said my dad. I hadn't even realized he was on the line too. My mom must have had me on speakerphone. Bailey and Teddy and the dogs were all probably listening in, too, snickering and showing their sharp little teeth.

"Bye."

Now I was all rattled up inside. I took a deep breath, looking down at my phone. I really wanted a soothing voice, caring words, a hug in a sound.

Instead of my old nanny, my phone flashed with MOM again. I sighed. "Hello?"

All I heard on the other end was shuffling, some murmured sounds I couldn't make out. A butt dial, I realized after a few more attempts at a greeting. Which wasn't uncommon for my mom. I should probably realize it by now and not just pick up whenever she called me right back. Only I knew that if I did that, the next time she called me right back would be legit and she'd lambaste me for ignoring her. So be it. I hung up on her butt.

On to my old nanny. Andrea picked up after only two rings, even though I hadn't called her in . . . had it really been five years, since I told her about my college graduation? My whole body was tense, and I didn't realize it until I relaxed with her warm "Pom, how are you doing? I saw the news, and I've been thinking of you and your family."

So what if, as Nicholas had never let me forget, she had been paid to look after me? She wasn't being paid to talk to me now. That was something. I let myself confess, "I don't know what to do."

"Breathe, first of all," she said.

Right. She didn't know about the account freezing and everything. So I spilled. She listened, mm-hmm'ing just often enough that I knew she was listening. When I finished, she said immediately, "Well, keep breathing. You will be okay, I promise you. No matter what happens."

How could she know that? She couldn't. Not at all.

"Do you need somewhere to go?" she continued. "My son's roommate just moved out all of a sudden, and he needs someone to replace her. It's a nice place—a little smaller than you're used to, but the price is good, and there aren't any roaches or mice. And I bet he could help get you set up with a job. He's good at that sort of thing."

I shuddered. If "no roaches and mice" was a main selling point, I'd hate to see what the rest of it looked like. "That's very kind of you, but my plan is to stay right now with my brother and his girlfriend. And I can take on an influencer campaign or two if I need money." Saying that felt so crass, like I'd just stood up at the dinner table and farted. "I still have all my followers."

"That's something," she said. "You call me if you change your mind. You're strong, Pom. And you're good, and smart, and capable. Don't forget that."

I rolled my eyes. I didn't believe a word of what she was saying, but I knew better than to argue with her. She would never let me hear the end of it. "I'll try not to." I stopped in front of Jessica's building, a big prewar construction a few blocks too far from Central Park for comfort. At least I wouldn't have to leave my neighborhood altogether. To be fair, that was probably the only reason she and Nicholas have lasted as long as they have—he works too much to spend time going back and forth to a farther neighborhood. "I have to go."

"Big imaginary hug to you, Pom."

I tried to feel it as I buzzed my way in, walking past the empty desk where a doorman might sit if they had one, and took a quick trip upstairs in the elevator. The ceilings were kind of low, and the hallways dark. The building was crumbling a little bit at the edges.

I would *never* say that Jessica didn't come from the right kind of family. It was my mom and my grandma who'd said that. Jessica had never been anything but kind to me, and she loved Nicholas in a way that made her eyes glow when she looked at him. They'd been glowing together for over a year and a half now. So what if her parents were teachers in Ohio and she'd once shown up at a gala in a dress from Target? I mean, I'd done my best not to be seen with her, but I hadn't made fun of her behind her back with Opal and Millicent and Coriander. And it was my grandma who'd declared that she'd never be invited to a gala again, not me. It wasn't like I was the one sitting on the planning committee. I couldn't naysay her.

"Pom, I'm sorry," Jessica said when she answered the door, pulling me in for an embrace that smelled like baked apples. "You can stay here as long as you need."

I was soothed a little bit by her hug, only to catch Nicholas's stern glare from behind her when she backed away. The nose we'd both inherited from our mother's family might have been "unseemly" on me, but on him it was considered strong, made his glare seem more intense.

"As long as you need to get on your feet," he clarified. "You can't just be sitting around doing nothing all day. You need to look for a job or something."

"Give her a few days," Jessica said over her shoulder. "Her entire life just got turned upside down."

Nicholas grumbled, but didn't launch into his "do something with yourself, Pom" speech. I gave Jessica a grateful smile, feeling a little bad about not defending her after the gala to either my friends or my grandma. So what if her brown hair was a little flat and could use highlights? And so what if her cheeks were a little too round to be fashionable? Buccal fat removal just made you look old after a few years, as Coriander had discovered.

To be fair, I had at least tried later on to go up against my grandma. She and I had shared a car home from the gala; she'd insisted on it, and I figured I could just go out later from the hotel. In the car, I'd broached the subject. "Maybe I could take Jessica shopping sometime, go with her to the salon for some subtle highlights and makeup tips, and then she could come to a gala again?" I said meekly. "Nicholas really seems to like her. She might be around for a while."

Grandma had shaken her head. "Not if I have anything to say about it," she grumbled in her voice that, no matter how much work she'd had done on her face and her neck, tattled on her smoking habit of many years. "Nicholas is going to be the head of *my* company someday. He needs a girl with proper instincts at his side if he's going to keep it going and help it thrive. She can't be showing up at fundraisers with a Tupperware of macaroni salad like it's a potluck or teaching their children Marxism."

Jessica hadn't done either of those things, but okay. There would be no arguing with Grandma about that. Still, I said, "I just think she's nice."

"Lots of things are nice, Pomona. Mimosas are nice. Bulldogs are nice. That doesn't mean you marry one."

Jessica went beyond nice that night I showed up at her door, though. Along with Nicholas, she helped me send out responses to companies who'd emailed or DMed me in the past looking to collaborate on an influencer campaign; I selected a designer I'd worn before and felt good about recommending to my followers, even though I was being paid for it. We set up the payment along with days and times they wanted me to post, and approved the content, and by the time we were done, it was dark outside. (Well, it got dark early in Jessica's apartment, considering it was on a low floor.)

"You're doing great!" Jessica enthused. Nicholas had said something to her about potentially being able to get me a job wherever she worked—it was something in advertising, or marketing, or were they the same thing?—but she'd said there weren't any openings. Which was a relief. There was no sense in me going out and getting a real job when everything would surely be fixed within a few weeks. "Here, we can set up the couch for you."

I blinked. "Set up the couch for what?"

Jessica laughed, as if I'd been making a joke. "For sleeping. I only have one bedroom."

I'd slept on a couch plenty of times in my life, though never intentionally like this. But to protest would be rude. Besides, what else was I going to do, curl up in bed between her and my brother? "Thanks," I said through a frozen smile.

And the week went downhill from there. I woke up one morning, a crick in my back, to the sound of Jessica bumping around in the kitchen. I sat up, yawning, only for her to poke her head out with an apologetic grin, a knife in her hand. My breath caught in my throat before I realized she was chopping bananas for her morning smoothie. "Oh, sorry. I was trying to be quiet, but I have to get ready for work."

For someone who was trying to be quiet, she wasn't doing a very good job at it, considering she woke me up every single morning.

At least I'd soon have enough money coming in from influencing where I could probably move out soon and sublet somewhere until everything was fixed, I consoled myself.

But as soon as the first photo from the campaign—me posing in a crosswalk in a chic LBD, sunglasses, and bright yellow heels that echoed the classic New York City taxi—posted, the comments started pouring in. Omg, your GRANDMA just got murdered and you're posting pics like this??? Wtf, how callous can you be? Wow, I knew Pom was low, but not THAT low.

And naturally the think pieces followed. I was a heartless monster. I was an airheaded idiot who was trying to profit off her own family member's brutal murder. I'm not saying she had anything to do with it, because that would be libel, but something like this really makes you think.

The designer pulled their campaign the next day. Sorry, Pom! We misjudged the timing. Maybe we can work together again in the future.

After a few more days of sleeping on Jessica's uncomfortable couch and getting woken up by her early each morning, and also each time she got up in the middle of the night to use the bathroom (seriously, how much water did this girl drink?), I gave Opal a call. Which made me realize, as the phone was ringing in my ear, that I hadn't heard from Opal at all since I lost everything. She'd texted me her condolences when she heard about my grandma's death, had posted a selfie looking somber with black netting over her face at the back of the memorial service, but nothing since.

My call went to a recording that Opal's voicemail was full. Irritated, I called again. This time she picked up. "Hello?"

"Hey," I said. "Any chance I could crash with you for a bit?" Opal's place wasn't quite as nice as mine, and it didn't have a great view of the park, but, crucially, it did have an extra bedroom with an en suite bathroom. I'd had about enough of Nicholas banging on the door whenever I'd been in the shower for more than twenty minutes. "Sleeping on Jessica's couch is wearing a bit thin."

She was silent for so long I actually took the phone off my ear and checked to make sure it hadn't dropped the signal. "Oh, wow, that's a fun idea," she said finally. "It's too bad it won't work, though. Um, I've been using the spare room as an office."

I bit my lower lip. An office for what? She didn't work. "You can't maybe put the office in your living room or bedroom until I get back on my feet? It's not going to be very long." A beat of silence. "I'd do it for you, Opal. You know I would."

"I know," she said. Her voice was low and subdued, almost like she was trying not to cry. "But I can't. I'm really sorry, Pom. I . . . I need the space."

When she hung up, I stared at the phone for a moment. Something was off with her. I considered checking her shared location so I could track her down and confront her, but I didn't have the mental energy to expend on her or that now. Who else to call? Millicent lived with her obnoxious boyfriend. Coriander lived in a studio (a big one, but still, no privacy). And Vienna . . .

I couldn't call Vienna.

No matter how much I wished I could.

Maybe I could have stuck it out at Nicholas and Jessica's if there were any sign the investigation was progressing. But every time I called Mom and Dad, they hadn't heard anything. The news coverage dwindled from the front page to the occasional online "no news" update. It seemed like it was stalling. No wonder, according to people on Reddit who seemed to have nothing better to do than speculate about the case. Everyone associated with the Aftons is lawyered up to the hilt. There's no way anyone's getting close to them.

It has to be one of them, right? Like u/Looking4TheEnd said, there was no sign of a break-in, and the only people with access to the apartment were either associated with the family or with the company.

I wanted to put my face through the computer screen and shout at them. *If you random people on Reddit know so much, solve it. Solve it so I can get my life back.*

"What was that, Pom?" Nicholas leaned over me. Jessica followed, looking down on me with concern. I'd spoken aloud, it seemed. Their shadows fell over me, making me feel like a little kid again, afraid of monsters in the dark.

Last night, I'd overheard a few scraps of whispered conversation filtered through the crack beneath their bedroom door. While I couldn't confirm for sure, it was pretty obvious they were talking about me. *Spoiled. Layabout. Not enough space here.* Most of it in Nicholas's voice.

"I'm going to get some air." My voice made me sound like I was being strangled.

Being outside in the early spring chill didn't help all that much; it just replaced the falling shadows of Nicholas and Jessica with the shadows of the buildings surrounding me. Even going all the way over to Central Park and sitting on one of the benches overlooking Fifth Avenue wasn't a big help, though that probably had more to do with the flock of pigeons ready to tear each other apart around my feet over some spilled french fries. (To be fair, after days of Jessica's extremely healthy meal prep, I would also draw blood for some fries.)

I hadn't even thought about the murder going unsolved. I hadn't thought about any of it, really, which felt stupid and silly now. I'd thought about it mostly in regard to the threat to myself, first to my life, and then, well, to my *life*. And probably I should have been more upset about the murder of a blood relative going unsolved and the murderer facing no justice, but, well. This wasn't an interview with the press. I didn't have to pretend.

I took a deep breath. Yanked my foot out of the way of a pigeon dive-bomb. Pulled out my phone and pressed the contact.

"Pom, hello!" Andrea said cheerfully into my ear. "Is everything okay?"

"No," I said, and took another deep breath. "Is that room in your son's apartment still open?"

Beside me, feathers flew.

CHAPTER

Five

The next day, I stepped out of Jessica's building with my bag slung over my shoulder, sporty sneakers on my feet, my hair tied up in a tight ponytail. Face scrubbed clean of makeup (except my usual waterproof foundation), plain oversize white T-shirt over a hot pink sports bra. Unless anybody really squinted their eyes at the monogram on my bag, nobody would recognize me.

Which was exactly how I wanted it as I marched east. It was a good thing Andrea had given me the details of my new living situation over the phone, because I hadn't been able to hide the dismay on my face when she told me its location. It was even farther east than Jessica's apartment, which was already too far east for my comfort. Was it even still the Upper East Side that close to the river?

At least it wasn't in Queens. Or worse, New Jersey.

I was already past the elegant buildings of Park Avenue, but now I was really leaving them behind. At the corner of Lexington people spilled over the sidewalk from the underground subway entrance; I sidestepped them and nearly got slammed by an e-bike going the wrong way on this one-way road.

The street grew livelier as I continued east, stores turning into bars and restaurants that almost definitely had sticky floors and laminated menus. I was debating just continuing on east until the river, where I could fall in and drown, but part of the river was technically Queens, and there was no way I was ever going to let my body be found in Queens. So.

Nicholas and Jessica hadn't been all that sad to see me leave. They'd pretended, of course, but that was just courtesy. "I'm always here for you," Nicholas said, punctuated by Jessica chopping something in the background. It was a bigger knife than the one I'd seen her with before. How many knives could one girl have?

Whatever. I stopped in front of the address, checking and double-checking it against the text on my phone. This would work out. It had to. And in a month, when I was telling the other girls about my grand adventure where I thought I'd lost everything but had actually risen from the ashes like a fiery phoenix, Opal could go home alone and puke on her own pillow.

The address was correct, I was unenthused to discover. My new home was in a small, dumpy building, the concrete steps crumbling at the edges. The fire escape crawling down the side of the building was rusty and janky. I shook my head as I gingerly climbed the steps, catching in my peripheral vision something with a long tail skittering away into the shadow. Wonderful.

No doorman, I was unenthused yet not surprised to discover. Before I could buzz Andrea's son with this complicated-looking device, someone cleared their throat behind me. "Excuse me."

I moved to the side as another girl, her hair in a ponytail like mine, unlocked the door and pulled it open. I followed her in past a row of mailboxes set in the wall and through another locked glass door.

The lobby was dim and smelled musty, if you could even call it a lobby; it was more of a wide hallway with a stairway in it. The stairs were covered in tatty carpet, probably where the smell was coming from.

I took a deep breath, squaring my shoulders. I could do this. I could. *Just get in the elevator upstairs and out of public view.* I peered around the side of the stairwell to find only an apartment door. Of course. There was no elevator either.

Up the stairs, then, lugging my bag with me. On the top floor, a slick of sweat beneath my underarms, I knocked on the door of 4A. The last thing I felt like doing was smiling brightly, but I smiled brightly anyway as the door swung open.

The guy who opened the door did not smile brightly in response. In fact, he didn't smile at all. A smile would have added some warmth to the angles of his face: square jaw; high cheekbones; strong brow. His dark eyes smoldered as he said, "It's you."

"It's me!" I chirped. I waited for him to stand aside and let me in, but he didn't move, blocking the narrow doorway with his broad shoulders and long legs, lithe and muscular in the gym shorts he was wearing.

He'd smile now, surely. He was looking for a roommate. Here I was, his roommate. Surely he'd been told to expect me? When he still didn't move, I said, "I'm rather tired after lugging this thing halfway across town and climbing all these stairs, so if you wouldn't mind showing me to my room . . ."

Now he smiled—no, he was grinding his teeth. "You've got to be kidding me," he forced out through them. "*You're* the new roommate my mom found?"

My smile faltered in response. Suddenly the smoldering of his eyes took on a new light. You can smolder with sexiness. You can also smolder with anger. Or annoyance. Or irritation. "She didn't tell you I was coming?"

He ran a hand over his thick brows, strong nose, dark dusting of stubble. "She told me she'd found me a roommate," he said, voice muffled through his hand. He dropped it. "But she wouldn't tell me who it was. I assumed my cousin was coming back to town and they wanted to surprise me. I don't know why."

He *still* didn't move. I pushed my shoulders back and said, in a haughty voice like that of my mom on a bad day, "Well, I'm not your cousin. But your mom sent me here to live, so unless you'd like to take it up with her, please let me in."

His eyes widened, but he did finally move aside. I stepped in, feeling vaguely insulted. It really felt like he didn't want me here, but I didn't understand why. And it wasn't like I could just ask him. That would be rude.

The door didn't open into a main foyer but rather into a combination kitchen and living room: the oven, fridge, and stove sat in a neat line at one end, with a beat-up couch that looked like it had been plucked from the curb across from a crooked TV at the other. The entire room was about the size of my kitchen, which didn't have to share space with any other rooms. I mean, Jessica's apartment hadn't been much bigger, but I hadn't thought I'd actually be living *there* long-term.

I took a deep, soothing breath. *You can survive this, Pom.* I dropped my bag on the floor. It slid a few inches. The floor sat at a slant. Everything was crooked.

Just like my life.

I pasted that bright smile back on my face. "It's quite charming," I said, even though it was nothing of the sort. "Where's my room?"

Suffice it to say that my room was exactly what I'd expected, looking at the rest of the apartment. And the bathroom was shared. I stood in the doorway of the tiny, damp, mildewy room, staring at the litter box on the ground, and tried not to cry.

"What is it?" called my new roommate. It might have been my imagination, but he sounded a little bit . . . smug? "My place not up to your high expectations? Not enough Italian marble and gold plate for you?"

Deep breath, Pom. I turned around, telling myself I was going to deliver a speech on how I was tough and everything and I didn't own anything gold-plated, it was all pure gold, but my eyes fell on something behind him and I immediately forgot what I wanted to say.

It was a cat, something I probably should have expected from the litter box in the bathroom. He had crept out from under the couch, where he had been hiding upon the introduction of someone new and potentially scary, only to emerge once he realized I wasn't a threat.

I knew this because he was *my cat.*

It was impossible, and yet somehow it was true. That blocky square head, the fuzzy black fur, the bright green eyes, the crooked front fang that always protruded from his lip. The tears that sprang to my eyes this time were happy ones. "Squeaky?"

I fell to the floor and upon him, showering him with kisses and love, scratching those spots behind his ears that always made his butt stick up high in the air with delight. I totally forgot someone else was even there until my new roommate cleared his throat behind me. "His name is Meatball, actually."

I suddenly realized my own butt was sticking up in the air like my cat's. I scooted around into a seated position on the floor and pulled Squeaky into my lap, where he relaxed into me with a rusty purr. I didn't even care that, at this angle, I could see the buildup of dust under the couch. Whoever he hired to clean this place was not doing a very good job. "No, it's not. This is Squeaky. How did you—"

"His name is Meatball." My new roommate's voice was loud. "My mom brought him home almost ten years ago. He's been my cat for ten years."

That was when Squeaky had run away. Which was weird. Had my former nanny *stolen* him?

No. She wouldn't do that. Wires must have gotten crossed somewhere. Maybe my parents asked her to take care of him while I was away at college, and she'd thought that meant taking him home, and then my parents had forgotten. That was a plausible explanation. I could go ask my parents if that had been what happened, but something in me didn't want to.

I sniffled, wiping my hand across my face. Bits of black fuzz stuck to my upper lip, making my nose twitch. "That's exactly when my cat disappeared. My parents told me he ran away. So you see . . ." I went to say my new roommate's name, then realized I didn't know it. Which seemed wrong. I should know his name, not just because he was the person I was going to be living with, but because he was the son of someone very important to me. Was it Caleb? Somehow I thought I remembered my nanny talking about someone named Caleb.

"Look, it's fine," said maybe-Caleb, his voice softening. His eyes softened a bit too as I kissed Squeaky's head, buying a little time. "Whatever happened, I'm glad you get to see him again. And you're right, we both live here now, so he can be both of ours. At least for now."

An olive branch. I'd take it. "Thanks, Caleb."

And his face hardened again. "My name's not Caleb." His voice turned frosty. "Caleb is my brother. Did my mom tell you you'd be living with Caleb?" He muttered something indistinguishable under his breath.

Really, Andrea should have told me who I'd be living with. This was *her* fault. "No," I said. "She just said I'd be living with her son. I assumed."

"Well, I'm her other son. What's my name?"

I opened my mouth. Nothing came to mind. I closed it. Again, *her* fault.

Not-Caleb scoffed. "I mean, you only spent all day, every day for what, eleven years? Twelve years? With my mother. Nobody could possibly have expected you to pick up such esoteric information as *the names of her children*."

"Well, I didn't. I'm sorry," I said. "So you can either tell me your name or I can call her and tell you how . . . how unchivalrous you're being."

He rolled his eyes. "Yeah. Sure." But then he said, "My name is Gabe. Short for Gabriel. *Not* Caleb. Can you remember that?"

Perhaps unnerved by our argument, Squeaky hopped off my lap and hightailed it into the bedroom. Not my bedroom, Gabe's bedroom, which kind of stung to see. Gabe's room was his place of safety.

Like it didn't bother me, I stood up and stepped closer to Gabe, tilting my head up. I'd actually stepped a little too close, probably. I could feel the heat radiating off him through his T-shirt as he crossed his arms, glaring down at me. If those dark eyes had been smoldering before, the spark had caught now.

I spoke frostily, trying to tamp it down. "I think I can handle it." This was getting off to a bad start. *Quick, Pom, play the murdered-grandmother card.* "Though my head's been all over the place lately, considering I'm the one who found my grandma dead."

That did the trick. He ran a hand down his face, sighing. "Yes. Sorry. My mom would be pissed about how I'm acting." He shook his head. This close I caught a drift of coffee and soap. "Even though your grandmother's death affected her as much as it did you."

My tears dried up. A surge of curiosity took their place. "What do you mean?" If my grandma's own family wasn't mourning her, surely her employees weren't either. Grandma wasn't nice to us, but she was nicer to us than she was to them. I'd seen her use Rosa, her housekeeper, as a footrest. She'd made her chef—she called him Gordon, though his name was Peter, because if you squinted he looked kind of like Gordon Ramsay—miss his son's middle school graduation to cook for my grandma's book club.

Gabe's hand, now resting on his chest, balled into a fist. "My mom worked for your family for over fifteen years, missing her own children's lives . . . nannying all those little Aftons to adulthood. It was hard, thankless, endless work." Part of me withered hearing the process of raising me described as hard and thankless and endless. "Your grandmother dangled a huge reward in front of her for *years*. Every time my mom was on the verge of leaving, your grandma would suck her back in again with the promise of a free apartment and a massive retirement and provisions for her kids in your grandma's will."

"The will that's been frozen," I said.

A muscle twitched in his jaw. "The will that's been frozen. At least, until they find the killer."

A breeze from the nearby kitchen window rustled my hair. Which was a bad sign, considering the window was currently closed. "They're not going to—" My throat was so dry I couldn't force the words out. I swallowed hard and tried again. My stomach flipped over as they finally came out, because it was a little like I was hearing them for the first time too. "They're not going to find the killer. Whoever killed her was either family or close to the family, protected by money and a hundred lawyers throwing up walls and thorns in front of them."

"The money's all frozen," said Gabe. "How are they paying for these lawyers?"

"Loans, I assume." I depended on my trust fund, but my parents and others who were heavily invested in the business would take out loans against their holdings, then pay the loans back each year with stock earnings and the like. "My parents have money that isn't tied to the business or my grandma, both from other holdings and some money from my mom's family. I assume people like the CFO do too. They'll have to be conservative with them, since obviously they won't get anything else approved if the business doesn't . . . if it never . . ."

I was one of the only ones who didn't, because I'd never diversified. I just took the money that got deposited into my account each month without questioning it or thinking about it, just racked up bills on the credit cards and sent them to my grandmother to pay off, just woke up every day in an apartment that had never really been mine.

And now I was paying for it. Would my parents give me more money eventually? Probably. But right now they were—understandably—tied up in their own stuff, trying to figure themselves out. And whatever they'd be able to give me would pale in comparison to what I was used to. For now, I was on my own.

Which meant . . . "Gabe. Your mom said you might be able to help me get . . . a job?"

His brows furrowed. "I don't know what she told you, but I don't think I'd be able to help you with anything you'd want to do."

"I don't mind starting from the bottom," I said earnestly. My hands clasped themselves together in front of me. "Like, I don't need to head the acquisition of a corporate art collection, you know? I could just advise on what to buy. Or assist with the search."

Gabe looked at me as if I'd plucked a giant cockroach from the floor and handed it to him like a prize hunting trophy. Which hopefully would never be a thing that happened in this apartment. "What are you talking about? Who said anything about an art collection?"

"Well, nobody," I said. "That was just an example. Like, if you need someone to design a new collection for the fall season, I don't need to be the actual designer. I could help out and pick out fabrics or advise on cuts or something."

Now he looked at me like I'd taken a big bite out of that cockroach.

"Pom, I manage a coffee shop while I get my master's degree at night. I'd be hiring you on at the coffee shop."

I furrowed my brow. "Like, to pick out the art collection for its walls?"

"What is it with you and art collections? No. To make coffee."

A tinny ringing started in my ears. The building should probably get that looked at. I pictured mice shimmying up and down the pipes in the walls, their tiny claws tinging against the metal.

It had probably kept me from hearing Gabe right. "What did you say?"

"If I hired you at the coffee shop, you'd be behind the counter, making people's coffees and ringing up their orders," he said. "Putting the baked goods they order in bags. Writing their names on paper cups. You know. The usual things that go on behind the counter at a coffee shop."

I had no idea what usually went on behind the counter at a coffee shop. When I was out and I'd stop at a coffee shop to pick something up, I was usually too focused on my phone to notice what was going on behind the counter. Half the time the person would recognize me when I told them my name and give me my coffee for free, which was great, since I didn't have to deal with getting my card out of that annoying slot in my wallet. I'd just take the cup handed to me and leave without looking back.

Which, thinking about it for the first time, seemed maybe a little bit rude.

"Are you okay?" asked Gabe. I realized I was breathing very fast and very shallowly.

"No," I blurted. I was going to have a heart attack. Or panic attack. One of those.

What had made me think I could do this? I couldn't do this. Not this way.

"I have to go," I said, already moving toward the door.

CHAPTER

Six

'd left my bag behind. My bag containing all of my worldly posses-
sions. Which meant I'd have to go back up there.

But I couldn't think about that now. Not while I paced back and
forth next to the East River, a chilly wind whipping through my hair.
All I knew was that I'd made a huge mistake.

Deep breath in. Deep breath out. Phone to my ear. My mom answered. "Oh, Pom!" she said sprightly, as if her life was just fine and
dandy. Something yelped in the background. I was worried for a second before I remembered she was sharing her friends' beach house
with some spoiled dogs. "How are you? Nicholas said you were moving in with some random man."

If that was the case, shouldn't she sound at least a little worried
about me? "He's not some random man. He's Andrea's son."

"Andrea?"

I ground my teeth. "Andrea, my old nanny. You know. Who spent
every day with me for twelve years?"

"Oh, right. I didn't realize you were still in contact," Mom said
breezily.

"Well, we are," I replied. "Though I don't think I'll be living with
him much longer. That's what I was calling about, actually." Some guy
rattled by me on a skateboard, so close it made me jump. *Chill out,
Pom.* "Is there still room at the Hamptons house? For me?" And
Squeaky, I thought. Surely I could take my old cat. Gabe might have
owned him longer than I had, but he'd been mine first.

My mom cackled in my ear, which made me jump again. "Richard!" she shouted, also in my ear. I heard footsteps thumping through the line, my dad coming to answer her call. "You owe me an hour massage!"

My dad cursed in the background as I said, "What are you talking about?"

Mom's cackle had turned into a chortle by the time she answered. "Your father and I made a bet. I said you would last a night in the real world once you left Nicholas and Jessica's; he said you would last a week."

"She didn't even make it a night," I heard my dad yell. "So you didn't really win."

The wind was slapping my cheeks, making them sting. "Neither of you thought I could do this?"

"Oh, Pom," Mom said. "It's all in good fun."

Was it, though? Because it didn't feel fun. It felt a little bit like they'd each taken turns kicking me in the stomach, actually.

And I couldn't let them feel all victorious about it. "You know, never mind," I said. "I'll be fine. I don't mind the new apartment so much." The words kept spilling out. "You know who's there, right? Not just Andrea's son, but my old cat, Squeaky. Remember? You told me he ran away."

I didn't know what I wanted her to say. Whether I wanted her to apologize for giving my cat away without telling me, for letting me cry myself to sleep for weeks as I missed him, for continuing to lie to me for years.

All I knew, suddenly, was that I didn't want to hear it. So I hung up. I stared at my phone for a few seconds after clicking the red button. Maybe she'd call me back to apologize. Maybe.

Sure enough, as if I'd willed it, my phone began to buzz again. MOM flashed on the screen. I went to pick up, then made myself stop, wait three whole rings to show I wasn't too eager. "Hello?" I said, sounding bored, like my heart wasn't thumping.

Rustling sounds came from the other end. "Hello?" I said again, hopes falling. Of course she wasn't calling to apologize. It was just another butt dial. I should've known, I thought as I hung up. I shouldn't be feeling this disappointed. It wasn't like Mom ever apologized, not even the time when she'd lost a libel lawsuit that required her to admit wrongdoing. Every word had been carefully planned through gritted teeth. *I acknowledge that I was not technically correct when I told multiple news outlets that Gretchen Neiman stole the name and branding of her skin-care line from an entry in my diary. I acknowledge that I do not keep a diary.*

Whatever. *Put her out of your mind, Pom.* I squared my shoulders, drawing in a big breath of salty river air. It had a tinge of murk to it, probably thanks to its border with Queens. If I was going to make a go at this real-world thing, surely I could do it with a better job than working at a coffee shop.

So my next call was to Nicholas. Back when he was working fourteen hours a day it always took him ages to call me back, if he did at all, but now he picked up on the second ring. "Hello?"

"Hey," I said.

"Who is this?"

I rolled my eyes. "It said my name when you picked up, you jerk," I said. And then, just in case it actually hadn't, "It's Pom. Look, I need your help. You've been telling me for years I should get a job or something. Now I want to get a job. Okay?"

"Okay," said Nicholas. His voice was abrupt, like I'd interrupted him in the middle of something. "I think it'll be good for you."

I wasn't sure about that, but whatever. "Can you help me? Maybe give one of your art gallery owner friends or fashion designer buddies a call?"

Nicholas barked a laugh in my ear, which was getting tired of having people laughing in it when its owner wasn't trying to be funny, thank you very much. "Pom, who do you think I am? I don't live downtown, I don't have any artsy connections, and I assume you don't want to work at another hotel or real estate business. Assuming any of them would hire one of us with what's going on. And assuming they'd hire someone who has a totally empty résumé.

"What about your friend Vienna?" he continued. "Doesn't she have a foundation where you can answer phones or something? Or your friends' parents, aren't they all on boards at museums? They can probably get you a job giving tours or ringing things up in the gift shop."

I shuddered, first at the thought of asking Vienna for anything, then at the thought of begging my friends' parents for a job. The word would ripple through our circle, going outward and eventually reaching even the most peripheral members, who would revel in getting to laugh at me. The stain such a job gave me would never fade, not if they all knew about it, and they all would know about it if one of them got it for me. Years later, once this was all over and I was restored to my rightful position, Millicent or Coriander would make a crack about how good I was at answering phones and I'd be able to see them all laughing at me even through the Botox.

And that was assuming any of them would pick up a call from me. My parents were in the Hamptons during the *off-season*, for God's sake. And look at how Opal had responded to me when I asked her to stay over. The only thing worse than them responding and giving me some sort of menial job would be them not responding at all.

Nicholas was still talking. He finished with "Good luck."

"You told me you'd always be there for me," I said, stung by the brusqueness in his tone. "Remember? Like, hours ago?"

"I don't have time for this right now," he said. "Part of being out in the real world is being able to cut it on your own."

"Hypocrite," I said, the sting digging deeper into a bite. "Cut it on my own? Have you ever cut it on your own? You've spent your life working for the family business. You think that's—"

"It'll be good for you," he said, then hung up. I stared down at my phone as it beeped. The empty screen stung even more. What had stuck *that* stick up his butt?

I was still wondering that when Gabe opened the door to me. I'd slunk back to his building with my tail between my legs. At least the sight of Squeaky peering up at me from the couch lifted my spirits a bit.

"You're back," Gabe said, stepping back so that I could step in. Was it my imagination, or did he look faintly impressed?

Bluff, Pom. Don't let him see you sweat. "Of course I'm back," I said, sweeping in and lifting my chin. If I couldn't feel powerful, at least I'd look it. "I was just going for a walk. Checking out the new neighborhood. What, did you think I'd gone for good?"

"Kind of," Gabe said, shutting the door behind me. I watched as he hustled around me and to the kitchen area, where something was hissing and spitting on the stove. And smelling good too. I wandered in that direction and saw that it was mushrooms and zucchini browning in a pan. Behind it burbled a pot of boiling water.

"What are you making?"

"Pasta," he said, somehow dumping a spoonful of chopped garlic into the pan of vegetables and a bunch of dried pasta into the boiling water at the same time.

I opened my mouth, ready to thank him for making us food though unfortunately I was gluten-free right now and couldn't eat it . . . but the garlic smelled so good that my stomach growled, and I kind of forgot about the whole gluten-free thing. "Yum," I said. "I can't wait."

He glanced over his shoulder at me, that crease between his eyebrows back. He should be careful with that—he was going to get wrinkles. "I didn't really plan—" And then he sighed. "You know what, okay. New start. Let's eat together."

New start, I told myself as I watched him finish up his cooking and ladle the finished pasta on mismatched porcelain plates. This would be a new start for me too. I was stuck here, maybe forever. I might as well make the best of it.

A sentiment that lasted until I forked the first bite of pasta into my mouth, actually moaned out loud, and didn't even care that I should be embarrassed for it. "This is literally the best thing I've ever put in my mouth since your mom stopped cooking for me," I said. "What's even in here?"

A pleased expression ironed out that eyebrow crease, which accentuated the long, dark lashes around his eyes. "It's just pasta with mushrooms and zucchini," he said. "What makes it good is all the garlic and cream and Parmesan."

Oh. I could practically hear my mom tutting at me. But I was mad at her right now, so I pushed her voice away and took another big bite of the pasta.

"I'm glad you like it. My mom taught me how to cook. She didn't teach you?" Gabe said, those long-lashed eyes settling on my lips for a moment, watching me chew. Then he blinked, shaking his head just a moment, like he was clearing his eyes. "By the way, Pom. I was thinking about what you were saying earlier. You know, about your grandmother's killer. About how they'll go free."

I swallowed hard, feeling the pasta fall like a rock into my stomach. "Wow, subject change." I'd rather talk about his mom teaching me how to cook, which she'd tried. We'd gotten in a few lessons, mostly baking-related: simple things like brownies, cookies, easy cakes. My mom hadn't approved. When I asked her if I could keep trying even after Andrea left, she'd said dismissively, *It's for the best. You don't want to keep eating things like that anyway. You won't fit into sample sizes anymore.*

"Sorry," he said, but he didn't change it back. "It's just that, how can you accept it? That your grandma won't get justice? That my mom will never get what she deserves, and the killer won't either?"

I couldn't think of it like that. I shook my head, flattening my lips into a grim line. "Because there's nothing I can do about it. The police won't be able to get close enough to my family. If someone had even the slightest chance of solving the murder, they would need to be someone who could slide in there and ask questions and dig around without anyone getting suspicious."

"I was thinking about that." Gabe's eyes narrowed. "That's someone like you."

A laugh burst from my mouth, thankfully not spraying any pasta with it. He leaned back as if it had. "What? No! It couldn't be me." It had to be someone *like* me, was what I meant. But someone who was smarter, and better at things than I was. Imagine me investigating a murder? My grandma would laugh. My parents would laugh and probably place bets on whether I'd wind up murdered too. Nicholas would laugh. Jessica wouldn't laugh, but only because she was too polite.

"Why not?" He leaned forward again. This close, I could smell him—coffee and soap—and could pinpoint the specific soap to sandal-wood and lemon. "I really want to help my mom. I could help. I mean, we're stuck here together already."

I allowed myself to entertain the idea for a moment. Me and Gabe, diving into the darkness side by side. The smell of sandalwood and lemon in my nose as I cry, "That's it! That's the killer!" The feeling of triumph. I imagined it would feel good.

But, as quickly as it had come, the idea flitted off and popped like a bubble. "You have many strengths," I could practically hear my mom say. "But this isn't one of them." I'd heard it so many times before. Curiously, nobody ever specified what those "many strengths" actually were.

I shook my head and watched Gabe's face fall. Better it fall now than fall later, when he realized I couldn't ever possibly do something that big. "It's just not a good idea," I said. I mean, I was always surprised by the twists on *Here to Slay*. Surely, if I was good at investigating, I'd be able to see them coming. "But I was thinking about what you said about the job. You know, at the coffee shop. Is that still on the table?"

There was that faintly impressed look again. "Sure, if you think you can handle it."

"I can handle it," I said, projecting confidence. This would be an adventure. A grand adventure I could write into my memoir when I was old, after this was all fixed. Maybe it would even be fun.

CHAPTER

Seven

I t was not fun.

The next morning, I was wearing a dark green apron behind the counter of a small, bright coffee shop. The main space of the café, which was scattered with clean wooden tables and a chalkboard wall with the menu scrawled on it, smelled strongly of coffee beans and hot milk and baked blueberry muffins, which were currently being loaded into the glass-front counter. I guess I knew now where Gabe got his coffee scent from.

I was not doing the loading. I was standing, my arms wrapped around myself, trying to control the panic that came from everything in my life moving so fast. A panic that burst out of me when Gabe, also wearing a dark green apron, handed me something that stabbed my finger. "Ouch!"

"Sorry. Why did you grab the pin side?" Gabe cast me a bemused look. I looked down to find that the pin hadn't pierced the skin and that it belonged to a plastic tag crying out that my name was POMONA. "You're welcome to add pronouns if you want to."

My breath was suddenly short in my chest, though maybe it wasn't sudden; maybe it had been that way for a week and this was just the first I was noticing it. "Do I have to wear this?"

"We all wear name tags," Gabe said, waving his arm around as if to gesture at invisible people. As the manager, he was the first one in at this ungodly early hour. As the manager's pity tagalong who apparently could not be trusted to get here safely by myself, I was second.

(To be fair, I would also not trust myself to get here safely on the subway, which I'd previously mainly used for photo ops or high school party games, when we'd dare each other to take the train to our next locale instead of a car.)

Anyway, I didn't want to identify myself, but I fastened the badge onto my stiff polyester apron anyway. I felt smaller with it on my chest, like the eyes of the whole world were watching me, waiting to see how I'd mess up, their phones at the ready to capture it. This whole thing was supposed to be anonymous. My friends were never supposed to know about it.

The door swung open and two other workers streamed in. Both young, probably college-aged, and both feminine-presenting. They had their heads down, tying on their aprons, but when they raised them, their eyes indeed immediately fell on me. Then down to my name tag. Then up to my face.

"Oh my God," said one, whose name tag said SAGE, THEY/THEM. "Pomona? Like, Pom Afton?"

The other—ELLIE, SHE/HER—snorted with laughter. "Are you kidding? Why would Pom Afton be working in a coffee shop? She doesn't even look like her." But her eyes landed on my face, crawled over it like flies, tiny legs poking and crawling over my distinctive nose and real lashes and into my pores.

"Because of the scandal?" Sage said. "Haven't you heard about it?" And their eyes joined Ellie's, and they were everywhere, and I felt like I might throw up. I spun and rushed into the back, which somehow I'd expected to be a big, stainless-steel kitchen but was actually a small cramped break room stuffed with shelves and a few chairs and a microwave that emitted the odor of popcorn.

I took a deep breath. It didn't make me feel better. It just made me want popcorn.

The door opened after me and Gabe stepped in. His expression was somber. "Sorry about that," he said. "I'll talk to them."

I shook my head. "It doesn't matter. I can't do this." I couldn't. I really couldn't. I couldn't work the complicated-looking machines and deal with everybody's eyes on me, staring at me without my makeup and snickering behind their hands about how far I'd fallen, and I couldn't make small talk with these people who didn't know me but thought they did even though they'd never even seen me without falsies, and—

Gabe handed me another badge. This time I didn't grab it by the pin end. I turned it over in my hand and studied it. This one said RACHEL. He said, "Rachel quit a few days ago. I haven't gotten rid of her name badge yet. Do you want to wear this one instead?"

The tension in my shoulders loosened as I unpinned the POMONA badge and tossed it onto the table like it had stung me, which it kind of had, and put on the new one. Rachel. I whispered the name to myself, tested out how it felt on my lips and tongue. Not bad. "Do you have a hat?"

A few minutes later, I was back out in front, introducing myself to Sage and Ellie. With no makeup on my face, my hair stuffed up into this green baseball cap, and my badge proclaiming me Rachel, all talk of me being Pom Afton dissipated like the milk on top of a cappuccino. "Sorry, I hadn't realized I'd grabbed the wrong name tag," I said breezily. "I'm Rachel. Rachel Sparks. I work here because I need money for handbags and rent."

I thought I'd done a convincing-enough representation of a normal coffee shop worker, but the way Sage and Ellie looked at me through slightly narrowed eyes made me quail. But it didn't matter. I was Rachel Sparks now. Those eyes couldn't hurt me.

And then they shrugged. "Okay. Nice to meet you, Rachel."

I had no idea if they actually believed me, but it didn't seem to matter either way. They weren't going to press it if they weren't absolutely, positively sure, and hopefully that meant they wouldn't spread the word. People saw what they wanted to see. They didn't like to look too hard, or think too hard. They liked to do what was easiest.

Which, as it turned out, did not include working at a coffee shop. After a slight disaster with the milk-steaming machine that left me with a shiny red welt on my forearm, I was banished to the register, which beeped alarmingly every time I pressed something. My heart hammered in my throat with the stress, with the beeping and the line of people shifting impatiently before me and the realization that I had no idea what I was doing. I glanced behind me, beseeching Gabe for help, but he was in the back somewhere doing businessy things. Ellie and Sage were both flipping levers and filling cups. I didn't want to distract them and give them burns too.

Deep breath. *You can do this, Rachel.* Maybe Pom couldn't, but Rachel certainly could. I thrust my shoulders back, fixing a winning smile on my face.

The guy at the front of the line did not look impressed. After waiting a beat—was I supposed to say something?—he grunted, "Americano, two shots."

I did not know what that was. All the coffee drinks I ordered from shops like these had various types of syrup involved and consisted of no fewer than five words. But it couldn't be that hard to punch it into the register. Dizziness swept over me as I looked at the screen, at all the buttons and words and lights flashing everywhere. All I had to do was input the order. It couldn't be that hard.

The guy sighed.

Pressure rose in my throat. So much pressure. When was the last time I'd done something like this? Something with actual consequences? I mean, it wasn't like I was a doctor scrubbing up for surgery. If I got this wrong, nobody would die. But Gabe could get in trouble. This guy could yell at me.

"Any day now," said the guy.

Focus. I jabbed at the button that said Americano, sweat prickling down the back of my exposed neck, and the total popped up. "Four ninety-five."

He frowned at me. "Are you sure? With the double shots it's supposed to be two dollars more."

The sweat was now trickling down my neck, pooling around my bra straps. Beside me Ellie popped over, hopefully unable to smell me over the coffee. "Yeah, it's supposed to be two dollars more."

"What do I press?"

The line of people behind the guy were shifting and sighing, checking their phones and looking over their shoulders. One actually stepped out of line and left. I hoped Gabe hadn't seen. I was already disappointing him. Disappointing everyone.

"Here." Ellie walked me through it quickly, jabbing the buttons so fast I could hardly tell which ones she'd pressed. In the meantime Sage was making the coffee, and right as the guy pulled his card away, they were passing the warm cup to me.

I handed it to the guy, trying as hard as I could to muster up a smile. "Here you go. Two shots."

He nodded and took it, slipping his card into his pocket as he left. No thank you? After all I'd been through? I glared after him. "You're welcome!" That nagging thought returned to me, though. Had I ever said thank you to a coffee shop worker?

But the next person was already stepping up, and I had to throw myself back into the whirlwind . . .

Something like seventeen hours later, Gabe materialized at my shoulder, as in one second I was looking at empty air, the next I looked back and there he was. I took a deep breath, somehow soothed by the notes of sandalwood floating beneath the strong coffee scent. "Is the day over?"

The corner of his lip just barely turned up. "No, it's time for your break. You can grab a pastry from the case if you want."

Seamlessly, Gabe stepped in front of me and took control of the register. It was like a weight lifted off my shoulders as I stepped away and grabbed the first thing I saw behind the counter. Some kind of Danish. I hadn't realized it until now, but I was practically hollow with hunger—I would literally eat one of the cardboard coffee cups I'd been handing out. I crammed the Danish in my mouth.

And immediately wanted to spit it out again. It was cold and stale and tasted like wet paper. "This is terrible," I said through pastry.

Gabe didn't even stop moving. "If you're going to insult the merchandise, please do so in the back room, where customers can't hear you."

I shriveled under the disappointment as I walked away. But it was nothing compared to the shriveled husk I felt like at the end of the day, after I'd been running from case to machine to register for hours. My feet throbbed like somebody had been chewing on them (did once at a massage parlor, do not recommend). Sweat soaked my shirt and even the hideous apron. My hat was still crammed around my ears, keeping anyone from recognizing me but also slowly steaming me pink and soft. The wet newspaper Danish had left remnants in my mouth. The aftertaste reminded me of cough syrup.

I sat on a stool in the customer area as Gabe cleaned around me. I couldn't bear to move anymore, and he was kind enough not to make me (though he did make me lift my feet when he came around with the mop, which, rude). He asked me, "So how was your trial by fire? Do you feel ready to do it all again tomorrow?"

Something within me snapped at that moment, clean in half, a moment of resolution. This could not be my life. I could not do this every day for the next week, let alone the next year. I couldn't do it. I just couldn't.

I turned to Gabe, lifting my chin, projecting fierceness, a model out to trip her rival on the runway (which Doe had used as evidence on *Here to Slay* about who wanted Danica dead, but I'd tried to trip plenty of people I didn't want to kill; usually I ended up chickening out because I felt too bad, though). "Okay."

He stopped mopping, propping it on the floor and leaning on the top. His white T-shirt lifted, exposing a slice of firm tan hip. My eyes focused on it, lifting only when he said, "Okay, you're ready to hop back on that register?"

I couldn't stop the shudder running through me. "God, no. I'm ready to do whatever it takes so that I'll never have to do that again."

"Meaning?"

That slice of hip was *really* distracting. When had my eyes fallen back down? I raised them again, meeting his with something like a click. "Let's solve a murder."

CHAPTER

Eight

So the thing about deciding that you're ready to solve a murder is that the decision really doesn't give you any actual knowledge about how to solve a murder. The only crime I had experience with was tax evasion, and I didn't think you could solve a murder by snooping through a bunch of numbers. "I kind of hoped you'd know what we're doing," I told Gabe as we sat side by side on his sad beat-up couch, a notebook and pen before him and the Notes app open on my phone in my hand. "Considering you're in grad school and all."

I wasn't looking at him, but I could practically hear the eyebrow wrinkle in his voice. "Pom, I'm in grad school to become a teacher."

Honestly, that threw me a bit. I gazed at him through newly curious eyes. I'd never met a teacher before. I mean, obviously I'd met a teacher before—I'd gone to school (our claim to fame was that they'd based *Gossip Girl* on us). But I didn't know any teachers who were my peers. None of my friends had become teachers. "Really? Why?"

He scratched the back of his head with the hand holding the pen. "Because I want to help kids the way my teachers helped me."

That was very sweet. "How long is teacher school? Aren't you, like, my age?"

"I'm twenty-eight," Gabe said. His hand with the pen fell back to his lap, dotting his jeans. "It took me a couple extra years to graduate from CUNY, and then I took a break for another couple years to fig-ure out exactly what I wanted to do and save money for tuition. Do you think that all grad school programs teach you how to solve a murder?"

"Of course not." I'd kind of hoped he was in grad school for something relevant. Criminology, or something. That would've been convenient. "But going to grad school means you're smart." I made myself laugh. The back of my neck itched with the effort. "*One* of us should be smart if we're going to do this."

"Going to grad school does not mean I'm any smarter than some-one who didn't go to grad school," he said. "Have you tried googling 'how to solve a murder'?"

"No." I googled "how to solve a murder." It was not helpful. "What about true crime? Do you listen to any helpful podcasts or anything?"

"No, I find them too morbid. Do you?"

"Yeah, sometimes," I said, but it wasn't like I could email Doe for help—once I'd emailed her to ask if she was including me in the pit of vipers, and she hadn't even responded—and she'd started off with a bunch of clues in easy reach, anyway. Not like us.

"My brother, Caleb, is a detective, but it's not like that's helped either," Gabe said.

My mouth dropped open. "What do you mean, it hasn't helped? Go call him and ask him how to solve a murder!"

He snorted. "If I did that, he'd immediately ask me why, then call our mom and have me shut down. He won't be any help. Besides, he's in a totally different department, and it's not like he can give me any insider information on the case. It's all confidential. Don't you have an assigned police officer you can call or something?"

"I don't think so," I said. "The last I heard from the police is that they tried getting DNA off the wineglasses left on the table and didn't find anything usable, and that was ages ago. There's the guy who in-terrogated me, but it's not like he gave me any tips on how to do it my-self. And if I wanted to get someone else's info, I'd have to get it from my parents. And they'd probably think I knew something and was rat-ting somebody out." I sighed. "No, we're on our own."

"Okay," he said. "Well, we know that the person who did it is probably someone in your circle, right? Someone with access to her apartment. So why don't we make a list of people we think might have done it? We can start talking to them and narrowing it down."

"Based on what, gut feelings?" I'd never been able to trust my gut. Even after I started eating gluten-free. My gut never seemed to have any better ideas on what to do than my head did.

"Maybe. Or alibis. Or motives. I don't know. We have to start somewhere."

Neither of us could agree on who should be the keeper of the list, so we both made lists, me on my phone and Gabe in his notebook. After an hour or so of debate, my list read like this:

1. Fred—company CFO, was going to see Grandma the day she died with some secret mission, looked nervous and sweaty (is always a little sweaty though???)

2. Rosa—Grandma's housekeeper who hated Grandma (can't blame her, Grandma sometimes made her stay awake all night to see if Grandma talked in her sleep and said anything genius), had access, maybe finally snapped???

3. Dad/Mom—I disagree but Gabe said we had to include them because maybe Dad was sick of waiting for Grandma to die so that he could take over the company

4. Farrah/Jordan—Cannot picture my cousins killing anyone, but it is awfully convenient/suspicious for them to turn up in town right before their estranged relative is murdered

5. Nicholas—same as Mom/Dad, except I could potentially picture Nicholas killing someone (probably me if I took too long in the shower one more time)

I sat back and grimaced at it. A few notifications popped up on the screen, but I swiped them away without reading them. "This sucks."

"I know," said Gabe. "I'm sorry. It can't be easy to have your family members on a list like this."

I grimaced harder, then pulled back. I could practically hear my mom: *Wrinkles, Pom.* "No, I'm not talking about that. I'm talking about the list. It's useless! I was kind of hoping listing out all our options would give us more clarity on where to start, but I can't see any of these people as a killer."

"If you could see who was a killer, it would make solving a murder much easier."

I tapped the side of his head. His hair was softer and silkier than I thought it would be. "See, you are smart."

"Whatever you say." But he looked pleased. "We have to start somewhere, right? Who's the easiest person to get time with on this list?"

Probably Nicholas, but I didn't particularly want to see him after the way he'd snubbed me, and then my parents, but I didn't particularly want to see them either. What if they found out what I was trying to do? How many bets would they make on me? "Farrah and Jordan probably blocked me, and I have no idea how to reach Rosa either," I said. "But I can try Fred. I'm not sure if he'll pick up."

Fred picked up on the first ring. "Pomona!" he cried into my ear. I cringed, lowering the phone and putting it on speaker. "How are you? Do you realize you're the first person from your family I've heard from since . . . well, since the tragic incident that left us all jobless?"

"Wow, I can't believe it." I totally could believe it. Afton Hotels wasn't a family company in that all of its employees became family. It was a family company in that the family was in charge and nobody else mattered.

Which, come to think of it, was motivation. Fred had been at Afton Hotels for . . . like, longer than I'd been alive. And yet he'd never be able to advance higher than his current position. In fact, Nicholas, something like forty years his junior and way less experienced, held a higher position than him solely because of his last name. That had to grate on a man.

Fred continued, "I don't blame any of you, of course. I hope you
didn't take it that way. I know you're all grieving your grandmother."

"Yeah, that's definitely it," I said as earnestly as I could. "But you
know, just because we're family doesn't mean our grief is greater than
yours. You knew her for a long time, right?"

"I was the first employee your grandparents hired almost fifty
years ago," he said.

I glanced over at Gabe, mouthing exaggeratedly, *There's the motive.* I expected Gabe to snap his fingers, maybe nod sagely. Instead
he just wrinkled his forehead and mouthed, *What?*

Whatever. It didn't matter. "Let's get coffee and talk about her," I
said, which, yes, was technically what I wanted to do. "I want to make
sure you're okay."

With most people I wouldn't go all the way in on the obvious pity,
but I knew Fred well enough to have an idea that the strategy would
work. "I'd love to, Pom," he said. "How about tomorrow afternoon?"

Gabe was mouthing something else at me now, but he'd been so
bad at reading my own lips that I purposefully ignored him. "Three
o'clock?" I asked, so Fred couldn't possibly interpret this as me wanting to have a meal with him. He affirmed, and I quickly named a coffee
shop I'd passed on my way here so that I wouldn't have to go all the
way to where Fred lived. Wherever that was. He didn't strike me as
the Upper East Side type, and now that I didn't have a driver anymore
or money to afford car service, I was not eager to adventure too far
on the subway.

Gabe was staring at me as I hung up, feeling very pleased with
myself. "There we go," I said. "Should we come up with questions
we want to ask him, or should we just wing it so that it doesn't feel
forced?"

"Pom, I have a shift tomorrow afternoon," he said. "And you do
too. I thought we'd consult with each other before picking a date and
time."

Well, that wasn't my fault. He should've told me. If he had told me, he should've made sure I noted it down somewhere in my phone. "What's more important, getting people coffee or solving a murder?"

He let out a long, low breath, eyes turning up to the ceiling as if asking a higher power for strength. I knew this because his mother had frequently done the same thing when I was growing up, only she'd mutter *Ay, dios mío* under her breath. It would have been funny to see the commonality, if Andrea hadn't only done it when I'd done something that tested her patience.

"We can call out sick this one time, right?" I said. It really shouldn't be that big a deal. That small coffee shop didn't actually need four people behind the counter. We'd just gotten in each other's way. Well, it had been mostly me getting in other people's way, but that wasn't relevant.

He sighed. Something creaked in the walls, as if the apartment were listening to him. "Fine. I'll ask Ellie if she can cover me. But in the future, Pom, we've got to consult better if you want me along for the ride. I've got work at the coffee shop, plus school at night, plus my volunteer work."

"You have school at night? It's night right now."

"It's mostly virtual," he said. "And most of the classes are independent study at this stage. But it's still a lot."

"I'm sure," I said. I was not. Every time I let my schoolwork at college get a little bit away from me, like when I decided to go to Paris for Fashion Week instead of studying for my midterms, a call from my mom (and probably a nice check) took care of it. If I ever fell, there was a cushion waiting for me on the floor. Someone was always there to scoop me up and kiss any bruise.

Until now. Now, who knew what lurked beneath? A pit of spikes? Hot coals?

"Are you okay?" Gabe asked. "You look like you've got a headache."

My entire life right now was a headache, but I wasn't going to let him see that. Maybe we'd get lucky tomorrow and Fred would immediately confess to the murder, which naturally I would be recording on my phone and could send right away to the police and they'd be so grateful for my hard work that they wouldn't just reinstate all my credit cards and my trust fund, but they'd give a press conference singing all my praises, one that would go viral all over social media and rub Vienna's and Opal's and Nicholas's and Jessica's and everyone's faces in how good and competent I was.

"I'll be fine," I said. "Don't worry about me. Let's worry about what we're going to ask Fred tomorrow." Because, if we were lucky, that would be the end of this investigation.

Nine

W e were not lucky.

Upon arrival at the coffee shop, ten minutes late to ensure I wouldn't have to waste any time waiting around for Fred to get here, he leaped up from his chair to greet me. Then winced in pain, because if my grandparents hired him fifty years ago, he had to be in his seventies, or at least his late sixties. "Pom! It's wonderful to see you."

I sat at the table he'd selected, with my back to the door, and let Gabe go order me a drink. This coffee shop wasn't much more upscale than the one Gabe—and I guess *I*—worked in. A menu scrawled on a chalkboard wall, funky paintings by local artists decorating the walls, a cacophony of buzzing and hissing behind the counter, both from the machines making drinks and the two guys working there, who were glaring at and bumping into each other in a way that said either bad breakup or one had murdered the other's parents and vowed revenge. Relatable.

I figured I'd use the time while Gabe was in line to soften Fred up with memories of happier days. "It's really good to see you, too," I said, giving him a gentle, demure smile. "It feels like it was just yesterday when you were sneaking me hard candies under the table at board meetings."

They'd been cinnamon, which had been way too spicy, and literally dusty. The candies had made up part of a game I'd played with Farrah and Jordan and a few other board members' children or grandchildren—Nicholas had been too dignified, obviously—to see how much stuff we could collect from all the old people talking about business.

As I'd hoped, Fred's face melted into a nostalgic smile. "We were opening hotels in Monte Carlo and Tulum and Toronto. What an exciting time."

"Unlike recently," I said. I had no idea if that was true, but if it was, it might have something to do with his last-minute meeting with my grandma.

His smile only stiffened a bit. "Unlike recently."

He didn't go on. He would need more buttering up, then, to get him talking about things he probably shouldn't be talking about. "Right," I said, nodding. "Well, if the business was getting stressful, it must be at least a little bit nice to have some time off now, right? With your . . . family?" I thought he had a family. I hoped he had a family. There had definitely been at least one executive in the business who lived in a town house with a passel of ferrets. Grandpa always said it wasn't true, but I knew it was. I could smell it. "I bet they want you to retire after all these years!"

Fred heaved a sigh. "Don't you know it," he said. "Marjorie's always after me to retire. 'What's the use of all that money if you never have time to spend it?' 'Can't we move to Florida?'" He leaned in so that I could smell his everything-bagel breath. "Never move to Florida, Pom. It's all alligators and old people."

"Grandma would have fit right in, then," I said. "Haven't you ever seen those teeth of hers rip someone to shreds?"

He laughed. He actually laughed with his mouth open, which meant I could see the poppy seeds stuck between his teeth. "She was a bit of a metaphorical alligator, that woman. I think we've all been on the receiving end of those teeth. I certainly was. Just the day before she died, I . . ."

He trailed off, but now I had the thread. I leaned in myself, so close I could've kissed him if I wanted to. (I would rather have kissed an alligator, and not the metaphorical kind.) "The day before she died? That was the morning I saw you in the lobby, right?" I made my brow wrinkle in a sympathetic way, which I couldn't have done if I'd started my mom's recommended preventative Botox regimen. If this sympathetic forehead wrinkle ended up being the key to cracking this entire case, I couldn't wait to rub my mom's (admittedly wrinkle-free) face in it. "What did she say to you?"

Gabe chose this moment to pop back up at our table, his fists full of paper coffee cups. "They're so disorganized back there. Whoever's managing it needs to take a firmer hand." He set the coffees down on the table. The scent of lavender drifted up from mine. Millicent and Coriander both recently had posted shots of their own lavender lattes—apparently they'd become the hot new thing sometime during my fall from grace—so I'd wanted to give it a try, but it smelled like my grandma's foot cream.

That could be a natural segue back into our previous topic. I parroted my thoughts, which made Fred laugh again. I didn't just see poppy seeds this time: my eyeballs got sesame seeds in molars. Score. I continued, "So, what you were saying before about her . . ."

Gabe's chair screeched against the concrete floor as he sat down. Both Fred and I winced. "Sorry about that," Gabe said, then stuck out his hand. "I realized I never got to introduce myself. I'm Gabe. Pom's—"

"Friend," I interrupted, right as he said, "Partner."

"He means partner in a friendlike way," I said hastily. "Not in any investigative sort of way, because that would be weird." Maybe I should've just let him go work his shift while I did this on my own. It seemed like I'd been doing better before he showed up. "Anyway. What you were saying . . ."

Fred shot Gabe a dubious glance. "Are you sure you want to talk about this here? In front of your friend?"

Maybe I should send Gabe away again. For sugar, or milk, or literally anything to water down the strong taste of soap in my coffee.

No, I told myself. *He's here for a reason. You need him to figure this out. You can't do this on your own.*

I smoothed out the sympathetic wrinkle and propped my chin on my hand. "Oh, Gabe's a very close friend. You know how it is. I tell him everything."

Fred raised his eyebrows, then gave me a knowing nod. "I see how it is. Kids these days. You date, but you don't want to call it dating."

This time, Gabe said, "No," as I said, "Yes." I glared at him. He glared back.

He lowered his eyes, which meant I won the staring contest and the right to speak next. "We're totally dating," I said, sighing and fluttering my lashes. I assumed it wouldn't have as much of an effect as the move did when I had my falsies on, but it would do the job well enough. In his eyes I was now young and shy, innocent and sweet. "Why do men have such trouble talking about their feelings?" Fred was nodding, as if he weren't one of those men. "Maybe you can give him tips. You were just going to talk about what happened the day before my grandma died, right? That must have been so hard."

This time, Gabe blessedly kept his mouth shut. Fred said, "Thank you for acknowledging that, Pom. It means a lot. I've known your grandma and grandpa longer than I haven't known them. I watched your dad grow up. I feel like we're family, almost."

"I feel that way, too," I lied.

Fred's face softened into such a delighted expression—so happy to hear those words from me—that for a moment I felt like I hadn't lied. I wasn't sure if any member of my actual family had ever felt so much joy upon me saying *anything*.

But then it darkened. "You're the only one, then. That's what we were arguing about. I'm sure you knew about the troubles."

"There are so many troubles in our lives," I said, turning away from Gabe's skeptical expression. "Which one are you referring to, specifically?"

"The ones with the business, of course," he said. "That's what I was originally going to see your grandmother about that morning. We'd just gotten word that creditors were going to start trying to fore-close upon the San Francisco location, and construction upon the newest spot in London had stalled." A storm crossed over his face, hooding his eyes and flaring his nostrils. "But the discussion quickly turned into something else."

"Like what?" Gabe jumped in, maybe to feel useful. I tensed up for a moment, hoping he hadn't ruined my careful softening of the old man, but Fred had already fallen over the edge of sharing.

"Pom, you know I care deeply about your father and about Nicholas. About all of you," Fred said. "But as of late, your grandmother had been giving more of the business operations over to your father to prepare him for her inevitable . . . well. And, to be blunt, he wasn't up to the task."

I should probably have felt betrayed at this admission, but I didn't feel any special loyalty toward my father's business skills. If anything, I felt a grim kind of camaraderie. *At least I'm not the only one people look down on.*

"So I broached the subject to your grandmother about how maybe I could step up and take more of a role," Fred continued. "I've been with the business longer than anyone else, and to be blunt, again, I know what I'm doing. I'm very good at this job. But your grandmother sneered at me. Asked me who I thought I was. If I thought my last name was Afton. 'This is as high as you go,' she said. All these years of work, and this is what I got?"

I studied his expression. He looked upset. Aggrieved. Betrayed. How would a killer look? Probably furious. Maybe a little bit satisfied, because he'd gotten his revenge.

I didn't think Fred was a killer.

Which wasn't all that surprising. I mean, he was an old man. It wouldn't take a lot of strength to overpower an elderly woman too short to go on many roller coasters, but she probably would've been able to put up more of a fight against someone as frail as he was.

That didn't mean he didn't know something, though. "Did she say anything while you were up there? Anything that sounds suspicious with what happened to her later?"

"I told the police everything I could," Fred said immediately. "I wasn't there for long, and most of it was her lecturing me and then throwing me out. There was only one thing that struck me."

He paused. Gabe and I both waited, our coffees cooling on the table between us. Mine probably tasted even more like liquid soap now, but I reached out to take a long sip, just in case anyone who recognized me might be snapping a picture. Had to make sure I was staying current in the eyes of the public.

Fred said, "She went on for quite a while. But one thing she said that stuck with me is that me 'trying to overthrow the company' was too much to handle in addition to that 'young woman threatening her.' I didn't think to ask her about it, given everything else going on. I probably wouldn't have thought twice about it if it weren't for . . . well, what happened later." His pause was heavy in the air. "Do you know who that young woman could have been?"

Gabe gave me a significant look. "If someone had been threatening her right before her murder . . ."

He didn't have to spell it out for me. I wasn't *that* stupid. "She didn't give any indication who this person might be?"

Fred shook his head. "Unfortunately not. I'm sorry I can't be of more help." And he actually looked sorry.

Impulsively, I said, "You would've been a great CEO, you know."

I wasn't sure whether I wanted him to give me a hug or not. But it didn't matter, because Gabe immediately ruined the moment by saying, "What did you end up doing after your meeting? Like, that night?"

Fred stiffened in his seat. "What are you implying?"

"He's not implying anything," I said, but it was too late. Gabe was speaking again.

"But, well . . . the two of you had just argued, and then she was murdered. It can't be that surprising that people might think—"

"Might think what, exactly?" Fred was already standing up, his chest puffed out like a bird preparing to fight. "Is that why you asked me here? Because you thought I might have killed her?"

"I definitely do not think that," I said hastily, standing too and shooting a sharp look at Gabe. "I think there might have been a misunderstanding—"

"I should have figured. Marjorie said something was amiss when you wanted to meet with me. None of you have ever given me the time of day; why should now be any different?" His lips curled with disgust. "Is this guy even your boyfriend, or is he an undercover cop?"

"He's not an undercover cop," I said meekly, shrinking back in my seat. I waited for Fred to rage at me, tell me what a bad person I was.

But he only shook his head, and, somehow, that look of disappointment hit harder than the reaming I would've gotten from my parents. "I don't care if it means I've lost my job. I hope you Aftons lose everything." He tossed a twenty onto the table. "That's for my coffee. Keep the change. You need it more than I do."

It was amazing that a man in an ill-fitting pair of khakis and a blazer that pouched open in front could manage to sweep away, but he did. Fred swept out of the coffee shop with his shiny head held high, leaving me and Gabe staring after him.

When I finally turned my head away from the door through which Fred had made his dramatic exit, it felt like breaking a spell. That sick feeling left by Fred's disappointment vanished. What replaced it wasn't quite fury, but it was definitely more than annoyance. "What was that?"

"What was what?" Gabe spread his hands before him, appearing baffled. Which only made my anger heat up a notch on the thermometer.

"I had him spilling, and you barged in and ruined it."

His lips flattened into a thin line. "I thought we were playing good cop, bad cop. You were the one softening him up, and I was the one swooping in for the kill."

That was news to me. "We weren't playing cops at all! What the fuck, Gabe? Is that how you're going to talk to your future students? Just, like, telling them you think they cheated on a test or, I don't know, killed someone very important to them without literally *any* evidence? Because that's going to make you a terrible teacher."

It wasn't just his lips that flattened this time. It was his entire face. It was like a door closed over it, shutting any hint of emotion down. "Wow. Okay."

Maybe I'd gone too far. Pulled a Gabe, if you will. "I shouldn't have said that," I said hastily. Somehow I'd known exactly what to say with Fred, exactly how to pull all of his little strings to make him dance, and here? Nope. "I'm sure you'll be a great teacher. And we got some good information from Fred. We can follow up on the young woman who was supposedly threatening my—"

"I think I'm going to go for a walk." His lips barely moved as he spoke. "Maybe this whole thing was a bad idea."

He moved to go, but I stepped in his way. "What do you mean, this whole thing?"

"This . . . investigation. This living situation. All of it." He put his hands firmly on my shoulders, and for just a moment, I got the bizarre thought that he was going to kiss me.

But he only used his strong grip to move me gently to the side and step past me. "I'm going. You've got your keys, right?"

I nodded, and then he was gone.

CHAPTER

Ten

W hen I unlocked the door and shoved my way in (the lock stuck, Gabe had told me on our way out), I found Squeaky sitting atop the couch, watching the door, the tip of his tail twitching in the air. "Hey there, bud," I said, moving forward in a crouch, hand out-stretched for a pat.

He blinked those huge green eyes at me accusingly and let out a rusty meow, then leaped gracefully off the couch and scurried into Gabe's room. It made sense, logically. He hadn't seen me in years, more than half his life. I was basically a stranger. In his tiny mind, I had abandoned him. Why should he want to hang out with me? Why should anyone want to hang out with me?

Vienna had always wanted to hang out with me. If our friendship hadn't broken up, she wouldn't have blown me off like Opal or gotten distant and noncommittal like Millicent and Coriander and, like, every-one else I used to go out with.

I didn't even remember the first time Vienna and I met. In my mind, we'd always been friends. We'd run around the same playgrounds in preschool, worn the same itchy wool skirts and starched blouses in kin-dergarten, done drama and poetry club together in middle school. We'd taken our first sips of alcohol together in our sophomore year of high school. I'd persuaded her to sneak into a bar with me using some fake ID's I'd bought off some guy in the Fourteenth Street subway passage-way despite her doubts; she'd cut me off before I threw up.

My lips twitched in a smile at the memory of us leaving the bar together, arms wrapped around each other, singing some Rihanna song at the top of our lungs and thinking we blended in so well with all the NYU kids out for the night . . . then the smile fell off at the memory of how our friendship ended. How she'd yelled at me. How I'd yelled back. How she'd slammed the front door of her town house in my face when I went after her because surely our fight had been a mistake, and, no matter how many times I pounded on it, she hadn't opened it back up. Maybe she'd retreated into the basement, where you couldn't hear the door, for a swim in the family pool.

What would she say right now if she were here? I pictured her sitting on the couch; she'd be grimacing at the mysterious stains on the seat and the way the cushions sagged the same way she'd grimaced at that first sip of straight vodka. *Pom*, she'd say, crossing her legs and her arms so that as little of herself touched the couch as possible. *You were kind of a jerk back there.* Vienna never cursed, not even when she was drunk. *You should say sorry, mostly because you don't want being a jerk to darken your aura, but also partly because you need a place to live and you need to solve this murder, and you need Gabe for both of those things.*

Fake Vienna paled in comparison to real Vienna. Once again, I fought back the urge to dial her number. She'd probably blocked me, anyway. But she was right. I had to make this right.

"If he's going for a walk to blow off steam, he's going to come back hungry for dinner, right?" I murmured, then nodded to myself. "So it would be thoughtful and considerate to have some food waiting for him when he gets back. A jerk wouldn't do that."

As if responding to me, Squeaky slunk through Gabe's half-open door, settling down onto the floor outside it and studying me curiously. I took that as agreement.

That good feeling lasted until I'd made the journey to the kitchen—approximately three medium-size steps—and realized that I'd never cooked anything in my life. I realize that sounds like an exaggeration. But neither of my parents ever cooked. When I popped my head into the kitchen as a kid, curious, my mom would pull me out and tell me it wasn't my place. They'd gifted me Lori's services as a graduation present when I got my own place in the hotel, so I'd never so much as turned on the stove before. And come on, I lived in Manhattan. Most nights I went out downtown. If I was hungry at home and Lori wasn't around, I could order delivery with a few clicks on my phone. I'd baked with Andrea when I was a kid, but baking was different than cooking.

I couldn't order delivery now, not without any money or a working credit card. I cast my eyes over the various pots hanging from hooks on Gabe's wall, the open pantry displaying various bags and cans and boxes of things I had no idea how to use. Did I have *any* practical skills?

It came to me, with an unsettling lurch in my stomach, that if there was ever some kind of global apocalypse that left all of humanity scrabbling in the dirt, my companions would probably vote to eat me first.

I let out a gusty sigh and shimmied my shoulders, trying to shake off the sense of impending doom. Hopefully the apocalypse would hold off for a while. "Little kids do this. I've seen it on TV," I murmured to myself. "And cooking can't be that different from baking. I can look up recipes on my phone and follow the steps exactly. How hard can it be?"

A little over an hour later, I was dripping sweat as I frantically waved a kitchen towel—which was now crusted with salsa and oil—at the smoke detector, which was shrieking like all of social media when I'd accidentally let a nip slip. Of course, this was the exact moment Gabe chose to come home.

"It's not what it looks like," I puffed, blowing a chunk of hair off where it had stuck on my forehead. Chilly air from the open window then hit it, making me shiver. "Nothing's actually on fire."

I'd googled "easy recipes for a first time cook" and picked nachos. How hard could they be? The recipe was basically just dumping a bunch of stuff in the oven and letting some cheese melt on top of it. And Gabe had all the ingredients—tortilla chips, cheese, salsa, some refried beans in a pouch. So I'd piled it all on top of a baking sheet and let it cook, opening the oven frequently to make sure I wasn't burning anything.

And I hadn't! "If you'd like to turn your eyes over to the table, you'll find a perfect pan of nachos," I told him. They'd come out of the oven a half hour ago and now the cheese was starting to congeal, which meant that maybe they weren't totally perfect anymore, but I was willing to fudge the truth a bit. "I wanted to make dinner for you. Like you made dinner for me."

Gabe's eyebrows rose as he regarded the table, which I hoped meant he was impressed and not that he was irritated. "They don't look burnt enough to set off the alarm."

My head was beginning to pulsate in time with the alarm, which was probably not a great sign. "So the thing is that then I may have gotten a little overconfident."

What had really happened: I'd pulled that perfect bubbling platter of nachos out of the oven and regarded it proudly, like I'd given birth to a baby that didn't look like a tiny wizened old-man alien the way most newborn babies did. I'd set it carefully down and turned to Squeaky, who had now progressed to watching me from the couch, where he'd tucked his paws neatly beneath him. "That was so easy. And it smells so good. What if this is my calling, and I just haven't realized it until now?" I'd asked him, my breaths quickening. Images of me assuredly stirring something on a stove beside Padma Lakshmi and throwing my head back in a laugh at something Ina Garten said flashed through my mind. She would seat me in the place of honor at her table, right next to Jeffrey. "Let's make something else."

To Gabe, I said, "So I thought you might want dessert. You know, a long walk burns a lot of calories. I decided, why not some classic brownies? I'd made them with your mom as a kid and remembered the steps vaguely, and, like, if I'd made them when I was eight or nine, it couldn't be harder than the nachos. I googled the best brownie recipes, which took me to Smitten Kitchen, which took me to . . ." I gestured at the smoking oven, then the fire alarm. "Anyway."

I expected Gabe to sigh in dismay and shake his head at me, but he didn't. If anything, a smile darted across his face before his jaw clenched, all business. "So are the brownies still in the oven?"

I nodded. Gabe grabbed the potholders, opened the oven door, and pulled the pan of brownies out. I crowded around him as he set them down on the stove. They were a little black around the edges, sure, but they actually didn't look too bad.

Gabe left them up there as he crouched, staring inside the oven. "Ah. There it is." He pointed at something on the bottom. I leaned forward, but didn't really want to get more smoke in my hair. It wasn't a wash day, and I'd left my favorite shampoo and conditioner (made from the oils of some flower that grew only in the Himalayas) back at the hotel anyway. "Some of the cheese from the nachos must have bubbled over and got on the bottom. That's what was burning."

As he stood, he turned the oven off. I probably should have done that initially. He followed up by smacking the smoke alarm, which finally stopped beeping. The silence that resulted was so loud I could hear it. "It's going to be annoying to clean, but you should get it done once the oven cools down or it'll get hard and stick," he said.

Me? *I* was going to have to clean it? I opened my mouth to argue, then closed it, chastened by my own brain. "Okay."

It was like he'd expected me to argue, because his eyebrows lifted again, this time in surprise. "Your brownies don't look bad. Maybe a little burned around the edges, but that's just because you forgot to turn the oven off," he said. "Do you want to eat?"

He wanted to eat with me. All was not lost.

Which left me to make the next move. I waited until we were seated around the little table, which rocked from side to side on uneven legs every time we moved. "Hey, I really am sorry about what I said," I told him after my first bite of nachos. They weren't bad. "I was lashing out because my feelings were hurt. I didn't mean it. If anything, I feel the opposite. I mean, you talked me into this investigation. You made me feel like maybe I could do it. So you need to work on how to interrogate a suspect a little, but you already know how to encourage someone and make them feel like they matter. That's going to make you an amazing teacher."

As I spoke, it was like the sun was rising over his face. When I finished, his eyes gleamed and his lips were wide in a smile. "I think that might be the nicest thing anyone's ever said to me."

"I wasn't saying it just to be nice," I said. "I was saying it because it's true." I took another bite of nacho. Could have used more cheese. Next time I'd be more careful about it bubbling over. Squeaky wound his way between my legs, maybe in agreement, maybe to beg for a cheese chunk.

Gabe leaned down to pet him. When he rose, he said, "You know, you were amazing in there. Maybe that's why I was so clumsy with my questioning, because you were knocking it out of the park and I felt like I had to do something to earn my place. Somehow you knew exactly how to talk to him to make him open up to you, exactly what to say to make him feel comfortable enough to share things he probably shouldn't have been sharing."

Maybe the sun actually *had* been rising over his face, because, with him looking at me like that, I was feeling a little sunburned. "It's not like it's a talent. Anyone can do that."

"That's not true," he said. "It's both a talent and a skill."

I laughed, a little self-consciously. "I don't think so. It's just talking to people. Everybody talks to people. Now, dancing on a table. That's a skill most people don't think is a skill."

He didn't laugh. "I'm serious. You should give yourself some credit."

"I'm serious too. You're teetering on a small surface high above the ground, usually while drunk and wearing very high heels. Lots of people fall off." He didn't seem impressed. Whatever. If he wanted to think I was good at something, I wasn't going to continue trying to convince him otherwise. "So are we back on?"

"We're back on. But before we start talking murder again, can we have some of those brownies?"

I might have been awkward about him praising me just now, but I wasn't at all awkward about accepting praise when I knew I deserved it. I nodded, pleased, as he said, "Okay, these are amazing."

"They are, aren't they?" They were chewy and chocolaty and bitter in a pleasant way along the burnt edges. "The recipe didn't say to add the chocolate chips. But I saw them in the pantry and decided to throw them in, because brownies can't have too much chocolate, right?"

He couldn't answer. His mouth was full. Which gave me the opportunity to continue talking. "These are way better than the baked goods at your coffee shop," I said, then realized I maybe should have asked who made them first so that I wasn't accidentally insulting Gabe. "Though I guess I did only try that one Danish. Maybe everything else you sell is better than that."

He finally swallowed. I was relieved to see him shake his head. "No, everything is pretty terrible. Corporate has them shipped over each morning. I don't even know where they get them from, but corporate must be getting kickbacks, right? Because nobody could think their food is good."

"How do they even sell?"

Gabe shrugged. "They don't sell to regulars. We throw away a lot of stuff at the end of the day."

"That's terrible."

He shrugged again. "It is what it is. It's not like I can change corporate's mind." He leaned down and picked up Squeaky, settling him on his lap. Squeaky rubbed his cheek against Gabe's chin. I smiled, trying to hide my jealousy. "Anyway, while I was on my walk, I realized something we were forgetting. Do we know the murder weapon?"

"She was stabbed," I said. "A lot of times." But . . . with what? "No. No, we don't know the murder weapon."

"Do the police?"

"I have no idea." I texted my dad, because if anyone would be up-to-date on the investigation, it would be the victim's son. I didn't have to wait long for a response. No. They haven't found it. They just know it was something small and sharp. I held my phone out so that

Gabe could read it. He ducked his head, making his shaggy dark hair fall over his eyes. I went to push it back, then stopped myself, my hand in the air. What was I doing? I couldn't touch him like that. That would have been so weird. "Something small and sharp," I said hastily, pushing my chair back so that I couldn't be tempted to reach out again. Not even to brush off the small smear of chocolate at the corner of his lips. "That could be anything."

"Well, anything small and sharp." He gave me a small smile. "What do you think about what Fred said at the coffee shop?"

What Fred said? A fresh wave of shame washed through me as I remembered his parting words.

But I wasn't here to feel bad about myself. I was here to solve a murder and get my life back. So I said, "About the 'young lady' threatening my grandma? I mean, we have no idea if she was the murderer, but at least it sounds like there's something there to check out. Maybe threatening turned into murdering. We can pull on that thread and see what unravels." That was how Doe on *Here to Slay* usually found her next suspect: following those little threads that came out of questioning. Sometimes they led somewhere, sometimes they didn't.

"True," Gabe mused. "It doesn't hurt to start there, at least. Let's make a list of all the young women in your grandma's life he could've been talking about."

That immediately killed most of our original list; Fred, Dad, and Nicholas were men, and Rosa couldn't be called young by the stretchiest Lycra of the imagination. She'd already been old when I was born. "So Farrah and Jordan," I said. "I guess this bumps them up to number one on the list then. And my mom could theoretically be considered young compared to my grandma."

Gabe pulled his notebook out of nowhere and scribbled something down. "Okay, so they can be our main suspects. What about widening the pool? Think about any young woman who would have had access to your grandma's suite."

I felt like I could have remembered all of this just fine, but I couldn't have Gabe making all these notes on his own. I pulled the note back up on my phone and made the necessary adjustments to our list, taking the men and Rosa off and bumping up Farrah, Jordan, and my mom. I hesitated over Nicholas's name. "I mean, Nicholas's girlfriend, Jessica, is a young woman, and she would've had access through Nicholas's apartment," I said. "I don't know about motive. My grandma didn't like her and had her blacklisted from all of her galas, but that also applies to half of our social circle. I don't think my grandma not liking her is enough of a motive to kill, do you?"

"Maybe she's a gold digger and wanted Nicholas to inherit the business sooner," Gabe said.

It wasn't like I hadn't heard the same sort of thing from my mom's mouth several times, but my stomach flipped a little anyway. Jessica might have been irritating during my brief stay at her apartment, but she'd been really nice to me when she didn't have to be. "I don't know. The business would go to my dad before Nicholas, anyway. But she did have access, so she goes on the list."

I added her, then said hesitantly, "As long as we're talking access with no motive, my friend Opal stays with me a lot and was with me the night of the murder. It's theoretically possible that she could've had access to my grandma's apartment."

"Can you think of any reason why she might want your grandma dead?"

I shook my head. "I mean, my grandma wasn't especially nice to her, but if being mean to someone was enough to get them to murder you, my grandma would've been dead ages ago from, again, half our social circle." I grimaced as my last conversation with Opal popped into my head. "And Opal's been kind of weird with me since the murder. I thought it was just because she's a snob and she doesn't want to associate with a broke person, but it's possible she could've gone up there for some reason and is now avoiding me out of guilt." Then again, Opal had been weird with me before, like that time we'd been sucked into a foam party in Ibiza, so it didn't necessarily mean anything.

"Okay, so Jessica and Opal go on the list. Anybody else?"

Most of the Afton executive staff close enough to Grandma to have access to her with a phone call were men, and the few women were either super old or not in the city. It was possible a hotel maid could be this "young woman," but I didn't think so. Grandma didn't tend to think of nonexecutives who worked for her as people. If a maid had been the one threatening her, she would've told Fred that and probably just had them fired. "I mean, it's always possible there could be someone I don't know about," I said. "But I think this is it for now. A good starting place."

"A good starting place," Gabe echoed. He reached down to scratch Squeaky's ears as the cat wound his way between his ankles. "Who first, you think? Your mom is probably easiest."

I had to hold back a snort. Only someone who'd never met my mom would ever call her easy. Unless maybe you were one of the guys she was photographed with during her self-proclaimed "wild phase" before she met my dad. "Farrah and Jordan were on the original list too. They probably blocked me, but let me give them a try."

I scrolled allllll the way down through my messages to our long-dormant group chat, which Jordan had lovingly nicknamed "Cuzzie Gals." Just seeing that silly name gave me a pang in my chest. I took a deep breath and held it, hoping the air would cushion me against the blow when my text inevitably rebounded. Hey, ladies! Sorry it's been soooo long. Heard you were in town. Would love to meet up if you have time! No worries if not.

Send.

And the immediate buzz of me getting kicked from the group. I'd braced myself for it, but it still—wait. That wasn't a kick. That was a return text. Already. From Jordan. Apple Pie! Of course we have time! You name when and where.

Tears pricked my eyes upon seeing my old nickname. Farrah and Jordan had started calling me Apple Pie after we took a trip to Paris and learned that *apple* in French was *pomme*. Hearing it again felt like walking into your apartment after a long trip crossing five time zones and dropping your bags on the floor for Lori to unpack.

Something warm touched my arm. I almost jerked away before realizing that it was Gabe's hand, and he was frowning at me with concern. "They blocked you?"

I shook my head and sniffled. "No. The opposite."

"Why are you crying, then?"

I just shook my head again, swiping at my eyes with the arm Gabe wasn't touching. For some reason, I didn't want to shake him off. "I'm not." I blinked really fast, clearing away the tears that weren't there, and my eyes fell on the brownies. "Hey," I said. "Those brownies were pretty good, right? Do you think my skills are up for an apple pie?"

He looked dubious, but he shrugged. "There's only one way to find out."

Eleven

My baking skills were not quite up to apple pie level. Not yet. The apple filling tasted good, but it was kind of watery and the apples were too hard, and the crust ended up tough and chewy, even though I'd made pie crust with Andrea as a kid so knew the basic principles. However! I worked magic! Together, me and a YouTube wizard turned my failed pie into a tasty apple crumble. So it was with my apple crumble, tucked into Gabe's disposable foil dish, that I showed up to Farrah and Jordan's building.

"They're going to be so impressed," I said to Gabe, stepping over a group of particularly fearless pigeons fighting over some dropped falafel on the sidewalk. A guy walking past looked at me askance. Understandable, since it looked like I was talking to no one and nothing, thanks to the extremely tiny Bluetooth in my ear under my hair. Or maybe less understandable, because hey, this was New York. People talked to themselves in public all the time. "Do you think I should open up a bakery? It could turn out that I don't even *need* my trust fund anymore."

"Maybe give it a few more days," Gabe said dryly into my ear. I could barely hear him over the hustle and bustle and voices in the background; he was either on his way to work or there in the coffee shop. He couldn't take off again to come on this last-minute investigation with me—his manager was apparently coming in—which, honestly, was fine. After the way he'd bungled things with Fred, me taking the lead on this one seemed appropriate. And I could afford to take the time off—the money in my account from that long-ago sunglasses campaign would pay for several months of rent and living expenses as long as I was careful about my spending. I'd never been careful about spending before, so hopefully this would work out. Gabe had advised a spreadsheet, but I had zero desire to involve spreadsheets in my life.

Besides, I didn't really care that Fred would probably never want to speak to me again. But Farrah and Jordan? That was different.

"I just need to come up with my own thing," I mused, speeding up to make it across the street before the blinking red light went solid. "You know, like how Magnolia Bakery has their banana pudding and Milk Bar has their cake truffles. Obviously I need my baking to be delicious, but I also need it to be unique."

"I don't know if I've ever met anyone more unique than you."

"I'll take that as a compliment." I stopped in front of the apartment building on Central Park South where Farrah and Jordan were staying. I wasn't sure exactly whose apartment they were in, but I assumed it was a family friend's pied-à-terre or something. I was kind of surprised they weren't staying at the Afton to rub it in the rest of our faces that they could and we couldn't. "Okay, I'm going in."

"Good luck."

The doorman sent me right upstairs, hardly looking at my face. In the mirrored elevator I shifted from foot to foot, staring myself right in the eye. I'd left a lot of my usual makeup behind at the Afton in my rush to pack, and had been forced into the indignity of replacing it at the Duane Reade around the corner from Gabe's—my—apartment. Keeping one of Gabe's baseball caps pulled low over my forehead so that nobody would see me buying drugstore makeup, I had worried I'd look like an entirely new person.

But honestly, I didn't appear all that different. I'd still managed a pretty good classic no-makeup makeup look: neutral lip; rosy cheeks; slightly enhanced eyelashes. I admired the job I'd done until the doors slid open and allowed me into their hallway.

I didn't even have to figure out which apartment was theirs, because Jordan was hanging out the door, half into the hall. "Pom!" she shrieked, and threw herself at me. I barely maneuvered the apple crumble out of the way before she flung herself against my chest, wrapping her arms around my back and pulling me in tight. "I've missed you so much!"

Tears pricked my eyes. A lump rose in my throat. I barely managed to speak around it as I said, "I've missed you so much too." She looked exactly the same as when I'd seen her last—black hair ironed into a sleek bob; thick brows I'd always envied—which made it feel almost like no time had passed at all.

She backed away, grabbing my free hand. "You have to come in, at least for a minute. We booked time at the spa down the block, but Farrah's not ready yet. Farrah!" She was going to have the neighbors complaining to the doorman if she kept on being this loud. "Come on! Hurry up!"

She towed me inside and shut the door behind me. The apartment was sleek and modern, all spotless white and shiny chrome. Against that background, Jordan in her bright red leggings and red and yellow patterned tunic popped like a splatter of blood.

Really glad I didn't say that out loud. Gabe would definitely have judged me.

Her outfit did cause a little tingle of jealousy in my stomach, though. I recognized the tunic from Emblème's fall line, which had just been released. I had a similar one in blue and green buried in my closet at the Afton. I wondered if it was still there.

Honestly, I missed my closet with a physical ache. Lori'd fortunately had the wisdom from years of helping me arrange all my clothes to pack me an assortment of neutrals and pieces that could be worn together in a bunch of different ways, but every time I'd pair one of the same tops or dresses with the same pair of The Avenue leggings or Jane sneakers, my brain would immediately flash to the absolutely perfect patterned silk scarf or dangly earrings in my closet to finish off the outfit. So close, yet so far.

Also. Apparently most apartments in the city didn't even have laundry machines. Gabe's certainly didn't. When the time came where

I'd worn all my pieces as far as I could get them, he told me I'd have to lug them all the way downstairs into the basement, where there were two coin-operated washer-dryer stacks that "usually" worked. And he said we were lucky to have them in the building so that I didn't have to lug them all the way down the block to a *laundromat*, where you washed your delicates in full view of other people.

God, I hoped I'd be out of there before I had to do any of that.

"Oh, and I brought this for you!" I held out the pie plate like a contestant presenting their dish to be judged on one of those cooking shows. "I actually made it myself. I know, I'm impressed too."

"Wow, cool!" Jordan pulled up the side of the foil and took a sniff. "Apples. Nice. It smells really good."

"It *does* smell really good, doesn't it?" I said, mostly for Gabe's benefit. "I've actually been thinking that maybe my next move should be opening up a bakery. You know, starting fresh."

Jordan had her back turned to me as she put the crisp in the fridge, so I couldn't see the surely approving expression on her face, but Gabe blessed me with a snort loud enough to be heard over the commotion still going on in the background. "Unnecessary," I hissed.

Jordan turned back around, her dark eyes wide. "What?"

"Nothing," I said. "Hey, so . . ." The words died in my throat. I knew I had to clear the air about the entire year where I'd cowardly acted as though she and her sister didn't exist, but I had no idea what to say. "About last year . . ."

"Oh, Pom. We know you were in such a hard position," Jordan said, pressing her hands to her chest. Her scarlet manicure matched her outfit. "I mean, yeah, it hurt. But I understand."

"She might forgive you. But I don't."

Farrah's voice was decidedly chillier than her younger sister's. She'd stepped out of a room at the end of the hall, braids tied up in a bun at the top of her head, light brown skin glowing even without makeup. I held my breath as she continued. "As soon as Grandma told my parents that we were out, you vanished. There's no excuse for that."

I shriveled beneath her glare. "No excuse," I said meekly. "I was wrong. And I'm sorry."

"See, Farrah?" Jordan interjected. "She's sorry!"

The gossip rags had speculated for ages over the cause of the estrangement. After all, said DeuxMoi and its hundreds of anonymous submissions, anything that cut the younger Afton son and his entire family out of not just the business and the will but the family altogether, sending them fleeing in disgrace to *Florida*, home of alligators and old people, had to be juicy and scandalous. Maybe an affair between the Afton patriarch and his daughter-in-law. Or the family had been embezzling, and the matriarch had cut a deal that she wouldn't press charges as long as they left without a fuss.

The truth, as it so often is, was way less exciting. Grandma had refused to explain herself, telling me only that sometimes you needed to cut a dying branch off before it made the whole tree rot from the inside out, but of course Mom had sniffed out the truth and bowed heads with me over high tea at Bloomie's. Grandma and my uncle had disagreed over a number of boring business decisions. He'd refused to apologize. His kids and wife took his side. Grandma couldn't handle it and went nuclear.

Farrah snorted. "She's only crawling back now that Grandma's dead and she doesn't have to worry about facing her wrath," she said to her sister like I wasn't even here. As if she heard me think that, she spun to me with a smug smile. "Though who has the last laugh now that you've lost everything anyway?"

I didn't know what else to say. I'd apologized. I'd said I was wrong. What else was there to do? Maybe Farrah would come around over the course of our spa day, though she definitely wouldn't if she knew that the real reason I'd reached out was to investigate her for murder.

I should've reached out sooner. I really should've.

"I'm just glad you're in the same room speaking to me." I made myself smile, even though it wasn't nearly enough, and decided not to remind her that I would definitely be getting everything back. "So. Spa day?"

Farrah rolled her eyes. "I guess."

As we marched down the sidewalk to the unassuming spa building, the bustling noises of Gabe at the coffee shop blended with the
street noise. I probably should have texted him to mute himself unless
he was speaking, but I kind of liked this little auditory window into a
normal day when the stakes were so high on my side. Every time Farrah shot me a needle-eyed glance from the side, Gabe would say
something boring like "Two shots of espresso with that?" or "Did you
say oat milk or goat milk?" and keep me from wanting to crawl out of
my skin.

I'd been to this spa many times before, so I moved through the entrance automatically, barely registering the calming cedar scent or
soothing bell music piped through unseen speakers as I followed Jordan and Farrah into our usual private room. We dumped our bags
there in the dim, bare space and took our comfy chairs beside the
pool. Unlike most pools, it didn't smell even the slightest bit like chlo-
rine. "Manis, pedis, and facials?" Jordan asked, as if the answer
weren't obvious. I nodded.

It was hard to talk while skilled workers were scouring your face
with salt and sand and then slathering it up with something moisturiz-
ing and plumping that smelled like the ocean, which was great, because
it (fingers crossed) gave Farrah some time to cool off and (toes crossed)
gave me some time to figure out the right questions to ask afterward.

That is, when Gabe wasn't making some comment in my ear.
"That music sounds like you're on a spaceship," he said at one point.
Was he talking to me? I couldn't ask without inviting suspicion from
Farrah and Jordan.

After a relaxing and delightful half hour of stuff on my face, the
attendants toweled it off. I blinked my eyes open, feeling cool and refreshed, and watched the water lapping at the sides of the pool while
Farrah and Jordan picked their nail polish colors. I didn't even need to
think about it—I picked the one I always picked when I didn't have an
outfit in mind to pair it with, an almost neutral pale pink with the
glossy shine of the inside of a seashell. It wasn't like I could come back

in a few days and pick out a new one. This would have to last me for at least a week or two, so it had to go with everything.

The sobering thought was cold in my stomach, brought me back to reality. "So!" I chirped as the attendant knelt before me, ready to buff my feet. "I was so happy when Nicholas told me you two were back in town. He said you were here for some art gallery thing?"

I'd plunked myself in the chair between the two sisters, which I'd figured would give me maximum advantage, but which actually made judging their reactions more difficult as I had to glance back and forth between the two of them to catch the looks on their faces. Both were currently serene, but then Farrah broke her peaceful expression to crack one eye open and scowl at me. "Our cousin on our mom's side had the opening of her first gallery show, yes. It was a very big deal for her."

"Congratulations to her," I said. I only half meant it. I'd talked to their other cousins occasionally at family events, and they'd always struck me as stuck-up. "How long are you here? Anything else fun you're getting up to?"

Fortunately, it was Jordan who answered me this time. "We actually came up two days before . . . well, before you know what happened. We were supposed to—"

"Jordan!" Farrah said sharply.

Gabe murmured in my ear, "There's something there."

I had no idea if he was talking to me or if he was helping someone clean gross stuff off the bathroom walls, but I didn't need it either way. "You were supposed to what?"

"Dad told us not to mention it to anyone," Farrah said, her voice a razor.

"Yeah, but Pom isn't just anyone," said Jordan. "And maybe she'll have details! Farrah, you have to admit you've been dying to know why Grandma summoned us back here after not talking to us for a year."

"There it is," said Gabe.

I had no idea how he was getting away with this during his workday, if his coworkers thought he was talking to them or if customers were thinking he'd lost his mind. It didn't matter. "Wow, really?" I said slowly, mind buzzing with the best way to go about this. I obviously had to press, but not so hard it would spook them. "What did she say?"

"Jordan," Farrah warned, but Jordan waved her off. Literally, which meant she came frighteningly close to whapping her pedicurist in the head.

"Nothing other than that. I actually ignored her first email; we figured it was some weirdo posing as her prying for information. But then she called. Told us she had to speak to us about something important, and it had to be in person, and it had to be very soon."

Something important, in person, and very soon. And, most importantly, secret.

I had to find out what it was.

"Ask them more questions," Gabe was hissing, but I ignored him, which was easy to do when he wasn't here lumbering around in person like a human wrecking ball.

"So weird," I said, and flinched as the pedicurist filed a little too hard. She murmured an apology. "I wish I knew what it was." If I gave them a little bit of something secret, maybe Farrah would chill out more. "The only thing I know is that there were troubles with the business." I turned in Farrah's direction and gave her a small, wry smile I hoped would disguise the fact that I was talking entirely out of my ass. Well, I guess not *entirely*, considering what I'd learned from Fred. "I think she was regretting exiling your dad. Maybe she was starting to realize she was wrong and she wanted to bring you back in."

"I don't think the business had anything to do with it," said Farrah. "I think it was just an excuse. I don't think she loved having Black family members. You know she told my dad not to marry our mom?"

"Obviously not the same thing, but she said something very similar to my dad," I said. "At least in that case, she got over it. Mostly. Well, kind of. As much as she could."

"She never stopped hating your mom, and you know it," Farrah said darkly. I snuck a glance over at Jordan, who was staring down at her feet. Her toenails were half electric blue. "Do you know it wasn't even her who banished us? My dad quit and we left with him. We were done with her and her mind games. She was just trying to save face by saying she was the one who initiated it."

"I didn't know," I said quietly. But now that Farrah had started, she was on a roll.

"It was what she said during their last fight that really sealed the deal. 'How do you know they're even real Aftons?' Like my mom had cheated on my dad!" From the way Farrah was tensing all her muscles, I was getting nervous she might accidentally kick her pedicurist in the face. "My mom had been staying out of the whole thing. You know her, she's not one for drama. But Jordan and I stewed over it for months before we finally got one of those ancestry DNA kits. We didn't doubt our parents, but remember, Grandma did the kit a couple years ago? We knew she'd get a notification when we popped up as relatives. I wanted her to see it and know how wrong she'd been."

"We thought that maybe that's why she was reaching out. She saw that she was wrong and had decided to be the bigger person," Jordan said quietly. "But I guess we'll never know."

"Your grandma sounds like a bitch. I kind of want to kill her. Oh, wait," Gabe said. I barely managed in time to turn my extremely inappropriate laugh into a sneeze.

"Bless you," Jordan said.

"Thank you," I said weakly. I couldn't believe I hadn't known any of this. I couldn't believe I'd taken my grandma at her word when I knew how terrible she was. I couldn't believe I hadn't reached out to Farrah and Jordan sooner to hear their side.

My eyes were tearing up. I reached up to swipe the moisture away before it could spill onto my cheeks and ruin the effects of my facial. So much for the cooling cream they'd put on my eyes.

Farrah and Jordan were right. My apology wasn't enough. Not when I'd caused this much hurt.

I took a deep breath. "I know I already said it, but I'm sorry. I wish there was something I could do to make things right, but I know

I can't. I hope you'll give me the chance to prove how much I love you and want you in my life."

"Whatever," Farrah said, but she sounded less adamant about it than before. "I'm just glad they can't pin the murder on us. We were at the gallery opening all night, with plenty of photographic and video evidence. And then the doorman here saw us coming back for the night."

It was helpful of her to come straight out and tell me that. Not that I'd thought they'd killed her, but it was a relief to hear they had an alibi anyway. Still, I made a mental note to verify.

"Anyway, enough depressing stuff," said Jordan. "Pom, tell us about what you've been doing since the family's fall from grace. Throw in enough sad details of how much your life sucks now and maybe Farrah will feel sorry for you."

"I will not," said Farrah.

"She will."

"Will not."

"I live with a roommate and I have to share a bathroom now," I said quickly before they could lean over me and start pulling each other's hair. "Remember Andrea? I actually moved in with Andrea's son." And then, because I could, "He says I'm the best roommate he's ever had. Just an absolute joy to live with."

"What was that?" Gabe said. "Oh, sorry, I didn't hear that last bit. Busy drowning myself in some boiling milk."

"Ooh, Andrea's son," Jordan said, waggling her eyebrows. "Wait, which one? The hot one or the funny-looking one?"

Gabe this morning briefly flashed into my mind: a towel around his waist, a few drops from the shower still glistening on his bare chest, wet hair curling over his sleepy, half-lidded eyes.

My cheeks were warm. I said quickly, "Definitely the funny-looking one."

"Ooh, Caleb?" Farrah said, like she'd forgotten for a moment to be mad at me. I'd take it. "Those thick glasses always made him look like a bug. Gabe, on the other hand? Whew. I'd live with *him* anytime."

Oh, God. Gabe was going to be insufferable tonight. He was already cackling on the other end of the line. I said, quickly, "I think you're probably mixing them up," but it was too late.

"Definitely not," said Farrah. "I always had a little crush on him. Not a major one, though. Don't let it stop you."

"Stop me from what?" I said, but as she began responding, badmouthing basically every guy I'd ever dated (which, fair, they were almost all terrible), I heard a sharp voice on the other end of the line.

"Gabe, can you step back here with me for a moment?" I didn't recognize the voice, but it sounded like an older guy, not a customer or a fellow coffee shop worker. Maybe his boss? Right. He'd mentioned earlier that he especially couldn't miss work today because the district manager was going to be at his store.

Some shuffling, and the sound of a door closing hard. The background noise ebbed away. I tuned back to Farrah for a moment—she was now monologuing on Tristan Burns, my longest-lasting ex at nearly a whole year and who broke up with me by posting a photo of him making out with some new girl at a club, so she could trash him as much as she wanted to—and then Gabe was speaking. "Sir, did you have a chance to look at my email about changing my hours?"

Honestly, it felt a little awkward to be listening to this conversation, like I was skulking on the other side of the office door. But I couldn't turn it off without showing Farrah and Jordan that I had this earpiece in, which would invite all sorts of questions from them. Maybe even shrivel our budding re-relationship. So I didn't have much of a choice. At least that's what I told myself.

"I did." The manager's voice was brusque. "I'm afraid it's a no-go. We can't afford to shift your hours around at this point in time."

I was annoyed on Gabe's behalf already—surely if he'd asked for a change in hours, he should get one. Gabe said, "But I need to take this seminar on Tuesday and Thursday mornings. It's the only time my school offers it."

"I'm sorry. Tuesday and Thursday mornings are some of our busiest days. And we can't afford to hire anyone to cover them." There was a shuffling noise, like he was playing with a stack of papers. "And speaking of what we can afford, I'm also afraid we can't afford the raise you asked for. Our profit margins are tight and it's just not in the budget."

I pictured Gabe lighting up with a fiery speech, storming out, quitting. Which would be cool, since it would give us more time for our investigating.

But he only said, quietly, "Are you sure? I've been working here for almost four years and have never received a raise greater than cost of living."

Indignation flared within me as he named the hourly wage he was making, which was less than I paid for a cab ride home from the yoga studio when I felt too stretched out to walk eight blocks. Absurd. He deserved so much more than that. Anyone working as hard as he did deserved so much more than that.

But the manager was unmoved. He rebuffed Gabe's reasoning with nothing language like "state of the market" and "flat profits" and made an excuse to leave. The door opened and closed again. He sighed into the earpiece. "Pom, did you hear that?"

"I heard it," I said without thinking, stopping Farrah midsentence.

"We all heard it," she said. "I mean, that asshole was so fucking loud I think the whole city heard it."

She had to be talking about my ex Thad, who screamed when he heard that Novak Djokovic surprise-lost at Wimbledon. Which fine, whatever, except that it was in the middle of my surprise birthday party, just when everybody was quieting down, ready to yell surprise. It had kind of ruined the whole thing. Even if Millicent had already accidentally let the surprise part slip that morning when she asked me for a ride to my party later.

"Anyway," Farrah continued. "I think the lesson we've all learned is that you could do worse than Gabe."

"Point taken," I said. The manicurist stood up, asking me with raised eyebrows for my approval. I held out my fingers and toes, wiggling them. "Looks great." She nodded and went to leave without any further interaction. Which seemed wrong. I mean, she'd almost been conked on the head as she worked on some of the smellier parts of the human anatomy, and it was hard to imagine she was making much more money than Gabe was. "Thank you."

This time, her raised eyebrows weren't asking for approval. They seemed like surprise, actually. Which was fair, because neither Farrah nor Jordan thanked theirs as they moved away.

It was how we'd always done things. But maybe how we'd always done things wasn't the right way.

"Don't worry about the cost," Jordan said. I hadn't worried about the cost, because I hadn't even thought about it. Now I was thinking about it, though. If she hadn't said not to worry, I'd be panicking. I had no idea what the services here cost—they'd always just gone on my card—but if I couldn't afford a driver anymore, I probably couldn't afford this spa day. "I'll put them on our tab. I'm glad we got all our money out of the company when we did." She giggled, but there was a note of darkness to it. "I hope there's an afterlife just so that Grandma can see that *we're* the richest Aftons left."

If being a ghost didn't mean she was already dead, *that* definitely would've killed her.

CHAPTER

Twelve

As much as I'd loved reconnecting with my cousins, I begged off lunch after our spa treatments. For one, I didn't want to feel like a charity case again, and I certainly couldn't afford what the furtively googled menu told me our usual prix-fixe lunch at our favorite spot cost (more than I made in an entire day of aching feet and hissing steam and relentless coffee smell!). For two, I was tired. I'd forgotten how exhausting relaxing at a spa could be. So we hugged goodbye outside the spa—Jordan enthusiastically; Farrah stiffly—and promised to get together again before they went back to Florida.

Without a driver or cab fare, I was left to walk back uptown, tired or not. At least the sun was out and the breeze was mild, and I had a good pair of sunglasses to keep anyone from recognizing me. My recent influencer campaign might have been cut short, but at least they'd let me keep the merchandise. "I'm heading back home," I reported to Gabe through my earpiece, feeling kind of dashing, a CIA agent in disguise. "I checked on social media just now, and yup, they were both featured in a bunch of posts the night of the murder. Unless they're lying about their doorman seeing them come home later, and I imagine the police would've confirmed it, it couldn't have been them."

"Bummer," Gabe said. His background noise had died out; maybe he was outside taking his break in the park. "I mean, not bummer. I know you care about them and I'm glad they're not murderers. But—"

"I know what you meant," I said. I inhaled deeply as I passed one of the vibrantly colored tulip gardens in the median of Park Avenue.

Opal and I used to stop by these on our way to her place and some-times illicitly pick one or two as a memento. "It would've been nice to solve the crime so quickly."

Wait. Not one of these—this specific median, with the ombré color scheme stretching from red tulips at the top to pale yellow at the other end. Maybe my subconscious had done this on purpose, I thought as I gazed up at Opal's building, which was your classic Park Avenue co-op made of gleaming white stone and elaborately carved cornices.

Or maybe it wasn't my subconscious. Maybe it was fate.

Gabe was blabbing in my ear about our next steps and how maybe I should call my mom up next and blah blah blah as I marched across the street and into Opal's gleaming black-and-white marble lobby. Stan was on duty, which was good. I knew Stan. I raised my sunglasses so he could see my face and flashed him a gleaming smile. "Hi, Stan."

He didn't smile back at me. Seriously? Him too? "Hello, Miss Afton. How can I help you?"

There was no way *Stan* could be snubbing me in his little black cap and baggy off-the-rack suit. I fought to keep that gleaming smile on my face, because if there was one thing I'd learned over the course of my life, you could be rude to pretty much everybody but the doormen. The doormen were basically the gods of a building. There were rumors of people who'd skimped on tips and then ended up moving out of the building when they got stuck in elevator after elevator and found their packages mysteriously disappearing. "Just the usual. Here to see Opal."

At this, surprise flitted over Stan's face, ruffling his mustache. "Miss Sterling? You must know she doesn't live here anymore."

If I had a mustache, my own surprise would have blown it clean off my face. "What? Opal moved?" But I'd just talked to her and she hadn't said anything about it. She'd claimed she was in the same place she always was, using her second bedroom as an "office" for her "job." "When? Where?"

"You know I can't tell you that."

Right. It was against the doorman code. Privacy above all else.

Something I valued in my own doormen. Less so in Opal's right now. "What about Jim and Lucy? Her parents? Are they home? I'd love to see them."

I wouldn't actually love to see them. That wasn't quite fair—it wasn't like I'd hate to see them. Opal's parents were perfectly nice people, about the same age as my own and just as enmeshed in the social scene. I was used to cheek-kissing her mom at galas, breathing in her scent of Chanel No. 5 and complimenting her latest clutch, which was usually shaped like some kind of animal. At the gala the night of the murder (the murder gala?) she'd really gone all out and come with a clutch shaped with a rhinoceros. If my grandma hadn't gone and gotten murdered that night, Mom would've been gossiping about it the next day, half saying how tacky it was and half buzzing with envy that she hadn't thought of it first.

"Mr. and Mrs. Sterling also no longer live here." Stan was unmoved. I wondered briefly if he would take a bribe, then remembered I had nothing to bribe him with.

I could try pity. I lowered my eyelashes, trying to channel the pathetic look of a dog begging for dinner. "It's just that . . . as you probably know, I've lost everything. If Opal and her family are in that same situation, I want to be able to help her. They might be too embarrassed to say anything first."

I didn't honestly think Opal and her family might be in the same situation. They'd probably just moved to another building in the area, thanks to bad neighbors or a good deal elsewhere.

But Stan's response intrigued me. "I wish I could help you. I'm sure Miss Sterling would love your help. But I can't. I'd get fired."

And no matter how pathetically I gazed up at him through my lashes, he wouldn't budge after that. "Right," I said. "Well. Okay. I guess I'll go." I lingered, pretending to search my bag for something in case he relented, but nothing. "Okay. Bye. Nice seeing you, Stan."

"You too, Miss Afton."

Back out into the sunshine. "Did you hear that?" I murmured to Gabe.

"Yeah, but I'm not entirely sure what happened." His background was entirely quiet now.

"Are you still at work?"

"No, I have a class. I'm at home working on an essay."

So I'd see him shortly. The thought actually kind of lifted my heart, as corny as it sounded. Still, I told him exactly what had gone down so that we didn't waste any time. He said, "So Opal lied?"

"Yes! Isn't that weird?"

"Weird as in potentially making her a murderer, though?" Gabe sounded skeptical. Too skeptical.

So I hung up. Let him think we lost connection. We'd see each other in a little bit, anyway.

If I was tired after the spa, I was plain exhausted after lugging myself up three flights of stairs to my new apartment. I pushed open the door, bracing myself for the slope of the floorboards, and then Squeaky came running at me with his signature rusty meow.

That jolted new life into me. I leaned over to pick him up, hugging him tight against my chest. He squirmed, so I only made him endure my love for a few seconds before letting him jump back down and pad away to where Gabe was sitting on the couch. "Oh, hey," I said. "Barely saw you there."

"Understandable. This fellow is the apple of everyone's eye." Gabe leaned down to scratch the cat as he wound his way between his ankles. "I really have to do this essay, so let's cut right to the chase. Do you actually think your friend could be the murderer?"

I'd been teeing up a speech the whole way back, mouthing the words and everything, about how Opal's behavior was suspicious, but the direct question sent it all scattering apart. "I mean, it's possible," I said. "And the fact that she lied to me like this makes it suspicious. We've been friends for years. I thought she was being a snob and ditching me because I lost my money, but hearing that she moved without telling anyone means it could be something else. What if she fled the country?"

"I guess," Gabe said doubtfully. "I don't know. I mean, you know them all better than I do, but your mom must know more than anyone else. Maybe you should give her a call next?"

Or, if I could find the killer before calling my mom, I would never *have* to call my mom. "But Opal lied. There's got to be something there."

"If you say so," Gabe said. "Can you call her and figure it out?"

"No, I can't just call her. I've tried to call her. She won't pick up." I pulled up Opal's social media. She'd been posting less than normal since that pic of her posing at my grandma's memorial, but she'd still been posting. An artfully filtered shot of her with some blooming cherry blossom trees (which in real life made her sneeze until her eyes were watery and her nose was red, hence the filter). Another shot of her biting into a massive croissant (I could guarantee that the one bite was all she took and the rest either went to her dining companion or to the New York City rats who scavenged the trash).

One pic smiling with her parents, all three of them dressed up for some gala or event or other. Opal was basically a younger twin of her mom, sharing her green eyes and auburn hair and narrow face, and her mom was carrying . . . was that a pigeon clutch? I knew I'd seen that before. The New York Public Library benefit gala last year? This picture was old, but it wasn't like it was uncommon or weird to post a throwback where you looked good. "Things look normal enough. It seems like she's still in the city."

Gabe snorted. "You can't tell anything from social media. It's all fake."

"I think you can tell a lot more about someone than you think. Do you even have social media?"

From the way he rolled his eyes, I could tell the answer was no. "I used to have it, and it made me sick. All these people competing to show how great their lives are. No, not just how great their lives are— how much better their lives are than everybody else's. And in the meantime, they're so busy hunting for that perfect shot and getting take after take that they miss out on real life."

It was my turn to roll my eyes. "You think I haven't heard that before?" We both jumped at the sound of an ambulance siren wailing outside. I wasn't used to being this close to street noise, but Gabe had no excuse. "Of course you can't look at someone's social media and expect to see their real life. You have to be able to remind yourself that you're looking through someone's highlight reel, not their actual day-to-day. It's another way to present yourself to the world the way you want to be presented. You're already doing that. You pick out your clothes based on what people will think of you in them, you phrase things for public consumption. It's just another tool. You have to think about it like you're seeing them how they want most to be seen, and go from there."

Gabe clearly hadn't been expecting me to argue back with such passion, because his response was to blink a few times in silence. "Okay. Yeah, I guess I can see that. I hadn't thought about it like that before."

I'd returned to Opal's profile, scrolling through to see if I could catch anything that felt off. "She used to post pictures taken all over the city, but all of Opal's recent shots were taken near her old haunts. The cherry blossoms are geotagged Central Park, and the croissant is from that new café near the Met. She's really driving home that she's in this area. Clearly she wants everybody to think that nothing's changed. Which means she's embarrassed about whatever caused her to move." Stan's weird answer after my pathetic display nagged at me again.

"Or she didn't move very far," Gabe countered. "Maybe it's not suspicious at all. Maybe she got a better deal on an apartment down the block."

I shrugged. "I don't know. I did think it, but thinking about it more on the walk back, the Sterlings aren't people who would move for a deal. They've lived in that apartment for years. Opal too. They wouldn't leave unless there was a reason. And if there was a simple reason and they're still nearby, why wouldn't she just have told me?"

Silence. I stood there staring down at my phone, gears turning in my head. Gabe, on the couch, stroked Squeaky's back as he stared off into space.

Then it hit me. "Location sharing."

"What?"

I was already clicking over to my message thread with Opal. "Location sharing. We used to share our location with each other whenever we went out, in case one of us got drunk and wandered off or went home with some sketchy guy, and if I'm lucky—yes! I'm lucky!"

Gabe raised his eyebrows. "She forgot to turn it off?"

"She forgot to turn it off." Triumphantly, I clicked. Opal's location loaded, placing her in a neighborhood called Rego Park. "Where is that?" I zoomed out. My jaw dropped. A roach could've jumped in and I wouldn't have noticed. "QUEENS?!"

It did not compute. I scrolled in and out, closed out of the app and reopened it. But no use. The blinking dot that indicated Opal's location—or at least Opal's phone's location—still sat in Queens. *Queens.* And not even the cool part of Queens, where I might not accept living but where I might accept visiting to get some food or go out.

"She certainly didn't show that on her profile," Gabe mused beside me. I jumped. I'd been so involved in my phone that I hadn't even seen him get up and come over, standing close to the point where I could feel the heat of him on my shoulder. "So what's the plan? Do we go out and confront her?"

I set my phone on the coffee table with a snap. Go out to Queens? How was I even supposed to get all the way out there? "Let's check again tomorrow," I decided. "Maybe she's just . . . visiting or something, I don't know. Or her phone was stolen and by tomorrow she'll have a new one."

"If you say so," Gabe replied. "How about in the meantime you call your mom and see if you can get anything out of her? You know, keep the investigation moving along."

He was suddenly way too close. I took a big step away, wrapping my arms around myself. "I think we should take things one at a time. You know. You keep from getting mixed up." So that he wouldn't get stuck on how that made no sense, I barreled on, changing the subject. "So what was up with your manager today? What a dick."

Now it was Gabe's turn to back away and wrap his own arms around himself. A body language expert would have a field day with us. Actually, they wouldn't need to be an expert—a body language amateur would be scribbling furiously in their notepad. "I didn't mean for you to hear that."

"Yeah, but I did," I said. A neighbor's door opened and closed in the hallway, so loud it was like they were opening and closing one of our bedroom doors. "And I'm annoyed on your behalf. No, outraged. I can't believe they're paying you that little!"

Gabe strode over to the kitchen and opened the refrigerator, sticking his face in. His voice was a little muffled when he said, "Gee, thanks."

It was hard to tell if he was being sarcastic or not when he wasn't looking at me, so I decided to continue under the assumption that he'd been speaking in good faith. "I think we should make a plan for how you're going to try again. Because you deserve more, and his reasons you're not getting it were total BS."

He rubbed the back of his head, his face still in the fridge. If he hadn't found what he wanted to eat by now, he wasn't going to find it. There was no Lori here to magically restock the food stores. "Lay off it, okay?"

"No way!" I said. My hands found their way to my hips. "I'm just getting started. I'm thinking that you shouldn't go back to him with an email, you should make sure to—"

"Pom!" Now he spun around, hands on his own hips. His face was red. "I told you to stop. I don't need your help with this."

"I mean, clearly you do."

That was clearly the wrong thing to say, because his cheeks darkened to a full-on brick red. "I can handle this myself. What do you know about situations like this, anyway? You've never even had a job, have you?"

Technically that depended on how you defined *job*. I'd done a few unpaid internships. "Maybe not the way you have, but I have lots of practice in demanding what I want," I said crisply. "And in getting it."

He shook his head. "Do you not understand that the world works differently for people like you and people like me?" He didn't wait for me to answer, which was good, because I had no idea what I was supposed to say to that. "Maybe in your life you've been used to getting whatever you want, but that's not how things work for me." He slammed the fridge shut. "I'm going to go work on my essay."

I stood there silent as he retreated to the couch to grab his laptop, then farther to his room. He held the door open for a moment, which confused me—did he want me to follow him in there? no, right?—but when Squeaky trotted in behind him and he closed it, I understood. He'd left me totally alone out here.

I'd only been trying to help. But fine. If he didn't want my help, then I couldn't force him to accept it. He could just languish in his job, getting paid less than he deserved and being given way less credit than he should.

My blood was pumping hot, though. I shook my hands out. I had to do something with them or I might climb out of my skin. Go for a run? I couldn't bear the thought of messing up my beautiful spa hair before I had to by sleeping on it. Go see a friend? I almost laughed at myself. What friend?

The thought of spending the night scrolling through my phone at all the fun people were having without me seemed so depressing.

Over to the kitchen. Gabe had been looking for something to eat, and he hadn't found it. I could bake something. One step closer to my own bakery chain and cooking show.

After googling the perfect recipe, I set about arranging all the ingredients on the counter—Andrea had always insisted we do that, both for the ease of keeping everything you'd need in reach and for making sure you weren't missing anything—and daydreaming about what I wanted my future show to look like. Obviously I would need to keep my hair tied back—nobody wanted to think about hair in their baked goods—but that didn't limit me. There were all sorts of ponytails and braids and updos I could do. And don't even get me started on the ribbons and scrunchies.

An hour or so later, I opened the oven to a cloud of fragrant choc-olaty steam. Potholder on hand, I carefully removed the tray and set it atop the oven, regarding it proudly. The chocolate chip cookies were puffy and a pale golden brown; they looked a little jiggly in the center, but I remembered Andrea insisting that they should look that way, since they'd finish cooking in the residual heat on the tray as they cooled. "Beautiful," I whispered, the same thing viewers would one day say about *Pomona's Kitchen* (that was my working title for my show).

Gabe's door cracked open, which was good, because if he hadn't emerged at this smell I'd have assumed he had keeled over and died. He didn't leave his doorway, though, as he asked, "What did you make?"

"Chocolate chip cookies," I said. He still didn't move. I sighed. "You should have some."

Now he bounded out. "Thanks." I thought he might dive right onto the sheet tray, smearing his face in cooling dough, but he stopped before me, looking chastened. "Hey, sorry for before. I didn't mean to get so defensive or insult you. I know you were only trying to help."

"Thank you," I said magnanimously. Maybe I'd let him come work on my cooking show. I'd pay him way more than they did at the coffee shop. "And hey. I know we've lived in very . . . different circum-stances. But I'm used to people underestimating me or thinking I'm not worth what I'm worth, and speaking up about it." To everybody except my family members, but I didn't have to bring that up. "So, you know. I do have some experience there."

He nodded once, jerkily. "Maybe you're right." And his eyes strayed over to the cookies.

"Go ahead," I said. "Try the first one."

He moaned. Actually moaned. "These are amazing."

"I know," I said, pleased. Now if only everything else would go as well as my baking.

CHAPTER

Thirteen

So, Queens smelled.

Good, mostly. Which was a big surprise.

Gabe and I went right there after our morning shift at the coffee shop, which left me sweaty, with achy feet, and fully determined never to set foot in there again. (Except maybe to check on how my licensed brand of baked goods was selling in place of the garbage corporate sent there now. I'd suggested bringing some of my cookies in, but Gabe had protested about all sorts of food safety laws and regulations I'd be breaking. *So what*, I told him. *They're breaking the laws and regulations of public decency by treating you like crap*. But he was not moved.)

Too exhausted to protest, I let him drag me on the subway. It was not an enjoyable experience. Somebody was clipping their fingernails on the bench across from me. Like, why? Just why?

Anyway, as horrified as I was to be voluntarily going to Queens, all the fingernail-clipping left me relieved to step onto such foreign concrete. The cars of Queens Boulevard zoomed around me, and the smell of halal chicken and rice filled the air. "Is that a sushi restaurant?" I said, surprised. "They have sushi here?"

"Looks like two sushi restaurants." Gabe stepped nimbly around me, pulling me to the side of the moving sea of people. "Yes, they have sushi here. Probably better sushi than in Manhattan."

I snorted. "Have you ever eaten at Sushi Noz? Or Yoshino? No? You're missing out." I consulted the location tracker on my phone.

Sadly for her, Opal's phone placed her in the same location she was in yesterday. "She's only a few blocks from here. Let's go."

My heart pounding, we followed the blinking cursor away from the highway lined with restaurants and shops and down a quieter residential street. Small detached houses lined up between large, boxy apartment buildings. Trees made the street green, and the occasional playground filled the air with the happy cries of children. It was so . . . ordinary. Nice, I supposed. But so dull. The dogs were all mutts. The people were all just outside walking around in jeans and T-shirts. Sometimes even sweatpants.

I did not belong. Even in my . . . "reduced state," as you might say, I'd made Gabe wait for me to change into a plain and only slightly smelly Emblème merino wool tunic (still working up the courage for that basement laundry trip). But I could see why some people might like it here.

"In there," I said, pointing as we approached Opal's location, one of the detached houses. It was squat and brick, a little shabby, lacking the cheerful flower gardens or brightly painted front doors of its neighbors. I couldn't picture my fashionable, snobby friend living there. "I guess we should like, go up and knock?"

Before we could get any closer, the front door swung open and somebody stepped outside. I gasped so big something small and fluttery—hopefully not a bug, please not a bug—got stuck in my throat.

Because there she was: Opal. But her existence in this place wasn't the only thing that made me gasp. I'd expected it, based on her phone location. It was what she'd done with herself. Or, to be more frank, what she hadn't done with herself. Her small, thin frame was practically swallowed up by an enormous hoodie emblazoned with the name of some tourist town in California; she'd tied her hair back in a not-cute-messy-but-real-messy ponytail and covered her eyes with big sunglasses. Her dishwater-brown roots were on full display. If she'd walked by me on the street and I hadn't actively been looking for her, I wouldn't even have recognized her.

"She's on the move," Gabe murmured. "Do we follow?"

We had to decide one way or the other immediately, because, after a moment of dawdling on her phone, she began walking toward us. "Yes!" I hissed. "But she can't see us yet!"

In one direction there was the road, lined by neatly parked cars. In the other was the courtyard of an apartment building, which had a few benches scattered around some wilting flowers. Since Gabe didn't seem capable of figuring it out himself, I shoved him toward the courtyard. He went tumbling toward a bench. Caught off-balance, I tumbled on top of him, straddling him.

His hands reached out to catch me by the waist before I could fall over. His heart thudded against mine. I could feel the definition of his pecs through his polo shirt.

It was . . . not unpleasant.

I held myself stock-still, afraid to move and call any attention to myself. That was entirely why, and it had nothing to do with the warmth creeping up the back of my neck.

After a few moments had passed, long enough where she was probably past us yet not so far that she'd be out of sight, I pushed myself off him, clearing my throat. "Okay. Well. Good. She didn't see us." I linked my elbow through Gabe's and pulled. My feet had been screaming in agony before from being on them all day at the coffee shop, but now I could barely feel them. Which, actually, was probably not a great sign. "Come on. After her!"

"Why are we hiding from her in the first place?" Gabe asked. "Aren't we here to confront her? Why don't we just do that now?"

That would've been a good thought to have occurred to me earlier, before I ended up on his lap. Because now I was buzzing all over, too frazzled to interrogate someone for murder. I had to walk some of it off. "Because . . ." I frantically scrolled through my mind. "Because we have to see where she's going. Maybe it'll give us a clue."

"What kind of clue? Do you think she's going to the river to throw in the bloody murder weapon?"

I shrugged. Doe on *Here to Slay* had done something similar, trailing after another model she suspected had something to do with

Danica's disappearance. The other model had led her to a secret club under a stuffy old-timey bar, where Doe had found her next clue. So you never knew. I started moving. Gabe had no choice but to follow me or else be abandoned alone on the mean streets of Queens.

Honestly, I took great delight in creeping down the street after Opal like we were FBI agents tailing a suspect. It was a little bit of a bummer that she didn't seem to have any idea she might be getting followed, keeping her eyes trained on her phone the entire walk back to the highway. I was actually kind of worried she might get hit by one of the e-bikers zooming past her on the sidewalk, but she made it whole and unbruised to the . . . Dunkin' Donuts? My eyes widened with horror as she walked through that pink and orange door.

This was worse than I thought, worse than her holding the bloody murder weapon. The sheer horror shocked the buzziness right out of my limbs. I couldn't let this drag on any longer. I centered myself on the sidewalk outside, ready to accost her when she emerged with her bitter, watered-down coffee (I'd become a bit of a coffee snob since Gabe).

She came out clutching not only a Dunkin' Donuts coffee cup—she wasn't even bothering to disguise she was drinking coffee from a chain that wasn't Starbucks—but also a crinkly paper bag containing what must have been, from the powdered sugar dusting her upper lip, a donut.

Their donuts weren't even that *good*.

Anyway, I didn't have to accost her—only lift my sunglasses to my forehead. She stuttered to a stop when she saw my face, and while I couldn't see her eyes under her own sunglasses, I was pretty sure they were so wide they might pop. "Pom? What . . ." She dropped the donut bag, like I might not have seen it. It landed with a crinkly thud on the pavement, where a guy race-walking to the train immediately stomped on it. "Wh-what are you doing here?"

There were several ways I could take this. I could be angry at her for lying to me and yell, or I could smirk at her for this downfall she was clearly on. But that's not how you get someone to open up to you. No matter how you really feel.

So I gave her a small, sympathetic smile. "I wanted to check on you. See how you were doing."

"How did you even . . . know . . ." A tear slipped out from beneath the rim of her sunglasses.

I looped an arm over her shoulders. Under the sweatshirt, her bones felt as fragile as a bird's. Most birds', anyway. If I'd learned anything living in New York City, it was that you could hit a pigeon with a taxi and the taxi would probably end up dented. "Come on. Let's go somewhere private."

She retraced our steps, though she walked us past her house and to a small park with triangles of benches. There wasn't much greenery here besides beaten-down grass and a few trees, and a guy smoking weed was taking up the most preferable triangle with the most shade, but it was quiet otherwise. She sat down on one of the benches. I sat next to her, and Gabe sat next to me.

Opal pursed her lips at him. "Who's this guy? I just assumed he was following us."

"And that didn't alarm you?" I said. She lifted her sunglasses and squinted at me, like I should take being followed as a compliment. "Opal, no. This is Gabe. My . . ." What should I even call him? My partner? My friend? The guy who made my insides melt a little when he touched me? "My new roommate," I said. I'd paused too long. Both Opal and Gabe were looking at me funny. "Anyway, he's supposed to be here. He's not a creepy stalker. At least, not that I know about."

"Hi," Gabe said, extending his hand. "Nice to meet you."

Opal just stared at his hand until he dropped it. "Okay."

She was being super rude, but if we focused on that, we might make her too defensive to open up to us. So I moved things along. "And Gabe, you already know this is my old friend Opal." I emphasized *old friend*, as if to remind her of all we'd been through together. "Opal, I stopped by your building to see you, and Stan told me you moved. Nobody knew where you went. I got worried." I patted her on the arm. She leaned into my touch, the bottom of her part auburn, part dishwater-brown ponytail—were those split ends?—brushing my shoulder. "What's going on?"

She stared down at her coffee cup. "Well. I guess there's no point in trying to hide things now. You always could see right through me."

"Because I'm your *old friend*," I said.

She sniffed. "I should've known I could trust you." She drew in a deep, shuddery breath. "It turned out that one of Daddy's biggest investments was a Ponzi scheme. We lost everything practically overnight." She paused for a moment, taking a slurp of her coffee. "Well, not everything. But everything that mattered. All of our holdings on the Upper East Side, and almost all of our liquid assets. We had to sell our apartments and move out here to one of the few holdings we had left."

I gave her a tight hug. "Why didn't you tell me? You know I'm in the same position. We could've supported each other."

She wiped her nose with the sleeve of her sweatshirt. "We're not in the same position, Pom. You're famous. You're from a famous family, and you might have lost a lot, but you still have plenty. We're new money, you know. My dad made all our money, not our great-great-grandparents. My mom doesn't come from Boston royalty like yours. We're nobodies. I just . . . I couldn't handle talking about it with you."

"Oh, Opal." My heart squeezed. I glanced over at Gabe to see him looking intently in the opposite direction, probably because he was rolling his eyes and didn't want us to see. At least he'd learned that much since Fred.

It made something flicker inside me at the thought that he was trusting me to take the lead. Pride? "So you've been pretending you're still living in your old apartment, doing all the same things, so that nobody finds out how far you've fallen."

She nodded. I wished she hadn't lied to me, but honestly, I understood. If I hadn't been "famous," as she said, with my family's misfortune blasted all over the place, I might have tried the same thing to save face. I told her so, and that was when she burst into tears.

"I'm so sorry, Pom," she wept. "I'm sorry I was behaving so weird. I'm sorry I stole your tracksuit after the gala because I was starting to need to repeat clothes not made out of polyester. I didn't mean to be a bad friend. I should have been there for you."

Her tears made tears well up in my own eyes. "I should have been there for you too. We can be there for each other now." We clung tight to each other, crying into each other's hair, as Gabe sat on the other end of the bench and probably wished he was literally anywhere else.

There's only so long you can cry for before your head starts to ache and the puffiness in your eyes won't go down even after a splash of cool water. We both knew that time period well, and so we separated at the same time, sniffling hard and tilting our heads back so that the tears would flow back into our eyes. "You won't tell anyone, right?" Opal asked.

"Of course not." I gave her arm a squeeze. "But I hope we can be honest with each other from now on." With everything except for me thinking she might potentially have murdered my grandmother, obviously. "And be there for each other."

Her big green eyes were shiny. "I'll be there for you."

"And I'll be there for you. Whenever you need me."

I didn't mean it literally, of course. I mean, it took an hour and two different subway lines to make it back to our apartment. By the time I had to haul myself up those stairs, my feet were throbbing again. I groaned just looking at the steps. "Any chance you want to carry me?"

"Zero chance," Gabe said. He'd been oddly quiet our whole trip back, even when we walked by multiple street carts selling fresh juices and churros, one of his favorite topics to expound upon. (He thought it should be easier to get a legal permit for people to sell their food. I agreed, mostly because it meant an easier start for my future bakery.)

I sighed dramatically. "Okay. But it feels kind of like we're about to climb Mount Everest." Which I'd never had the desire to do. Nicholas had gone with some friends in college and it had sounded depressing, hiking past dead bodies nobody was able to remove and hoping you wouldn't end up among them. Much better to climb an Alp via ski lift and spend your evenings sipping *vin chaud* under an enormous fuzzy blanket you half think might be made out of actual yeti fur. "Here we go."

Gabe still wasn't talking much when we reached our apartment. Typically I'd just let him have his space, but I was starting to become more attuned to his moods. "Hey," I said, once we had locked the door behind us and Squeaky was meowing about how happy he was that we were back. "Is everything okay? You seem kind of quiet."

He scratched behind Squeaky's ears, taking a deep breath before saying, "Pom, are you ashamed to be seen with me?"

"What? No." I didn't even have to think about it. "Of course not. You're my . . ." I was about to say "roommate" again, but somehow the word didn't feel right here. What did feel right was "my friend."

"I see." He helped himself to one of my cookies, so he couldn't have been that upset. "I just . . . maybe it's letting myself be biased by what I used to read and hear about you, but the way you were today with Opal . . ."

"She was being rude," I said immediately. "And usually I would've called her out, but I didn't want to compromise our investigation. You know?" I pulled out my phone and dangled it in the air. "But I'll call her right now and tell her I didn't like how she was acting around you. That just because she's poor now doesn't give her an excuse to be a snob."

Would I have been similarly rude to Gabe in the past? The thought unsettled me. I didn't think I'd be rude to him on purpose, or consciously think about how I was acting, but maybe that was the problem. Maybe it was that I hadn't consciously thought about how I acted around other people.

But then another thought hit me, a delayed analysis of what he'd said. "Wait," I said, kind of delighted. "You used to read about me? Like, before we knew each other?"

The tip of his nose flushed red, but he nodded. "I mean, my mom worked for your family. I was interested in who you were. What you were up to."

"Oh yeah?" I couldn't help but smirk. "What did you think about me?"

"Do you actually want me to answer that?"

Well, now I did. "Yes."

"Okay. You have to agree not to get mad, though. Because I don't feel that way anymore."

As if he sensed I needed him, Squeaky came trundling my way. He headbutted my calf, and I crouched down to give him attention. I took a deep breath, bracing myself to hear Gabe tell me he thought I was spoiled, selfish, vain, stupid, silly. All words I was used to seeing attached to my name. "Okay. I promise I won't get mad."

He started off the way I expected. "I didn't like you. At all." Then the way he continued made me blink in surprise. "But it had nothing to do with you personally. My mom spent so much more time with you and your family than she did with me and my family, and I took that personally. I knew it was her job, of course. That she got paid to take care of you. But I convinced myself it had to be because of some deficiency I had. That I wasn't a good enough son. And I took that out on you." I peeked up to see he was wearing a wry smile. "Thank my therapist for those excellent insights."

"That wasn't nearly as bad as what I thought you were going to say," I chirped. "And you said you do feel differently now. So you like me!"

He rolled his eyes. "Fine. Yes. I like you, Pom. I'm glad you moved in here and didn't give up your first night and go back to your brother's."

My brother's. I hadn't heard from Nicholas in a few days, which, while not unlike him, felt odd given our circumstances. Shouldn't he have at least checked in to see how his only sister was doing? To make sure I hadn't moved in with a cannibal ax murderer or one of those guys who played terrible saxophone in the park?

"I'm glad I moved in here, too," I told him. I took in another deep breath. He and his family had made sacrifices for me and mine. The least I could do for them was a small sacrifice of my own to further our search for the murderer. "And tomorrow I'll do it. I'll call my mom."

CHAPTER

Fourteen

G abe didn't understand why it was such a big deal for me to call
my mom, probably because he'd grown up with a loving mother
who praised him and did everything she could to build up his spirit and
confidence. I didn't want to get into it with him either, so I demurred,
said I was going to get ready for bed, and then got up in the middle of
the night to stress-bake a batch of brownies. I made sure to take them
out of the oven on time. They were delicious.

I woke up early the next morning, giving me enough time to see
Gabe out the door for work. When I padded out into the living room,
wrapped in the silky hotel robe I'd taken with me, he was squinting at
the Post-it note I'd left for him on the fridge. "Out of chocolate chips
and flour," he read to me, then turned in my direction. "You know
you could just go buy more, right?"

I blinked. I wasn't used to thinking about that; typically if I used
the last of something, I'd leave a note for Lori to pick it up. "Oh yeah.
Right. I'll do that."

"Just don't use it as an excuse not to call your mom," he said.

I blinked more. I hadn't even told him why I didn't want to call
her, but clearly he'd picked up on my attitude. "I won't. Though I'm
not sure when I was in a grocery store last. I might get lost in all the
aisles."

"I have faith in you," Gabe said as he walked out the door, and
even though I knew he meant it as a joke, it still made me go all warm
inside.

Not warm enough to listen to him, though. I knew I had to call my mom, but I had a ton of stuff to do first. Go to the grocery store, for one, where I picked up not only chocolate chips and flour but some other fun ingredients from the baking aisle: shredded coconut; malted milk powder; almond extract; instant yeast. Despite the fluorescent lighting that gave everything around me a sickly glow and was probably draining my life-force with each step, I also thoughtfully picked up some apples for Gabe, since I noticed he ate them daily and the fruit bowl was running low. Then I job-hunted, because if I was going to be stuck living this life for the foreseeable future, I could be doing something less taxing than working at a coffee shop. I didn't actually apply for anything, since I still had to write my résumé and a cover letter, but at least I got an idea of what was out there. Surely I could handle answering phones. As long as I could get off my feet.

Then lunchtime rolled around, and I had to eat food with fiber in it that wasn't just cookies and brownies, so I went out for a salad, and then I couldn't think of another excuse so I took a walk around the neighborhood, and then finally I returned home to find Gabe there munching on a brownie. "How did the call with your mom go?" he asked without even saying hello, which, rude.

"I'm going to do it right now," I said, and bolted for my bedroom, shutting the door behind me. It wasn't that I didn't want him to overhear our conversation. Okay, it was exactly that I didn't want him to overhear our conversation. He'd *just* admitted that he liked me and was happy that I'd moved in here. That we were friends.

I didn't want anything my mom said to or about me to make him reconsider that.

I gulped in a deep breath and hit Mom's contact, then speakerphone, since I'd left my headphones in the other room and I knew if I ended the call now, I'd chicken out. As soon as she trilled an "Oh, Pom, hello!" into the phone, I realized I'd made a huge mistake. I hadn't planned anything out. I had no idea what to say.

"Hi, Mom! So nice to hear your voice!" I said as enthusiastically as I could, because who didn't like thinking that someone was happy to speak with them? "How are you? What's new?"

She heaved a disgusted sigh so heavily in my ear I could practically smell her always-minty breath. "These dogs are getting on my last nerve. Every time one of them runs up to me yapping and wagging its stubby little tail, I'm tempted to kick it down the hall."

Just her mentioning the dogs made me think about my cat. Who she'd disposed of and told me ran away. Had Grandma ever done that to someone? Because that would be a totally understandable motive for murder. I took in another deep breath, trying to think less homicidal thoughts. "That sounds rough. At least you're right on the beach, though!"

"For what it's worth," Mom muttered, "I didn't realize their beach wasn't private, it's just beach access. So there are always other people around."

The horror. "Sounds rough," I said again, striving to sound sympathetic. *For your credit cards, Pom. For your beautiful apartment and for Lori. How is Lori doing now, anyway? No, focus.* "Have you heard if there are any updates on Grandma's case?"

"Keep that thing away from my purse!" my mom yelled. Then, to me, "Sorry, that dratted dog again. What was that?"

"Grandma's case," I repeated. "You know, the unsolved nature of which is keeping you trapped with those horrid dogs and beachgoing rabble?"

"Right," said Mom, still sounding as if she were only half paying attention. I could imagine her in a staring contest with some beady-eyed ball of fluff down the hall. "No, no news. They still don't seem to have any leads."

"Not even the murder weapon?" It seemed weird that they still hadn't found it, or at least figured out what it was. Doe on *Here to Slay* had been able to figure out that someone had hit Danica over the head with her Birkin bag before abducting her due to a specific pattern of dust and fibers on the floor. And on TV they always managed to take some detailed images of a distinctive nick in the wound and narrow it down pretty quickly. Though of course I knew TV wasn't reality. I'd been featured on enough shows where they cut the worst possible sound clips from me saying things like "I wouldn't say I think poor people deserve to be poor."

"No, not yet." A door slammed on the other side of the phone, probably my mom hiding from the dog. "You know, you really shouldn't worry your pretty little head about it so much. Look forward, not back."

This from the woman who'd recently anonymously sent her *Vogue* cover to the high school girls who'd friend-dumped her for wearing sweatpants to school one time. "I don't know, I'm having a hard time with it," I said, and since I was only saying it to get a reaction from her, I didn't even care that she would probably seize upon the opportunity to tell me I was weak. "I've been thinking a lot about who might have the motive to kill her. Can you imagine something as horrible as that? Stabbing a little old lady so many times with something small and sharp?"

Mom snorted, a very unladylike sound that, should it have come out of *my* nasal region, she would immediately have told me she'd disown me if I ever made again. "'A little old lady'? Come on, Pomona. Your grandmother wasn't some sweet, defenseless 'little old lady.' I know you have a brain in there, no matter how little you use it."

With every word she spoke, I could feel myself shrinking, my hands curling in on themselves like the legs of dead spiders. She went on: "Don't act like she was a saint just because she's dead. Hundreds of people had reasons to kill her, and all of those reasons were more than what I had. I mean, I wasn't going to kill her for trying to sabotage my arts gala or for continuing to tell your father he should divorce me even after twenty years and two beautiful children."

Beautiful. She'd called me beautiful. That was nice, right? Sometimes she could be nice.

"Anyway," Mom said, "I don't think we'll ever find out who did it, or even what they used. We should all start getting used to our new reality. I'm already apartment-hunting. I don't get my full trust from

Nana until she kicks it"—Nana being her mother, a faded socialite from a prominent Boston family—"but I got enough when Pop died that I can get something respectable to tide us over. And your father will find another job soon enough, as will Nicholas." She paused, then cleared her throat. "Don't worry, dear, I'm sure someone will hire you too. You still have so many followers, don't you? People appear to care about what you post, and that seems to be a viable career for those who don't have any other skills to use. Or you could marry a nice wealthy man. We know plenty, and you're young enough still where your looks will matter more than what's in your head."

I had withered so much at her words that I felt like a shadow, one who could only manage to push out a few words. "Oh. Maybe."

Barking sounded faintly in the background of her line. She cursed under her breath, something she'd always told me made me sound, to my horror, like a teenager from the suburbs. "Please tell me they haven't learned how to open doors. I have to go. Love you, dear."

"You, too," I said, but she'd already hung up.

Center yourself, Pom. The way I'd learned in yoga, I took deep breath after deep breath, pushing my shoulders back with each one, focusing on a different thing that brought me peace every time. A fitting room with gads of clothes ready to be tried on. The view of the city from the roof deck of Millicent's building at night, the streets of SoHo pulsing with light and movement. A fresh set of ingredients before me ready to be sculpted with my hands and made into something new, flour and butter and sugar.

That was a new one.

After a few moments—I had it down to a science at this point—I'd inflated myself back up enough to stand and go back out into the main area, where Gabe sat on the couch. He watched me come out of my room but tore his stare away and to the floor as soon as my eyes met his. "I, um," he said. "I should probably tell you that I overheard your conversation. I wasn't trying to," he added hastily. "But the walls here are thin. And your mom is, um, very loud."

My insides started to shrivel again, but I couldn't let it show on the outside. "Sorry," I said, keeping my tone carefully flat. "I'll try to keep it down in the future."

"That wasn't what I meant." He shook his head. "Pom, the way she talked to you? Unacceptable. No mother should speak to her child that way. No *person* should speak to another person that way."

"That's just the way she is. It's just the way she talks."

"It shouldn't be. It's not right," he said. "You deserve better than that."

I had to get off this topic. It was making my insides squeeze uncomfortably like they might all come spilling out my mouth. "Like you," I pointed out. "You deserve better from your boss."

We regarded each other, brown eyes into brown eyes. Finally he said, slowly, "Maybe you're right. Maybe we both deserve better."

It felt nice to have someone take me seriously. Like I'd put on a pair of platform shoes and now, instead of looking down on me, everybody had to look me in the eye.

Of course, my mom had to ruin it by calling me back. I grimaced to see her name pop up on my screen. "It's probably one of her typical butt dials."

"Or maybe it's not," Gabe said. "Maybe you could talk to her."

Before I could think too hard about it, I hit the answer button. Since it had been on speaker before, it automatically went to speaker now. I said, all in a rush, "Mom, I didn't think it was cool how you spoke to me just now."

No response. Or there was a response, but it wasn't to me. "Definitely a butt dial," I whispered to Gabe, since it was my mom and my dad talking faintly on the other end.

Mom's voice was as taut as hair wrapped around a curling iron. "—was asking questions," she said, her own voice hushed. I could barely hear her. "Too many questions. She's not usually this inquisitive. Do you think she knows?"

She had to be talking about me. Kindly, my dad confirmed it. "Pom barely knows how to spell her name. There's no way she knows."

My cheeks heated at the insult, but then I heard Gabe's voice in my head. *You deserve better.* Because, like, obviously I knew how to spell my name. I knew how to bake things and coax answers out of people who didn't want to give them. I *wasn't* a total fool.

"She was the one who found the body. She was in the apartment after the murder. What if she has the shoe and has just been waiting for me to confess?" Mom hissed. "Someone has it, or else the police would have figured it out."

The shoe? The police?

Wait. The murder weapon had been a small, sharp object. I'd almost lost a toe to Mom's famous stilettos. If they were sharp enough to pierce the skin and muscle of my foot, then surely they were sharp enough to stab a fragile old lady to death.

"Take a deep breath," said my dad. "If the police do show up, we have lawyers on retainer and plenty of cash on hand offshore. You'll be out on bail and then we'll figure it all out from there."

A dog started barking in the background, cutting off their conversation. My mom cursed, and then the phone hung up. Both Gabe and I sat there, stunned, staring at the blank black screen.

My mom. My mom was the killer. She'd stabbed my grandmother to death with her famous stiletto heel, before apparently dropping it at the murder scene and fleeing.

Which meant that I, Pomona Abigail Afton, was a murderer's daughter.

CHAPTER

Fifteen

Gabe was in favor of calling the police right away and telling them what we'd heard. "They can go and arrest her, and you'll get your life back. I can talk to my brother, Caleb—the detective. He might not be able to help with the investigation, but I know he'll pull some strings to make sure things are kept on the down-low until everything is absolutely certain."

But I was shaking my head before he'd even finished speaking. "You heard her. They've got the lawyers and money ready. We can't go to the police with some overheard gossip, not even if the police is your brother. We need real hard evidence."

Though, to be honest, that was as much a stalling tactic as anything else. I mean, terrible or not, she was my *mom*. The only one I had. The thought of turning her in felt like a betrayal, especially when I didn't know why she'd done it. And what would the rest of the family think of me? Obviously my mom would hate me. My dad would, too, out of loyalty. What about Nicholas?

At least Farrah would probably like me again.

I popped up from my seat on the couch, practically vibrating with anxiety. I considered baking something—maybe something with the yeast I'd bought, since I understood bread making required a lot of beating and smashing dough—but we already had the cookies and brownies I'd made. Anything more and we'd basically be laying out the red carpet for the mice. "I'm going to go for a walk."

"Want me to come with you?" Gabe asked, beginning to stand. I stopped him with a shake of my head.

"I just need to be alone for a bit."

Except that as soon as I was outside on the cloudy sidewalk, squinting at the extra-dim world through my giant sunglasses, the last thing I wanted was to be alone. From then on, it was like my feet started moving west on their own, weaving through the mobs of people emptying out of the Lexington Avenue subway stop and hardly even looking into the trendy coffee shops that had been popping up all over the place like designer boutiques during the Hamptons summer season.

Maybe fifteen minutes later I found myself standing in front of Jessica's building, staring up at the stained brick facade. I considered texting Nicholas and telling him I was here, or maybe ringing the buzzer like a normal person, but someone was coming out right then and very kindly held the door for me, or maybe it wasn't so kind considering I could have been there to steal all their packages, which would have been easy without a doorman to protect them. I barely spared the piles of packages a glance (seriously, it would've been so easy, but I doubted anything someone living in a nondoorman building had ordered would be worth my while, not that I was a thief even then) on my way to the elevator.

By the time Nicholas opened the door to their apartment, surprise written all over his face, I'd plastered on a huge smile. "Big brother!" I chirped, something I had never called Nicholas in my life. "I was just walking by and thought, Wow, it's sure been a long time since I've seen my favorite and only sibling, I should stop by and make sure he's still alive. Can I come in?"

I shouldered past him before he could answer. He needed some company, anyway, judging from how he looked: stubble shadowed his jaw, and he wore baggy sweatpants and a T-shirt so tight it might actually have been his girlfriend's. All of his were probably in a dirty pile on the floor until Jessica took pity on him and did his laundry. I didn't think he knew how to work a washing machine (to be fair, I didn't either). "Jessica home?" I asked, though it was clear she wasn't, considering the apartment was so small she would've been in sight or at least in earshot.

Nicholas shook his head anyway. "Haven't you heard of a phone?" he grumbled, though he didn't try to throw me out. "Maybe I was busy."

The TV, with one of the many *Law & Order* shows on, was playing in the background. "You can spare some time for your favorite and only sister," I said. "I wish I'd brought you some cookies or brownies. You know, I've started baking lately. I'm very good at it, as it turns out."

"That's great, Pom," Nicholas said absently, flicking off the TV. Our faces reflected in the empty black screen, and I marveled at how alike we looked (especially now that I was sans a twelve-step beauty routine): our long faces; our straight brown hair; our bow-shaped lips.

Surely he couldn't hate me when we were basically part of each other. And I knew that was a stupid thought, but it gave me hope anyway.

"Have you thought about job-hunting?" Nicholas was saying as I snapped back to attention.

"I have a job, actually," I said. "I'm working at a coffee shop for now."

His eyebrows practically levitated off his head. "A coffee shop? You're working at a coffee shop?"

"Why is that so crazy?" I asked, though I would probably have had the same reaction a few months ago if someone had mentioned to me that I'd be working at a coffee shop in the future. "I can handle it. I'm not too bad at it, actually."

His laugh was scornful. "Of course you're not bad at it. Any monkey could work at a coffee shop. I was asking if you'd thought about hunting for a *real* job."

Again, a few months ago, I probably would've nodded in agreement. But that was before multiple days behind the register had left me exhausted and unappreciated, singed by boiling milk and pained by aching feet. "Working in a coffee shop *is* a real job," I said. "And it's actually really hard. People are not that nice to you. And your feet hurt. And it's not easy remembering all the different drinks and how to make them, much less doing a good job at it."

Nicholas snorted. "Sure, okay. But let me know if you want help with your résumé. Such as it is. You can't have more than half a page, and I bet most of that is your contact information and social media handles."

Gabe's voice echoed through my head. *Maybe we both deserve better.* Pretend Gabe was right: I was better than this. Annoyance at what Nicholas had said sliced through me like a paper cut. "That wasn't very nice. Neither the thing about my job nor my résumé. You should apologize."

Nicholas blinked, rearing back a little as if in surprise. He probably was surprised: I'd never spoken to him, or any of my family members, like this before. "Okay." He paused for a moment, maybe thinking about it. "You know, you're right. I'm sorry, Pom." His eyelids drooped as if he couldn't hold them open a second longer. "It was uncalled for. No excuse, but I've been stressed-out lately. Jessica's been pulling all the weight in this relationship since we got kicked out of the Afton and I lost my job. I'm not used to depending on someone else like this."

I mean, he kind of was used to depending on our family and everything that being an Afton brought us. But I got what he meant. I took a seat on Jessica's couch, which was a nice soft blue velvety material that had been surprisingly comfortable to sleep on, and patted the cushion next to me. "It's okay. I forgive you."

He took a seat. Okay, now segue into the real meat of why I was here. "Speaking of forgiveness," I said casually, "do you think you could ever forgive someone who turned in a family member for murder? Just speaking, like, hypothetically."

Maybe he picked up on the fact that I was not at all speaking hypothetically, because his face immediately darkened, a storm passing through. "What are you talking about? What have you heard?"

I couldn't tell him about Mom. Not until I'd figured out what to do. "Like I said, just speaking hypothetically."

His voice lowered to a growl. The hairs on the back of my neck actually stood up. "I don't think you're speaking hypothetically, Pom. I'll ask you again: What have you heard?"

Jessica's couch wasn't feeling so comfortable anymore. I popped to my feet, trying to shake off the unease. "Why are you being so weird?"

He jumped to his feet, too, towering over me. "I'm not being weird. But I hope that you wouldn't accuse someone you care about of a horrendous crime without at least talking to them first."

He was right. I couldn't turn Mom in without talking to her and at least giving her a chance to defend herself. I needed to know why she did it.

"Do you promise, Pom?" Nicholas's voice had risen. If his face was a storm cloud, his voice was lightning.

Lightning that defused with the click of his front door opening. Jessica backed in, carrying a few bags and saying, "I stopped at the market on the way home and picked up some carrots for the—" She stopped as she turned around and noticed me. "Oh, Pom, hey!" she said brightly. "Do you want to stay for dinner? I'm making a chicken stir-fry."

Her smile faded as she glanced back and forth between me and Nicholas, probably due to the look on his face. "Is everything okay?"

"Everything's fine," I said hastily. "You look so cute, by the way!"

Her face lit up. "Thank you! I got this dress on sale! And it has pockets!"

Was getting the dress on sale supposed to be a good thing? From her tone, I guessed yes. "Well, I love it." That was a little hyperbolic, but the dress, a midcalf purple and yellow flowered cotton-blend thing with a gathered bust and flared skirt, was cute enough. "And thanks so much for the invitation."

"Pom was actually just leaving," Nicholas said.

I ignored him, instead giving Jessica a sunny smile. "How was work?"

"It was fine," she said, her own smile faltering. "Are you sure everything is okay?"

"Everything's fine," I said at the same time as Nicholas said, "Pom, I thought you had to go."

He was being so weird it made me want to stay, but I didn't want to make things even weirder between us by provoking him more. "Right, that's right. I do have to go."

"Oh, that's too bad," said Jessica, setting her bag down on the kitchen counter. "Come back soon, though! Don't be a stranger!" I hugged her goodbye—she hugged enthusiastically back—and then hugged my brother, which was like hugging a mannequin.

Of course, once they closed the door behind me and I'd done the obligatory walking-loudly-toward-the-elevator thing in case they were listening for me to leave, I tiptoed back over and plastered my ear to the metal below the peephole.

I couldn't hear much, and what I could hear was muffled. This door was thick, which was good for safety. But I could hear the two of them exchanging tense words. First Nicholas, then Jessica, then Nicholas again. "She knows something," I thought I heard. "What do we do?"

The voices went nearly silent after that, like the two had walked into the bedroom or kitchen. I gave it another minute in case they came back, then left. I spent my walk back to the apartment so deep in thought that I was lucky none of the sidewalk grates were open, because I definitely would've fallen in and been eaten by rats. Clearly, Nicholas knew something about the murder that he wasn't telling me. Could he possibly know what Mom had done? Could he be trying to cover it up?

It made sense, I guess. Nicholas had always been closer to Mom than I had. According to my mother, Nicholas could do no wrong. He was perfect, handsome, brilliant. It made sense that he would cover up a murder for someone who loved him like that. Or could he and Jessica have played some role? Maybe everybody in my immediate family except for me had taken part. Par for the course, really.

Back upstairs, Gabe was typing away on his laptop, probably working on an essay or some other project. "Hey," he said, looking at me over the screen. I expected him to ask me next what I had decided to do, but he looked way too enthusiastic for it to be that. "So I have a surprise for you."

I'd had just about enough of surprises for a while, thank you very much. "What?" I asked guardedly.

He turned his screen around to face me, a move which, if it was supposed to be climactic or something, failed dramatically, because all I could see was a white screen covered in tiny black font. "Your license got approved," he said, which was even less climactic, because I had no idea what he was talking about.

He seemed to see the cluelessness on my face. "So I did a little research when you mentioned selling your treats in the café," he said. "It turns out there aren't as many food safety regulations around it as I thought, at least when it comes to items that aren't highly perishable, like baked goods. All you have to do is apply for a license, which I did. And they already approved it. So you can sell your treats to the public now, as long as they don't need to be refrigerated."

Tears welled in my eyes, and I clasped my hands under my chin. I felt a little bit like I did when Vienna had persuaded her aunt, the owner of the one-of-a-kind ostrich feather Birkin, to let me borrow it for an event. Only better. Because back then, Vienna had only been trusting that I wouldn't destroy a handbag by the end of the night. Now Gabe was entrusting me with his job. With his stomach. He was telling me that he really believed in me. "I don't even know what to say."

"You could say thank you, for one." He turned his screen back around. "And that you'll bake something tonight to bring to the store for our shift tomorrow."

"Of course!" My mind was already whirring. I'd made the brownies twice and pretty much perfected them, so that was a safe bet. Or I could go daring and try something new. Maybe . . . oh. Wait. "And thank you! Thank you so much!"

"You're welcome, Pom." I could hear the amusement in his voice as he typed away. "I can't wait to see what you come up with."

I couldn't wait either.

Sixteen

The baking was a good distraction, at least, from the fact that I was the daughter of a murderer. Not just a murderer either. The murderer of a family member. I knew vaguely that patricide was the murder of a father. What was the murderer of a mother-in-law called? That sounded kind of like the opening of a joke.

I wished it were the opening of a joke.

And it wasn't simply that my mom was a murderer. It was that she'd been talking about it with my dad, which meant he knew his wife had murdered his own mother and was willing to cover it up. What did that make *him*?

I spent the night making two batches of my trusty brownies, plus testing out a cinnamon roll recipe that had to rise overnight. Of course, I miscalculated how much time I'd need to spend with them the next morning, which meant I was a few minutes late for my shift. Gabe had given up and left before me, leaving me to shell out some of my precious sunglasses savings to take a cab on my own.

"You're late," he said as I walked in, holding the platters.

"Not that late," I said. "Plus, I had to go slow to make sure these wouldn't get ruined."

He didn't press the issue, only helped me set up the brownies on the top—most desirable—shelf of the pastry case. Sage and Ellie, who were unstacking chairs and sweeping the floor in the main area, goggled at them. "Did you make those?"

"I did," I said proudly, attaching my RACHEL name tag to my

chest and pulling my green hat low over my forehead. After multiple shifts with nobody recognizing me, I was starting to feel confident in my role as Rachel Sparks. Maybe I should actually look into acting if the whole bakery line/cooking show thing didn't work out. I could picture myself on the *Today* show, sitting there in a tight white dress with my legs crossed over clear platforms with something quirky and fun in the soles—some jelly beans? a set of keys?—flashing the hosts and the audience a dazzling smile. *Why, yes! I took on the most challenging acting job of all—going undercover in the real world for a few months.*

I let the imaginary applause wash over me, keeping me from my own thoughts about tomorrow. When we were going to drive out to the Hamptons and confront my mom. My mom, the murderer.

It seemed as unreal as me on *Today*, prattling on about being undercover as if nothing had changed under my cover, laughing at myself like I didn't get the joke.

The morning sped by as usual. I was getting the hang of the register, and only lagged a little bit when making some of the less common specialty drinks. I even caught when Ellie accidentally mixed up oat milk and dairy milk before handing over the customer's oat milk latte. The customer thanked me profusely, adding all sorts of unnecessary details of what happened to her insides when she gave them dairy (I hadn't realized so many parts of the human anatomy could explode).

And my brownies! People snapped them up! The usual pastries were typically slow to go, probably because most of our customers were regulars here and the regulars were all wise to how terrible they were, but the brownies must have looked too delectable to pass up. It probably had something to do with the colorful plastic wrap and ribbons I'd packaged them in last night when I still couldn't sleep and ran out to the twenty-four-hour drugstore down the block, which, as it turned out, a whole different clientele frequented at night. I'd felt downright classy in my old sweats and greasy hair.

"Your cut won't be too bad," Gabe said, appearing behind me as if by magic during a lull in the line. I turned to him still smiling, and not even the fake customer service smile that Sage and Ellie had

counseled me to figure out early on. I didn't need a fake smile. This
job might be hard, but helping people and figuring out the system felt
good (though being thanked more often and not being yelled at if I
made a mistake would feel better).

"My cut?"

"Your cut. You get fifty percent of each sale," Gabe said. "Here's
what you're at so far." He named a figure that seemed pitifully small
out of context but felt larger when I realized that it amounted to three
hours of my pay here. "And then fifty percent goes to the café."

"What about you?" I asked. "I feel like you're, like, my agent. Or
my manager. You deserve something, too, because I definitely wouldn't
be doing this if you hadn't figured out all the licensing stuff."

"It's okay. You can buy the next round of groceries."

Seemed fair enough. The bell over the door tinkled and I turned to
the customer with a wide smile, ready to spark their daily joy with
some caffeine.

But the two girls who'd walked in didn't follow the usual customer
trajectory of scanning the menu, then marching up to the counter to
order, usually while scrolling their phone with a thumb. Their eyes lit
upon me, dug in so deep it felt kind of like they were scratching my
skin, and then they turned to each other as they whispered furiously. I
could only catch a few words. *She was right. That's totally her.*

Skin prickling, I pulled my cap lower on my forehead, as if that
would help now that my identity was apparently out. I had to get in
the back before they took a—

Nope. Too late. Both girls raised their phones in unison and
snapped pictures of me staring at them as if I were a model who'd
tripped on her first runway walk in front of Anna Wintour.

Well. If it was too late anyway, I might as well try to influence the
situation. Minimize the damage. This time the smile I flashed them
was fake, but it wasn't the measured customer service smile Sage and
Ellie had demonstrated for me—it was the dazzling fake smile I used
to use on old men who smelled like farts and leaned in too close when
they talked to me at galas, but were too rich for me to just walk away

from. "Hello there," I said, pretending I hadn't noticed what they'd done. "Can I help you?"

They shuffled closer, wide-eyed and gawking. "Are you Pomona Afton?" Girl One blurted.

I had a split second to decide: lie or tell the truth. It was possible I could get away with lying: my name tag said Rachel, after all, and I looked pretty different in this uniform without makeup. But it was risky. The girls had photos. If they had any sort of following—hell, even if they didn't—the photos could go viral, and someone who knew me could confirm. Even Sage and Ellie at least suspected, even if they were kind enough to pretend they didn't.

No. This was over. My identity was out. The only thing I could do was influence how the news went wide. I couldn't seem defensive, or the media would pounce on it. I couldn't look defeated. I had to be triumphant. Resilient. As if working here were totally my choice. "No comment," I said, giving them a wink. "But if I were, I'd be happy with how things are going. Turns out being in the real world is pretty refreshing."

Things spiraled from there. I lied and told them I wasn't allowed to take selfies while on the clock, but at least one of them must have been an influencer with a decent following or at least someone who knew how to work the hashtags, since by lunchtime people were flocking in not to buy coffee—though they did start after Gabe hung up a dubiously legal sign that said no hanging around without a purchase—but to gawk at me like I was the Hope Diamond. Only I wasn't protected behind glass; I was sitting on a stand out in the open where any random museumgoer could leave their grubby fingerprints all over me.

As a new crowd pushed their way through the door, filling the air with excited chatter, Gabe popped up beside me. "I know you said you were okay with all this, but I think maybe you should go home for the day," he murmured in my ear. His breath tickled my baby hairs. "This situation could get out of hand really fast."

"I can take the register," Sage volunteered. They and Ellie had stepped up during the onslaught, which touched me. They hadn't even asked for a selfie or anything.

"I don't mind," I said, but that changed as soon as the next person stepped up. She had pink hair and bright eyes and her phone screen held out in front of her. It was playing a video.

"Pom!" she chirped. "Do you have any comments on what Vienna said just now?"

My heart lurched at Vienna's name. Somehow meeting all these people at the coffee shop hadn't connected with the idea that people I knew—people like Vienna—would find out about my new circumstances. And while I could maybe make at least some of the public believe that I was where I wanted to be, that I was enjoying this new life, that it was my choice to be working at this coffee shop, my old friends wouldn't buy it. They'd laugh at me.

Suddenly I wasn't performing for an anonymous social media audience. I was performing for an audience of Vienna Soo.

A cold sweat broke out on the back of my neck. My ponytail was going to stick to it, and then people would come in and take pictures of me looking all matted and gross. "No comment," I said curtly, then looked over at Gabe, who was still hovering nearby. "I'm going on my break."

It wasn't my break time, but he nodded back. "Ellie, could you take register, please?"

Once I'd logged off I fled into the back room, where I tore my hat off and fanned myself with it. My underarms were sticky. *Don't look up what Vienna said "just now,"* I told myself, but my hand reached for my phone anyway.

Hashtag Vienna and Pom was trending. Heart lurching again, I pulled up the video, which seemed to have been taken by some random influencer who'd run into Vienna coming out of some art gallery, judging by the canvases covered by abstract paint splashes in the background. The way she'd done her black hair in an elegant French twist and casually thrown a colorful silk scarf over her tan pea coat made me even more witheringly self-conscious of my polyester uniform polo and sweaty ponytail. "Vienna! Vienna!" the girl who'd taken the video was saying behind the camera. "Did you hear that Pom Afton works at a coffee shop in Midtown now? What do you think about that?"

Vienna gave the camera a cautious, close-lipped smile. "I don't think about Pomona at all."

Ouch. Her words hit me like a kick to the stomach, which had happened a few times at the club (table-dancing space was at a premium). I actually staggered back a step or two, leaning up against the desk.

But the video wasn't over. The girl said, "Neither of you ever talked about your friend breakup. Now that it's in the past, can you tell us what happened and why the two of you stopped talking?"

Vienna's serene smile didn't change at all. I would almost have preferred her go big and toothy and triumphant. Because as it was, it felt a little like she was feeling sorry for me. "I don't have any comment. If you'll excuse me, I have an important appointment to get to." And she sailed away, the crowds of people on the sidewalk parting for her like the Red Sea.

An important appointment. I knew her well enough to know that she was probably going to a lunch or going home. I also knew her well enough to know that it was a dig at me. Because what important appointments did *I* have to go to these days?

Tears pricked my eyes. By the time Gabe walked into the back room, they had welled over. "Just wanted to check on you," Gabe said. "Hey, are you okay?"

I turned my head so that he wouldn't see my eyes go all red and puffy. My mom always said that crying gave me pig face. I didn't want—

You deserve better.

I consciously turned my face back toward him, feeling like I was pushing against a current. And I let him see me cry, pig face and all.

Gabe didn't respond with words; he just swooped in with a hug. I nestled my wet cheek against his polo. After all, it wasn't like the polo was silk and would stain. At the feeling of his heart beating against me, my own breathing slowed, calmed.

Honestly, I could have stood there forever. But after a bit, he backed away, holding me by the shoulders. "Are you okay? What happened?"

I shook my head, sniffing. "It's my ex–best friend, Vienna. You've probably heard of her. Vienna Soo?" He gave me a blank look in response. I kept pressing. "She runs an art gallery her parents bought her and started a charitable foundation supporting young up-and-coming artists of color? Her mother used to be an extremely famous Taiwanese pop star? Extremely gorgeous? Is known for the cute-but-not-objectionable quirk of only wearing comfortable shoes, no heels?"

The blank look didn't budge. I couldn't help but feel a little gratified, especially when he shook his head at the "gorgeous" part. It came to me then that I didn't want him thinking anyone else was gorgeous. Especially while I was standing here with pig face.

Anyway. Moving on. "Our split was a big deal when it happened. It was splashed everywhere. Even the *New York Times* did a write-up in the Style section speculating about it," I said. "Of course I said it was mutual. But it wasn't."

"People always say their breakups are mutual and they never are," Gabe said gravely.

I wondered what experience he had with breakups, mutual or not. It really wasn't any of my business. Only I kind of wanted to make it my business. I kind of wanted to step back up against him and not just hug him this time, but pull his face to mine.

What? Anyway. *Moving on, Pom.* "She dumped me. In a way that really hurt. That still really hurts, honestly." The pain was pulsing through my heart like a stab wound, which might have been a distasteful comparison to use given my family circumstances, but I didn't care. "And so seeing this video really, really hurt." I pulled up the video on my phone and showed it to him. Hearing Vienna's voice being so dismissive, even when I couldn't see her face, was a twist of the knife. Or stiletto heel, as it were. "So . . . yeah. That's why I'm crying."

"I'm sorry, Pom," Gabe said. "I can see why that would hurt." He was quiet for a moment. "Living well is the best revenge. Live so well that one day when someone asks you about her you can say you haven't thought about her in years."

Yeah. Easier said than done. But he meant well. "Maybe," I said. "In the meantime, I'm thinking I should probably go home. My presence here is no good for the shop."

Gabe was kind enough not to call me out on my blatant lie. "Go home, I'll cover for you. You should probably take off work for a bit while this all dies down. In the meantime, we can sell your treats here so you can keep money coming in."

"You know, now that my identity is out there," I said slowly, mind working, "I can post that I'm selling my homemade treats here. There are a lot of people who wanted to come in and laugh at me 'slumming it,' but I still have plenty of fans who would freak at the thought of getting to eat something I made with my own two hands."

Gabe nodded. "That would be good for both you and the café."

I raised my eyebrows. "Good enough, I would imagine, for the manager who hired me and began this program to go back to his boss and ask for a raise and more say in his schedule."

He didn't respond, and I began to worry I'd overplayed my hand. As I was about to apologize, he said, "You know, you're right. I'm going to give him a call."

I channeled my sad Vienna feelings and confused daughter-of-a-murderer feelings into my next batch of offerings for the café, which had to be extra good considering we were going to advertise them. When Gabe came home that night with the news that he'd gotten everything he asked for, I had batches of cinnamon buns, cranberry-orange breakfast rolls, and savory Parmesan twists ready to celebrate. Also a giant mess in the kitchen, but neither of us focused on that. At least, I didn't.

CHAPTER

Seventeen

The next morning dawned an ominous gray, storm clouds brewing in the sky and the electric charge of lightning tingling in the air. Actually, that was a lie—the next morning dawned bright and clear and sunny, the air unseasonably warm. It just felt more appropriate for today to be gray and stormy, given the task at hand: confronting my mother.

The murderer.

My mom and dad's current abode was way out in the Hamptons, meaning there was no train that would bring us directly there. We could either drive or take a bus.

Gabe was in favor of the bus. "No way," I said immediately. "The bus is a step too far."

"The bus is nice," he said. "It's air-conditioned. And there's a bathroom on board."

I shuddered. "Are those supposed to be selling points?"

In the end, I was able to convince Nicholas to let me borrow his car, which somehow hadn't gotten caught up in the Great Revocation (as nobody was calling it), so long as I was not the one who drove it. I was worried that calling him up and asking for a favor would be weird after what went down between us last time, but, if anything, he was extra gregarious and extra generous (though not to the point of letting me drive). Almost like he was making up for something.

I just hoped he wouldn't regret it when he found out why I needed it.

"Tell me again why I have to be the one to drive?" Gabe had checked and rechecked each mirror three times before pulling out of the garage at a crawl. I could have walked faster than he was driving. In case you think I'm exaggerating, we were literally passed by two different parents pushing strollers. "You can't be that bad a driver."

"I'm not," I said. I breathed in deep the leathery smell of the car, luxuriated in the feel of the heated seats even though it wasn't nearly chilly enough outside to truly need them. After spending most of the last couple of weeks traveling by subway, sitting in the passenger seat of a nice car felt glorious. "Most of the accidents I've been in weren't even my fault."

"Most? Accidents, plural?"

I shrugged. "Not my fault." I thought back. "Well, technically. The insurance company didn't always see it that way."

Gabe let out a disbelieving laugh, shaking his head. "No wonder you relied on a chauffeured car all the time."

I shrugged again. "Hey, it's not like I ever drove drunk or while texting. I'm not an idiot. Most were minor fender-benders. I kinda have trouble sometimes . . . judging perspective."

He kept his eyes fixed straight ahead. "I'm not even going to state the obvious."

"What?"

Over the next two and a half hours, the city streets turned into the suburbs of Long Island, which turned into the beach estates of the Hamptons. Everything looked a lot dirtier from this vantage point than it did from my usual helicopter. I chewed on the inside of my cheek as we turned into the ultra-exclusive hamlet currently housing my parents, their friends, and their friends' spoiled dogs. "Maybe I should've mentioned we were coming."

Gabe slammed on the brakes just in time to stop at a red light. "We drove all the way out here and they don't know we're coming? What if they're not home?"

"Where else would they be? Besides," I said in defense, "I didn't want to take the chance of tipping them off. I wouldn't put it past my mom to flee somewhere without an extradition treaty. I don't think she'd be that sad to live out her days in a luxurious Moroccan riad. She always said more buildings here should have courtyards. And she'd have to watch her drinking, but she could go to Bahrain. She's got some friends in the royal family there." I thought for a second. "Well, frenemies. Mom doesn't like it when other people get to wear a tiara and she doesn't."

Gabe glanced at me sidelong. "Do you know all the countries that don't have extradition treaties with the US off the top of your head?"

"Doesn't everyone?"

As it turned out, we didn't have to worry. I called my dad, who, despite being an accomplice to the murder, was less likely to play games with me or be away from his phone tormenting a tiny dog. He was delighted to let us in through the gate. He even met us outside on the long loop of a driveway. "Pom, so good of you to come all the way out here!" he said. "It's too bad Bailey and Teddy are out for the day. They went boating in the Sound." He leaned in and lowered his voice. "Actually, I think they wanted to get away from your mother for a bit. I'm just hoping they're not tempted to get away from her permanently and drown themselves."

"Sounds like there's a really healthy dynamic thriving around here," I said. "Dad, this is Gabe, Andrea's son and my new roommate."

He looked at me blankly. "Andrea?"

Only the woman who raised me for most of my childhood, I didn't say. "You remember Andrea. My old nanny," I said.

"Right!" said my dad, definitely lying. "Gabe, so good of you to drive our Pom out here. You may have heard about her track record with cars. The local Lexus store has an entire graveyard named after her."

To his credit, Gabe didn't laugh. "Nice to meet you, sir," he said, reaching out for a handshake. My dad was notorious for his finger-crunching grip, but judging by the determination on Gabe's face and the tension in his biceps (not like I'd been paying so much attention to his biceps or anything), he could handle it.

My dad dropped his hand first. "So, what brings you out here? I wish you'd let us know you were coming. We would've booked a table at the local seafood place. It's quite good, even if they don't serve their octopus live the way I like it."

"I actually had to talk to Mom," I said. "Is she around?"

Dad nodded. "She wanted to go with Bailey and Teddy, but I wouldn't let her. They probably would have come back without her and said a kraken sucked her overboard." Honestly, a fittingly dramatic end for my mother. She'd probably be thrilled by the news coverage. "I think she's napping. Come on in, we'll have lunch."

Bailey and Teddy's house was quintessential old-money Hamptons: cozy and cluttered with art and knickknacks they'd acquired abroad, with charming crown moldings marching along the ceilings and big windows looking out onto the sparkling water, where tiny triangles of sailboats bobbed. Signs of the dogs' presence abounded, from chew toys strewn about the floor to cashmere and merino wool dog beds tucked away in corners. "The burbling of all the dogs' water fountains drives your mother nuts," Dad said. "And she's tripped over multiple chew toys."

I only half listened to him as he listed all of Mom's complaints about the dogs. Gabe and I had agreed to both record whatever happened on our phones, so that, in case she did confess, we wouldn't be taking the chance of both our phones malfunctioning. I tripped on a chew toy or two myself, but by the time we made it to the combination family room and kitchen at the back of the house, where multiple sliding glass doors opened to a wooden deck overlooking the water, I was up and recording. I could only hope Gabe was too.

"Grace!" Dad called. "Pom's come to surprise us!"

If she really was napping, it might be a bit before she made it down. But I suspected otherwise, because she liked to tell people she was napping when actually she just wanted some time to herself. Sure enough, only a minute later she was padding into the room, not even bothering to give us an unconvincing squint as if she'd just woken up, or, God forbid, ruffle her hair.

She looked exactly like her usual Hamptons self: classic subtle makeup on, but even more toned down than she wore it in the city (neutral tones only); lounge pants woven from angora and cashmere; tiny gold hoops and pearls in her ears. I'd chosen correctly with my own outfit, which was pretty similar to hers, only black pants to her tan. "Oh, hello, Pom," she said. "What a pleasant surprise."

She didn't even glance over at Gabe, which I probably should have expected. "Mom, this is Gabe. You know, Andrea's son, and my new roommate."

"Right," she said. "Of course. Very nice to meet you, Gabe." She didn't extend her carefully manicured hand for a shake. Though . . . her hand didn't appear as carefully manicured as usual. Was that French manicure . . . growing out? Had she . . . chewed on her thumbnail?

I mentally cataloged this as evidence, though I knew no jury would accept it. "You look great," I said, because there was no more sure way to her heart than through complimenting her face. Sure enough, she preened. "Should we sit down? Maybe outside?"

Mom shuddered. "The wind is ghastly out there. And the noise of the ocean crashing on the beach over and over, all day. Terrible." She took a seat at the wooden table. An uneven leg knocked against the tile. She shuddered again.

"I'll throw together some lunch," Dad said. Usually I would've offered to help him, especially given the recent revelations about my skills in the kitchen, but I couldn't afford to waste any Mom time at the moment. "How do sandwiches sound? I hope good, because that's about all I can make."

"Do Bailey and Teddy not have someone to help with that?" I asked.

Mom shuddered once again. "No. They have someone who cleans once a week, but they do all their own cooking. Teddy claims to enjoy it."

Considering Mom mostly subsisted on olives, melon, and vodka, she was probably fine. But I formed my mouth into a sympathetic frown anyway. "Between the dogs and the cooking, it seems like you're dealing with a lot out here. It would be so nice if someone caught the murderer so you could get back to your old life."

Mom shrugged one shoulder casually, though her bottom lip tightened. "As soon as the Boston money comes through, we'll be out of here." She turned to Gabe. "So, you and my daughter. Are you dating?"

If I were drinking something, I would've choked on it. She wasn't usually this direct. The dogs and the "ghastly" beach noises had to be getting to her. Which was great, actually. Meant there would be a higher chance of getting a confession.

Gabe took the question in stride. "No, we're just friends," he said. "You raised a wonderful daughter."

I wondered if that was meant to be ironic, considering it was his own mother who had done most of my raising. But my mom looked satisfied anyway. "Thank you. If you think Pom is wonderful, you should meet my son, Nicholas."

And there it was.

Gabe opened his mouth, as if he was going to protest, but I didn't want to deal with the two of them arguing over me. What good would it do? Gabe could say all the kind things he wanted, but I'd still have to sit here and listen to whatever cutting comments my mom made in response. So I said, quickly, "Mom, while we're here, can I borrow a pair of your shoes?"

"Dear, aren't your feet a size larger?" she said. "I don't want you stretching them out."

"Our feet are the same size," I said, something I had to say every time I asked to borrow her shoes. "Did you bring them all with you here?" She looked bored, tracing one of the knots on the table with her fingertip. "How about your signature stilettos? You know, the ones that almost took off my toe?"

The effect of my words was immediate: she froze, eyes flying wide open, and her mouth opened, though no words came out. It was almost like the table knot had electrocuted her. "Those stilettos?" she repeated, her voice strangled. "Oh, no. I didn't bring them here. What's the point? There are no galas out here in the off-season."

She was rattled. Good. I couldn't give her the chance to get back on her feet. "So if I went back to the Afton, I'd find them in your closet."

"Of course you would." Mom gaped at me like a dying fish.

I folded my hands on the table, conscious that my phone was listening to everything I was saying. "I think you're lying." I felt a little bit like Doe in *Here to Slay*, who hammered her suspects until they broke into tears about how they'd bullied Danica, or spread false rumors behind her back.

"Why would I lie about something like that?" My mom's voice rose to a squawk.

I raised an eyebrow. This was it. This was the moment. "Because you used one of them to stab Grandma to death."

Silence. I held my breath. From the red-violet shade my mom's face was turning, I didn't think she was breathing either.

Dad cleared his throat. I hadn't even noticed him walk up next to the table, a tray in his arms. "Erm . . . sandwiches?"

Mom bared her teeth. "This is not the time for sandwiches, Richard."

I was pretty hungry at this point, but I hardly dared to stir, let alone take a sandwich. Gabe seemed to be of the same mindset, sitting stock-still beside me.

When Mom finally spoke again, her voice was low and deadly. If she was going to take a bite out of anything in this room with her sharp teeth, it wasn't going to be a sandwich. "I must have misheard you, Pomona. Because you can't possibly have accused me of killing your grandmother."

Doe never backed down. I wouldn't either. I lifted my chin. "You butt-dialed me after I called you the other day. I heard what you and Dad said about your shoe being the murder weapon. Are you going to claim that someone ripped it off your foot and used it to kill Grandma?"

Silence all around now. Mom's fingers flexed on the table, as if she was envisioning using them to strangle someone. Probably me. But no, right then she turned her deadly eyes on Dad. "I told you never to say anything like that aloud. Some digital device is always listening."

"It's not my fault you can't keep your ass from dialing the last person you spoke to," Dad hissed. He set the sandwiches down on the table, probably to keep them from tumbling onto the floor if Mom lunged at him. I had so many other things to focus on right now, but honestly, those sandwiches looked amazing: good fresh bread, thick slices of mozzarella, some leftover grilled vegetables with something dark and sweet drizzled over them.

Mom turned back to me. "Pomona, you must have misunderstood. It's not surprising, to be truthful. You've always had a habit of misunderstanding things even when they're plain as day."

I knew what I'd heard, yet I couldn't help but feel a spark of doubt. Maybe I had misunderstood somehow? She was correct: it wouldn't be the first time. Right?

But Gabe spoke up. "I was there, too, and I heard all of it along with her," he said firmly. "We didn't misinterpret anything."

Mom and Dad both stared at him. Thank goodness he was here. If it were just me, they'd probably tag-team me until I believed what I heard was something totally different.

Which, to be honest, *really pissed me off.* I lifted my chin even higher, so that I could look down my nose at her. "Don't try to gaslight me," I hissed. "I didn't misunderstand you, and I want to know the truth."

Something flashed in Mom's eyes that I wasn't used to seeing. Respect? "I can't believe you would think so poorly of your own mother," she said, but it was too late. I wasn't going to let her cow me. I only stared her in the eye, chin high in the air. She sighed. "Fine, Pomona. I was there that night, and I did leave my shoe behind, but I didn't *kill* her."

The shock waves reverberated through the room, practically shaking my chair. I looked up at Dad. He nodded grimly. "It's true. She's telling the truth."

Back to Mom. "You'd already left the gala. I'd pulled out my phone to see what people were saying about my outfit. You know, that darling pink dress you helped me pick out." That wasn't how I remembered it, but whatever. "And of course that troll was at it again. RibbetRabbit, posting all about how I resembled an, I quote, 'obese flamingo who choked on a wad of shrimp poop.'" What flashed in her eyes now was unmistakable: fury. "I couldn't let it stand a moment longer. I sent the account information to the family detective and he had an IP address for me within a half hour. And do you know what he found?

"The call was coming from inside the house."

I gasped. "RibbetRabbit was *Grandma*?"

Mom nodded. "How dare she. First she refused to attend any galas I threw. Then she actively tried to throw competing galas on the same nights as mine. But I guess that wasn't enough for her. She had to say all those nasty things behind my back. Obviously I left the gala to confront her."

It might be safe to take a sandwich now. Or not. It might sidetrack Mom and invite her to start making comments about what all the carbs would do to my hips. I folded my hands safely in my lap.

Mom continued, "As I'm sure you can imagine, our fight was not kind. She called me a homewrecking whore, simply because your father was already married when we met." Something I had not known, but we could pick up that thread later. "I called her a jealous old hag who insulted my clothes because she couldn't fit into hers anymore. She questioned your and Nicholas's paternity—apparently Farrah and Jordan had recently proven theirs to her with some ancestry test, and she wanted the same for you?—and that was enough. I'd had it. I'd taken my shoes off when I entered her apartment so that I wouldn't poke holes in the floor, but I'd held on to them so that she couldn't send Rosa to make them disappear.

"So, yes, I threw one at her. It hit her solidly on the side of the head, which, I have to admit, felt great." Mom bared her teeth in a vicious little grin. "I'm sure it hurt, and that it left a bruise, but it didn't break the skin. The shoe fell to the ground. She screamed at me to get out or she'd call security. Fine—I didn't want to be there anymore anyway. I stormed out, forgetting my shoe. I figured I'd send your father up for it the next day once she had a chance to cool down a bit."

Yes. It sounded like Grandma was the *only* one who needed to cool down. I didn't say that, though. Instead I said, evenly, "Is there anyone who can back that up?"

My mom stared me back down. "Are you serious, Pomona?"

My ankles quaked in my nonmurderous shoes, but my eyes held firm. "Yes."

She held eye contact for a moment longer, then sighed. "Only your father, which I suppose isn't good enough for you." She paused. "I didn't kill her, Pom. I might have wanted to for the past thirty years, but I wasn't going to prison for that hag. The ground would shake with how hard she'd be laughing in the pits of hell if I did."

I believed her. God help me, but I believed her. "How did you find out the shoe was the murder weapon?"

She looked at me like she couldn't believe she'd birthed such a stupid child, but she didn't voice that thought. I must have taken the fight out of her. Victory. "What else could it have been?" she asked. "A small, sharp object that tapered from root to tip. And it was missing later. Whoever killed your grandmother must have gone up after I left, picked up the shoe, used it to stab her, and taken it with them."

I let myself absorb her words for a moment. "You didn't tell this to the police?"

She rolled her eyes. "Of course not. I didn't want to bring negative attention onto myself." She glared at me. "I hope you won't tell them either. I don't need them trying to haul me in for questioning. We only have so much money for the lawyers right now."

So whoever killed Grandma must have the shoe. Or, more realistically, they'd burned it or tossed it in the ocean. If I'd killed someone, I certainly wouldn't hang on to the murder weapon for someone to find it.

"Anyway," Dad said, as if we'd been discussing a bad grade I'd gotten in school and not his mother's murder, "is anyone going to eat these sandwiches, or should I put them in the fridge to keep?"

Lunch was a solemn, silent affair, with Mom alternating between picking at bits of grilled vegetable and staring daggers (or stilettos) at me from across the table. Dad gamely kept trying to make conversation, asking Gabe about his master's program or what our apartment was like, but the conversations petered out when Dad didn't say anything in response but "Good, good." Gabe valiantly tried asking them questions about how they liked the Hamptons or how the local seafood place was but didn't get much more than pained smiles in return.

I didn't contribute much at all. Too busy thinking. We were at a dead end now. I mean, we still had suspects left. But, like, I'd thought we were at the finish line. And, as great as it was to know I didn't share half the genes of a murderer, I would at least have considered it an acceptable price to pay for getting my trust fund and apartment back.

"So, Gabe," my dad said. "That's a nice car you've got out there. Very nice."

"Oh, it's not mine," Gabe said. "I could never—"

"Nicholas lent us his car," I broke in before Gabe could say he could never afford a car like that. I didn't need my parents telling us all about how that wasn't true, he just needed to watch his spending on fancy coffees and be better at saving. Like they would know.

"Nicholas never would have accused me of murder," Mom muttered. "That's why I called him and not you that night."

I sat up straight in my chair, the last quarter of my sandwich falling back to my plate. "What? Nicholas was there that night? I thought you said Dad was the only one who could give you an alibi?"

Mom unwound the blistered skin from a piece of grilled zucchini, leaving the innards in a limp, pale pile on her plate. "He'd been staying at Jessica's that night, but because he's a *good* son, he came when I called. Both he and Jessica did. They knew I needed a soothing presence from a *loving* child."

"I would've come if you'd called me," I said, a little stung, even if that wasn't true, considering my phone had been off in my tossed-aside clutch while I danced at the club. I hadn't even gotten Grandma's calls.

Maybe that had been why she called me so many times. She knew Mom was going to bring Nicholas in, and she wanted to create an even playing field? It certainly wouldn't be above Grandma to pit one grandkid against the other. But that didn't explain why she'd urgently wanted to talk to me earlier that day.

"Sure," Mom said, voice heavy with sarcasm. For all her faults, she could tell when I was lying. "Usually I wouldn't have been thrilled that he brought that girlfriend of his along, but in this case it worked out well. Jessica could actually sympathize with me, since your grandmother was treating her much the same way she did me when your father and I first met."

I couldn't help but take a dig at her. "Though Nicholas wasn't married when they met, at least."

Mom rolled her eyes. "Your father's marriage was long over in spirit by the time we met. I was just the spur that got the paperwork done. Right, Richard?"

"Right," Dad said weakly.

Still curious, but it could wait. "When did they leave?"

Mom waved a hand in the air. "Oh, I don't know. At some point your father and I went to bed. They were gone when I woke up, though. They'd gone back to Jessica's place. I know because he barely made it back to the Afton in time to collect his things before he was barred from the premises."

I exchanged a glance with Gabe. He didn't have to say anything, because I knew he was thinking it too: What if Nicholas and Jessica had gone upstairs to confront Grandma about the fight, or about Grandma's behavior toward Jessica? The "young woman making threats" could have been Jessica—maybe she was upset about how Grandma was treating her. What if things had gotten heated, and one of them had grabbed the shoe and gone at it?

As much as I hated to think it, it did make Nicholas's weird behavior make sense. I'd purposefully been vague with who in the family I was considering reporting for murder. If he thought I was talking about him and Jessica . . .

But that meant he was already on alert. I couldn't just go and catch them off guard like I did with Mom. I needed some kind of proof.

Mom cast a disdainful eye at the remainder of my sandwich. "Are you sure you want to eat that? You don't exactly have the funds right now to buy an entire wardrobe in a larger size."

I had about a quarter left: the best bite I'd been saving for the end, the one with the perfect harmony of ingredients, the vegetables in balance with the cheese and bread. I stared at it. A month ago it would've transformed in my mind's eye into a giant writhing cockroach, and I would've dropped it on the plate in order to earn the slightest glint of approval in my mom's eye.

But this was now, and now I crammed the entire thing in my mouth at once. "Yum," I said around the mouthful of food so big I could barely even chew it. I could choke on it, and I'd die triumphant.

Eighteen

W ell, that was fun," I said as the house retreated behind us. Dad had seen us to the door and was waving goodbye in our rear-view mirror; Mom had retreated upstairs, claiming a headache. I feared for Bailey and Teddy when they got home.

Gabe was silent. I glanced at him to find him glancing at me, the caution on his face akin to him playing chicken with a giant rat at his door. I sighed. "I was being sarcastic."

He exhaled as he turned back to the road. "Thank God. That was the worst lunch of my life."

I snorted. "That was just another lunch with my parents." I cocked my head, considering. "Well. Except for all the murder talk." And the part where I'd stood up to my mom, but that didn't seem monumental enough to point out. Gabe probably stood up to his parents all the time. I'd certainly always talked back to Andrea, maybe because I knew deep down it wouldn't change how she felt about me. That, and she was paid to be there, so she couldn't leave.

"I'll come prepared with some topics to research before next time," Gabe said. "Like, there has to be something to keep your dad talking. What's a guy like him interested in? The stock market? Fancy watches?"

I laughed, trying to ignore the bubble in my chest that expanded when he said "next time." I kind of wanted to ask him what he meant by that, if he was picturing going home with me to "meet the parents" or if we were going to try accusing my dad of murder next, but I had to stay focused on the task at hand. "So, it sounds like our next step is my brother." Just saying the words twinged something inside me. I'd always looked up to Nicholas. Thinking of him as a potential murderer felt way more impactful than thinking of my mom that way. "And Jessica."

"Sounds that way," Gabe echoed. "So what's the plan? The same thing we did with your mom?"

I shook my head, then realized he was looking at the road and said, "No. We can't go to him without any evidence, since he already thinks I'm on to him. But what kind of evidence can we find without access to whatever the police have? I don't suppose Caleb . . ."

"No, I can't ask him to steal police files for us. If he even has access to these. I imagine they're kept locked up tight so that reporters can't sneak any of them out." Gabe was quiet for a while as we wound our way through the tony hamlets toward the highway. "Hotel staff, maybe? Could any of them have seen when Nicholas and Jessica came and left?"

"Maybe, but there's no way one of them will talk to us," I said. I barely even remembered any of their names, I thought with a pang. I'd known many of them for years. They'd taken care of me: cleaned my apartment; sent up room service when Lori was busy and I didn't feel like getting takeout; guarded my floor so that random fans couldn't get in. "We could break into their apartment and search for the shoe?"

"If I were the killer, that shoe would be at the bottom of the East River, tied to a barbell."

I pursed my lips, thinking hard. "Hmm."

We were almost back at the city before it came to me. "The security footage!"

A chorus of honks sounded behind us as Gabe slowed for a yellow light. "You mean from the hotel?"

"Yeah," I said. "There are cameras all over the place. I know the police probably have it, but they might not know who or what to look for. If we could get access to the footage . . ."

"But how?"

I wished I could say I had friends on the staff, but that wasn't true. I couldn't even bribe them. They'd laugh me out of the room with my brownie fund.

There was one advantage my exile couldn't take from me, though. "I spent most of my life in that hotel. My whole childhood I ran around through the employee hallways and the guest hallways, exploring all the rooms and passageways and nooks and crannies. So I know where all the security rooms are, and I know how to get there, and, assuming the systems are the same as they were a few years ago"—when I'd had to delete evidence of a particularly unsavory postclub hookup before the gossip blogs could get it—"which I'd bet they are, considering how cheap my grandma was, I can access the footage."

"But you're barred from the premises." Gabe coasted to a stop at a red light. I realized with a start that we were almost home. Well, not home. Almost back to Nicholas's garage. I went to text him that his car was home safe and unscratched, but hesitated. Didn't want to jinx the last few minutes of our journey when any taxi or e-scooter could sideswipe us.

"Right. So the main challenge would be getting inside without being noticed. Which, I mean, shouldn't be all that complicated, right? I put on a big pair of sunglasses and a hat—"

"Everybody who works at the hotel will know your face and your story," Gabe said dryly as he pulled into the garage. He handed the key, plus a cash tip, to the attendant. "And you always had a habit of wearing giant sunglasses. I think we'll need something more than that."

"Okay. Okay." We walked out of the garage, squinting into the sunlight. *That's why I always wore giant sunglasses, Gabe. It wasn't like it was just for the aesthetic.* "Well, we can spend the night planning. My cousins know the hotel as well as I do, so if they're still in the city I can rope them in. And Opal is probably desperate for any excuse to get back into the city proper."

"Actually, I can't tonight."

"What? Another essay? A seminar?"

Gabe rubbed the back of his neck with a sheepish smile. "No, actually. I, um, I have a date."

It felt a little like he'd dumped a bucket of cold water over my head, and not in the refreshing way I liked, when you were returning from a long soak in a New Zealand hot spring. I made myself smile so that he wouldn't see me shiver. "Oh! That's fun! Who with?" My fake enthusiasm should honestly win me an award.

"I haven't really been dating, you know, since I've been so busy with work and school, but my friend's been trying to set me up with his roommate's sister for ages, and we're finally both free on the same night, so . . ." He shrugged, palms up. "She's getting her master's in teaching, too, so we should have a lot to talk about."

We were almost back at the apartment. Thank God. "That's fun," I said again. "So fun. Well! I hope you have a fun time. The most fun."

"Thanks," he said, flashing me a little smile as we trudged up our stairs.

Fine. It was fine. It wasn't like I had time to date right now anyway, what with hunting down a murderer and starting a baking business and all. Besides, dating your roommate was ill-advised in all corners. Not that I'd be dating my roommate. Not that he wanted to date me. Gabe could date whoever and whenever he wanted.

So, as we got back and he proceeded to ready himself, taking a long shower and trying on a bunch of different shirts in the mirror (or so I imagined; I'd locked myself in my room so that I wouldn't have to be asked for my opinion), I texted my inner circle. Or at least the inner circle members I was pretty sure weren't murderers.

Farrah and Jordan hadn't returned to Florida yet, but they weren't eager to revisit the hotel. We did, however, make plans to hang out over the weekend and go gallery-hopping in Chelsea. I wouldn't be able to afford anything except appreciating the art, which was fine. The plans were made with Jordan, though Farrah gave the whole thing an emoji thumbs-up. Progress.

Opal, on the other hand, was ecstatic to help out. She didn't even

ask what we were doing or if she'd be breaking any laws before agree-
ing to come, just what neighborhood we'd be in. Given all the antics
we'd participated in at various clubs and parties, I knew she'd be an
excellent tool of distraction.

A little bit after six, I heard Gabe leave his room, then open and
close the front door behind him as he left the apartment. I waited a
minute in case he'd forgotten something, then left my own room.
Squeaky was sitting on the couch, his large, pathetic eyes trained on
the door. "Poor baby," I murmured, scooping him up and giving him a
big kiss on his block head. "Do you feel abandoned? Don't worry,
he'll be back later." Unless he went over to her place after their dinner,
I thought with an unpleasant lurch. Or—with an even more unpleasant lurch—he did come back here, but with her in tow.

I was overcome by the sudden urge to beat up some dough. I
mean, perfect my chocolate babka. The first batch of the sweet braided
bread had turned out glossy and gorgeous on the outside, even my
sloppy braiding unable to make it look unappetizing, but the inside
had been rubbery and underbaked. Something had gone wrong with
either the rising period or the baking period, and I was determined to
spend all my brainpower tonight figuring out which.

After a quick outfit change from the flared pants and light cashmere sweater I'd worn out to my parents into my cutest pair of black
yoga pants that made my butt look great and a crop top—hey, if Gabe
was going to bring back a guest, I wanted to make sure I looked
good—I started the babka dough. Sure enough, punching it felt great.
With each smack of my fist into the dough, I wondered what Gabe
was doing that moment. If his (surely beautiful) date was making stars
light up in his eyes. If his (surely very smart) date was engaging him in
fascinating conversation. If he was making excuses to brush against
her (surely perfectly manicured) hand while reaching for the menu, or
if they were playing footsie under the table.

So, apparently overkneading dough is a thing.

A second batch of babka dough later, I was letting it rise while I
worked on some sweet-roll dough I'd let rise overnight in the fridge,

and the lock clicked in the door. I jumped in place, dusting floury handprints against my black pants. Squeaky trotted toward the door, ears pricked.

The door opened. I held my breath.

Gabe entered.

Alone.

And closed the door behind him.

I exhaled in relief, shoulders sagging with the release of tension. "How was your date?" I asked, trying to sound breezier than a day on a yacht.

He shrugged off his jacket. "It was fine. She was nice."

"Nice? That's it?"

He shrugged for real. "She was a sweet person, and we had a lot to talk about between school and teaching, but I just didn't feel the chemistry. You can't win them all, right?"

I don't know. I kind of felt like I'd won.

CHAPTER

Nineteen

Though I knew Opal had fallen into reduced circumstances as well, I couldn't bear the thought of having her meet us at my apartment and see just how far I'd fallen. Besides, she might literally fall far herself, considering the high heels she often wore and the pitted slopes of our floors. So we decided to meet in Central Park near the zoo. There were benches where you could sit and spy on the trained sea lions that did laps around the elevated pool of water in its center without having to pay to enter or risk getting splashed.

Opal sashayed up fifteen minutes past our meeting time, casual but cute in a baggy white jumpsuit, denim jacket, and, unsurprisingly, four-inch wedge heels that had her tottering on the cobblestones. I offered to take some pics for her before she had to ask. We got a good number, and then she scrutinized them and asked if I'd take a few more from a different angle, and a few turned into a bunch, and Gabe didn't even once sigh in annoyance.

A good omen, I figured.

Once she'd fake-laughed and posed to her heart's content, we took up a bench and got to business, the sea lions splish-splashing in the background to the cheers of little kids. "Okay, so it's a long story as to why, but basically, we need to get into the Afton's security room, and we need the security guards in there to clear out for a bit, long enough for us to find some footage," I told her. She nodded intently, eyes hidden behind cat's-eye sunglasses. "I need to be in the room because I know how to get into the system, but nobody can see me since I'm banned from the hotel. So what I need from you is an epic distraction. Enough for Gabe to sneak me into the hotel and enough to draw the security guards out of their rooms."

Opal tilted her head, the sun gleaming off her lenses. "I assume you don't have the capital to bail me out if I get arrested."

"Absolutely not," I said. "Don't get arrested."

She sighed. "That really limits my options."

Gabe spoke up: "It shouldn't take anything too wild. We need a few minutes to sneak Pom past the security guards and the front desk workers into the employee halls, and then something big enough to call any security guards watching the video footage out of their room."

"Like I said," Opal replied, "really limits my options."

I ticked the options off on my fingers. "You could be a difficult guest that requires all the attention of everybody in the lobby. You could have some sort of medical emergency. You could make up some dramatic story about the terrible condition of your suite or say that you were robbed. You could—"

Opal stopped me by holding up her hand. She might be wearing a cute outfit from her old life, and she had clearly made an effort with her nails, but the slight smudges at their edges and the overgrown nature of her cuticles made it clear she'd done them herself. "Don't worry. I can handle it."

"Maybe you could share your plan with us, though," Gabe said. "So we can be prepared."

Opal flashed him a pointy grin. "You sound like you're doubting me. Don't worry. This'll be child's play compared to what Pom and I have gotten up to in the past. In fact, last year we—"

"It's just that this is super important," I interjected before she could tell Gabe about the time we'd sweet-talked our way into Coriander's ex-boyfriend's wedding so that we could steal the cake and take pictures of us all dropping it off the roof of the Afton. I didn't think he'd find it as funny as we did. Well, as I had at the time. It seemed a little immature now. The ex-boyfriend hadn't even done anything that terrible to Coriander, just broken up with her because he wasn't feeling the relationship anymore. "So we can't mess it up."

She lowered her sunglasses so that I couldn't miss her hurt look. "I won't mess it up. What do you need from the security room, anyway?"

I couldn't tell her that we suspected Nicholas and Jessica of the murder. But I could tell her about the investigation. "I have some questions about the night my grandma died. I want to see if anyone suspicious came into the hotel that night."

"Haven't the police already examined any footage?"

"I'm sure they have," I said. "But they're not operating with the same urgency that I am. They didn't lose their entire life."

"You didn't lose your life," Gabe said. "You're still alive. I mean, I think your life is pretty great still."

Opal's face contorted in a way that suggested he'd told her he thought all wine tasted the same. "What are you talking about? Are you worried that when Pom gets her trust fund and credit cards and apartment back, you'll never see her again?"

Gabe's face was stone. He didn't respond.

"That's ridiculous," I said. "Even if I did get everything back, we'd still be friends."

Gabe stood. "It doesn't matter. We should go."

He led the way to the hotel, speed-walking so that he stayed in front. No matter how much I tried to match his pace, I couldn't keep up. But he was right, I told myself. It didn't matter. What mattered was getting that security footage.

Opal managed to keep up with me in her heels, on surer footing now that we were on the mostly smooth surface of the sidewalk. "Can I tell you my theory?"

"About what?"

"About the murder," she said, and the casual tone in her voice made it sound kind of like she was talking about a murder on a TV show or in a movie. Even though it wasn't like I was out here weeping over my grandma or anything, it still rubbed me the wrong way. I'd been having nightmares at least every other night about the smell of blood and sense of shock I'd felt upon finding the body. Too bad I couldn't currently afford a session with my usual therapist, who only accepted payment via his own branded cryptocurrency.

Still, she'd come out of her way to help us. So I just said, "What is it?"

"I think it has to be the hotel staff," she said. "I mean, isn't that how it always works out? It's the people you least expect? And you know your grandma treated them all like shit. I wouldn't be surprised if she called up room service and made some ridiculous demands and they snapped."

It wasn't the worst idea in the world, in that it struck me as possible. I didn't think it fit with the "young woman threatening her," but I wasn't going to tell Opal about that. I couldn't, not without admitting we'd investigated her. "We'll keep an eye out for anything suspicious," I said. "Thanks."

She seemed very pleased with herself. "You're welcome. I'll keep an eye out when I'm in the hotel too."

It was strange how weird approaching the hotel felt, since I'd lived there all my life. It didn't feel like returning home. It felt like going back to your school a few years after you'd graduated, when you were like, have the bathrooms always been this small? Has the gym always smelled like horse blankets? Have the visiting chefs in the cafeteria always been this mid despite their Michelin stars? We stopped a half block away from the grand building, but even from here I was asking myself questions: Has the valet always scanned the street like he's keeping an eye out for infiltrators? Was that the lump of a gun in his pocket?

I slid on my big sunglasses and pulled my floppy hat down around my ears. It didn't help with any of those questions, but it kept people's eyes skating over me without settling.

If you were wondering why I'd spent time describing Opal's outfit earlier and not mine and also why I didn't ask her to reciprocate the picture-taking, it was because my clothes were deliberately terrible. In hopes that people would never think Pomona Afton would set foot in public looking unfashionable, I'd adorned myself in a hideous dress from a couple of seasons ago I didn't even know why Lori had thrown in my bag that sagged around my waist in a busy pattern of tiny bees and paired it with Gabe's beat-up sneakers (our feet were unsettlingly almost the same size). Between this and the hat and sunglasses combo, I hoped I'd be able to sneak through unscathed.

Gabe was just wearing a plain white T-shirt and jeans, by the way. A V-neck, so that a little bit of black chest hair curled out the top. Not that I was paying attention.

"Okay, so Opal, we'll send you in first," I said. "How long should we give you to sufficiently distract the entire lobby? Five minutes?"

"I can do it in two," she said confidently.

"Let's say three," I said. Impulsively, I leaned in and gave her a hug. She stiffened beneath my touch; I didn't squeeze her fragile bird bones too hard. "Thanks for helping us. It means a lot." I stepped back, hands on her shoulders, and looked her in the eye. Well, my sunglasses aimed in the direction of her sunglasses, so what I really saw was a reflection of myself. "You're a good friend."

For a moment she looked like she was going to cry. We never said things like this to each other unless we were drunk. She croaked, "You're a good friend, too, Pom."

And then she was off, clicking down the sidewalk, her stride straightening into what I recognized as my mother's: haughty rich lady ready to demand something unreasonable.

I told Siri to set a timer for three minutes, and Gabe and I settled up against the nearest brick facade to wait. A doorman stepped out and I worried for a moment that he'd look at us suspiciously, but he stared right through us. I wasn't used to this kind of anonymity.

"So how long have you and Opal known each other?" Gabe asked.

I had to think all the way back. "Since high school, I think? I mean, we've always moved in the same circles. Or I guess, past tense, we always moved in the same circles. Our families have known each other for years, but we didn't become actual friends until we took

French class together." A smile cracked at the memory. "The teacher was a total space case, so Opal and I used to tell her we had to miss class for our AP Philosophy study group. There was no AP Philosophy class, much less study group. But we'd go sit outside and vape whatever flavor cartridge was for sale that day." I wrinkled my nose. We didn't vape anymore. One of those things that were cool in high school and gross as an adult. Smoking was so bad for your skin. "She wasn't my best friend, though. She only became my best friend recently, after Vienna and I . . ."

My phone started chiming with the alarm. I jumped, but was grateful for it, glad I didn't have a chance to have that cold pit in my stomach open up all the way. "Let's go."

I could hear Opal pontificating loudly as we approached the entrance. The guy standing outside was still there, but he was no longer examining the people on the street; he was looking over his shoulder at the chaos erupting inside. I stood on the left side of Gabe, who, as a larger person everywhere but (unfortunately) his feet, was intended to block the view of the front desk workers on the right side of the room.

Inside the lobby, the marble floors gleamed just as brightly and the chandeliers glittered just as elegantly as when I'd left. I kept my head down, trying to duck beside Gabe without looking like I was ducking, but Opal's shrieks echoed throughout the room. "What do you *mean* you don't have a record of my reservation? Do you have any idea who I *am*?"

The front desk workers were occupied with her, and the one security guy lingering in the lobby had his eye on her, too, in case she started throwing crystal paperweights or potted plants. I said a silent thank-you as we easily passed behind her into the hallway beyond the lobby.

There the green patterned carpeting and generic landscapes on the walls made it clear this was a guest space. "We should be fine here," I said to Gabe in an undertone, my feet moving over the plush carpet with muscle memory. "But the security room is in one of the employee hallways. We probably won't see anyone but maids or porters, but we'll have to be very careful when Opal draws the security guy out of the security room. We probably won't have much time after that."

The entrances to the employee-only areas were behind doors that looked like guest rooms. I clicked the handle for room 123, inputting the code I remembered, and the door swung open, admitting us into the hallway beyond.

Every aspect of the employee areas was less luxurious than those for the guests: the carpet thin, brown, and industrial; the walls bare or hung with stern reminders to make sure to lock any personal items away in your locker and not to clock in late for your shift.

It occurred to me as we walked through the hall that, even if any maids or porters we ran into wouldn't recognize me, they would think it odd for guests to be wandering around back here, and would probably ask if we were lost or offer to escort us out. So it was really lucky that we didn't run into any employees.

Our luck ran out, though, as we approached the plain gray door to the security room. We stood across from it in the nook of another door, quietly debating. "We just have to wait until whoever's in there comes out because of whatever Opal does," I whispered.

"But what if the room is empty already?" Gabe whispered back. "Then we're standing here for no reason."

"It's probably not empty. There's usually someone in there monitoring the cameras."

"Probably. Usually. Not definitely or always."

Both points became moot as the door opened. A guy stood in the doorway, speaking into his radio. "Terrible reception in there," he said. "What was that?"

The voice that responded was crackly with static, cutting in and out. "Lady . . . threats . . . angry . . . climbing over the desk . . ."

The security guy must have heard more than I did, because he responded. "Roger that. I'll keep my eyes peeled on all the monitors."

I was holding my breath, as if that would keep him from noticing the two out-of-place people standing there right in front of him. Of course it didn't work. As soon as he raised his eyes from his radio, they settled on us. And narrowed.

Before I could even think about answering, Gabe was kissing me.

Honestly, I couldn't even appreciate it at first, because I was more shocked than anything. But the shock only lasted a split second, and then I could appreciate it all. The warmth and softness of his lips on mine. The pleasant scratch of his stubble. The gentle way his hand cupped my jawline as if he were afraid he might break it. How his delicious coffee and soap smell wrapped itself around me.

And then he broke away, stepped back a step, pressed a hand to his chest. "Oh, sir, I'm so sorry," he was saying. My head was still spinning, my heart thumping right under my skin. If anyone looked closely, they could probably see it in the roses of my cheeks. "We were just looking for a private place. Our families don't approve, but we're all staying here for the week, and we thought . . ."

The security guy held his hand up. "Say no more. I get it," he said, chuckling.

Oh. I got it. Gabe hadn't kissed me because he *wanted* to kiss me. He'd kissed me as an excuse for why we were here. As a reason to reduce suspicion on us.

As I ducked behind his shoulder, I felt a little like I was shrinking for real.

"Wait a second," the security guy said. Apparently I hadn't ducked far enough, because he was staring straight at me. "I know you."

I realized with an unpleasant lurch in my stomach that I knew him too. He was one of the security guys who'd accompanied Crooked Nose to my apartment when he evicted me.

I still didn't know his name. But he couldn't say the same. "You're Pomona Afton."

CHAPTER

Twenty

Y*ou're Pomona Afton.* The words seemed to echo through the
hallway, surely summoning distant security guards and hotel
managers like a bullhorn's call.

Gabe stood up straight, as if to protect me, but then glanced help-
lessly at me over his shoulder, like he realized he couldn't exactly fight
his way out. Not that I expected him to. I didn't clock him as much of
a fighter. A kisser, though . . .

No, Pom. Focus. I had only a split second to decide the best way
to handle this before the security guard surely called in reinforcements
to frog-march us out. Quick survey of this guy. I'd recognized him previously as someone who'd known me and my family a long time, but
his expression right now was inscrutable. He could have some fondness for us, or he could hate us. Had I been kind to him in the past? I
had no idea.

But being haughty definitely wasn't going to work, because I had
nothing to be haughty about anymore. I'd have to be pathetic and
hope he had some lingering fondness for me.

I lifted my sunglasses up to my forehead so that he could see my
wide, sad eyes. Hopefully they were shimmering with what could be
tears, but I didn't have the skill of crying on command. One point
against me becoming an actress one day. "I know I'm not supposed to
be here," I said, my voice trembling, half purposefully and half because I was legit afraid I was about to be arrested or something. "I'm
really sorry. I just . . . I just missed my home."

I cast my eyes down. Saying those words made me actually reflect on them. Did I actually miss the Afton? There were elements I did, without a doubt: the view; not having to share a bathroom; the luxury mattress instead of the lumpy bed that came with Gabe's apartment. And the freedom the money had given me was amazing. I appreciated it now, the ability to do whatever I wanted whenever I wanted without having to worry if I could afford it or if I'd be missing work.

But living here also came with my parents being a floor above, ready to pop in and criticize without a moment's notice. With the pressure to live up to my family name. My time as Rachel Sparks might be over, but it had been nice living without that pressure for a little while. Living just as me, as what I could do, rather than what people expected of Pomona Afton.

Okay, I'd been quiet for way too long. "It was a nostalgia thing. I wanted to show my new boyfriend where I used to live." I let my lower lip tremble. "I'm so sorry. I'll leave. Please don't get me in trouble."

The radio squawked again. The security guy glanced down at it, then back up at me. And—yessss—his face softened. "I don't think it was right what they did to you, kicking you out with no notice like that, but you'll get in legal trouble if they catch you here. Go on, go. If I see you again, I'll have to report you." Before I could thank him, he disappeared into the security room and closed the door firmly behind him.

Gabe shook his head. "The benefit of the doubt being a rich, pretty white woman gets you in this world."

"Aw, you think I'm pretty," I said. "Though I'm not that rich anymore."

He didn't laugh as I expected. "Pom, we're screwed. There's no way we're getting in there now." He paused. "Also, I'm sorry for kissing you like that without asking. It was the only way I could think of to throw them off."

"It's fine," I said, smiling tightly and ignoring how absolutely not sorry I was. He was right about us being screwed, though. We could try to hide out somewhere for a while and wait for the threat to pass, but I'd already been caught. If I got caught again, I'd be in major trouble. It seemed we were at a dead end.

Unless . . . I hadn't mentioned it to Gabe, just in case, but I'd thrown all my old keys and key cards into my bag as we ran out the door. I didn't think I'd need them, but figured it couldn't hurt.

I bent my head in toward Gabe, ignoring the way his smell washed over me again, made me think of his lips on mine. *It wasn't real, it was only a distraction, and he was sorry about it.* "There's another room where the security cameras feed. It's secret. I don't think even most of the employees know about it."

"Okay," Gabe said cautiously. "What's the catch?"

I pursed my lips. "It's in my grandma's apartment."

Silence. I added, "Back in the day, my grandpa wanted to know what was going on all the time, so he had the cameras feed there too. I don't know if my grandma ever actually used it. But it's all still there. I used to go in there as a kid to spy on what guests were doing around the hotel. You'd be surprised by how many people steal hotel art. Like, it's not even good art."

"Can we get up there?"

"As long as we don't get caught. Again."

He grabbed my hand and laced his fingers through mine. They were as warm as his lips, though rougher. *Stop it, Pom.* "Let's go, then."

Back in the guest areas, we didn't stand out as much. Opal was no longer shrieking in the lobby—I considered shooting her a quick text to assure her we were okay and had gone on to plan B, but didn't want to risk taking my eyes off the world around me for even a second. Gabe looped his arm around me and pulled me close against him as we waited on the second floor's elevator area—the first floor and the lobby carried too much risk with all the staff—but I wasn't fooled this time. He probably wanted to make sure we looked like a normal couple staying at the hotel to anyone who might walk by.

When the first elevator pulled up, it was full of people. Gabe went to get on, but I tugged him back, whispering into his ear, "We want to be alone when we insert the card to take us to the family floor. We can go up the stairs from there." Taking Grandma's private elevator wasn't worth the risk. They'd probably shut it down, anyway. Who was there to use it?

He nodded. I remained where I was for an extra minute. To hide my face from the people in the elevator, obviously, not to breathe in the smell of his skin. That would be weird.

The next one, fortunately, was empty. We hopped in and rode it up. When I was sure enough nobody else was going to get on on a higher floor, I inserted the card that would take us to the private floors, then ducked my face into Gabe's shoulder to hide it from any cameras in the elevator.

I was a little afraid there might be security guards on Grandma's floor, but why would there be? Nobody had been there since the murder, and nobody was supposed to be there now. I did, however, scan the ceiling for cameras. Grandma had explicitly forbidden them on the private floors, saying she didn't want to feel like she was living in a zoo, but that didn't mean the hotel hadn't put them up after she was dead. I couldn't see any, though. Good.

I held my breath as we entered Grandma's apartment, somehow afraid it would still smell like her death. Of course I couldn't hold it forever. When I did finally breathe in, the apartment just smelled stale, like air that hadn't moved in a long time. It made me sad somehow. Like her death should've left more of a mark on the place she'd lived most of her adult life.

I mean, it probably had. There was likely blood soaked into the bedroom floor. But I wasn't about to go check. "I'm sure we're okay, but there's a chance management might have been notified when we used the key to get up to this floor," I said, already moving through the living room. "So we should hurry."

Gabe obeyed, matching my pace, but his head was on a swivel the whole time, his eyes wide as we passed through the formal living room with its grand piano, pristine white furnishings, and floor-to-ceiling views of Central Park, the dining room with its fireplace and original

Picasso, the less formal living room with the not-as-grand piano that was still honestly pretty formal. "I can't believe your family actually lived here," he said, voice hushed, as if he were walking through a museum. "Was your own place like this?"

I didn't know why I was so uncomfortable with the question. Maybe because it felt like he was talking about me and my family like we were a different species or something. "My grandma's is way bigger," I nonanswered, rounding the corner into the hallway that contained the security room along with a bunch of storage closets and Rosa's room down at the end for when she stayed over. "And I didn't have a Picasso. It's one of these rooms . . . here!"

It didn't look any different from when I used to sneak in here as a kid. The room was a repurposed closet, with one wall covered in blank screens and an ancient computer sitting on an old, beat-up desk. I jiggled the mouse, and the computer screen lit up, asking for a password. "Let's hope she hasn't changed the password since my grandpa died. He always used their anniversary as the—phew. Okay, we're in."

The screens all lit up at once, rotating through grainy, flickering footage of all the hotel cameras. I caught the lobby, where a porter was pulling a big cart of luggage while a woman who might have been a B-list starlet watched him like a hawk, and one of the guest hallways, where a cleaner was picking up leftover room service trays. "So there aren't cameras on this floor, which means we won't be able to see who goes in and out of Grandma's room," I said.

"Solving the murder would be way easier if there were."

I sighed. "Grandma never was one for making things easy."

On the computer, I pulled up the records from the night of the murder. "I think we should start with the main entrance and look for Nicholas and Jessica, as well as any other members of the family, just in case. If we need to, we can branch out from there."

"Copy that," said Gabe.

I started up the footage. It was grainy and flickering, like the rest of the cameras; if I had been looking for the face of a stranger it wouldn't have been very helpful, but I could spot the people I knew so well. On fast-forward I found my parents coming home from the gala, Dad a step behind Mom, who was storming through the lobby so fast it was lucky no stray child got stabbed by her pounding feet. My eyes flitted to the time on-screen. It corresponded to what my mom had told me. "So she's going upstairs to yell at Grandma and throw her shoe," I murmured. "Then she'll head downstairs to her place and call Nicholas and Jessica."

Sure enough, Nicholas and Jessica showed up next, walking slowly, their hands entwined. How romantic. I watched him turn his head and brush a kiss against the top of her head. He really loved her. Enough to kill for her honor? Enough to cover up a murder she'd committed?

"So we have to wait and see when they leave," I said.

It took a while; we had to hit fast-forward to get us through a couple of hours. But eventually we caught them on their way out, still holding hands. I leaned in closer, squinting. It was hard to make out much on their faces, but was that Jessica swiping away a tear?

I should've known better than to trust Mom when she said they'd bonded over Grandma hating them both. Probably she'd piled on Jessica too and Jessica was now buried under twice the hate.

"So they left at 11:55 p.m.," Gabe said. "Is that past the time of the murder?"

My shoulders sagged. "No. Grandma's last call to me was after midnight. She's still alive at this point."

I'd been wrong. Nicholas and Jessica hadn't killed her. Which was good! I was glad my brother, who I loved very much, and his girlfriend, who was fine, didn't have blood on their hands!

It was good I hadn't just gone to him and made an accusation without any evidence. Our relationship might never have recovered. Gabe and I sat in silence for a bit, watching the events of the lobby that night swirl before us in fast-forward.

Still, this meant, "We're back to square one, then. Do we have any suspects left?"

Gabe pressed his lips together in thought. "Not on the list. Is there anyone else you can—wait, is that you?"

The video was still on fast-forward, but he pressed the button to make it go back to normal speed. The time stamp was now almost 2 a.m., and sure enough, there I was, wobbling over the marble as I leaned on Opal's shoulder. Opal was standing and walking straight, bearing my weight without falling over, which was impressive considering how drunk we'd both been, but I could barely tear my eyes off the way my head was tossed back in laughter. I couldn't remember this. Not at all.

I pushed back my chair, a sick sort of shame making me feel heavy. It wasn't shame at going out and having fun—I wasn't embarrassed about partying or anything. I felt that shame because, well . . . *had* it actually been fun? I'd had lots of fun at parties in the past (my twenty-first birthday party, when I called dibs on the family jet and club-hopped from Amsterdam to Paris to Barcelona, was maybe the most fun I'd ever had) but recently that fun had become . . . something else. And the drinking hadn't been to blur the lines around me and lower inhibitions, but to cover that *something else* up. "We should turn it off."

"No, wait, I want to see you finish your walk."

But I had no idea what I did next. What if I started stripping in the lobby and decorating the potted plants with my bra and underwear (Millicent's twenty-first birthday night)? Or I threw up in a potted plant (coming home from a gala aimed at saving some endangered marsupial last year)? Honestly, those poor potted plants. They just couldn't win. "I think we should turn it off."

Gabe was laughing like the whole thing was funny. "This is hilarious. You're so cute."

I took a deep breath, not even able to focus on the fact that he'd called me cute. "Please turn it off."

Now he looked over at me, and his eyes widened. "Pom, what's wrong?"

I wrapped my arms around myself as if I were cold, even though it was muggy-hot in this tiny room, the screens all giving off heat that had nowhere to go. I had no idea what I was going to say until it came out. "I don't like who I was back then."

His eyes darted back and forth between me and the screen. "This wasn't even that long ago."

"Yeah, well." My voice came out too loud. He probably would've taken a step back if there was any room to. "I've changed a lot in the last month. And now seeing who I used to be, what used to be important to me, thinking about how much I used to drink and why, is embarrassing. Can you please just turn it off?"

"Sure. Of course. Sorry." He went to hit the button. But as he did . . .

"Wait." I leaned in, squinting at the screen. A woman had entered the lobby, her shoulders hunched, her face covered by the brim of a large hat. But I knew her. I knew the way she moved. I'd just seen it on the footage.

Her name came out in an exhale. "Jessica."

CHAPTER

Twenty-One

So Jessica had returned to the Afton alone after she and Nicholas left. She'd snuck back in, trying to disguise her face from
the cameras—because why else would you wear a huge hat like that,
indoors, at night? My current huge hat was living proof—shortly before my grandma was murdered, shortly after she'd taken a bunch of
crap from my mom.

It wasn't irrefutable proof. But it was really, really suspicious.

And it meant that I was right.

Usually, being right made me feel great. Right now it only made
me feel a little nauseous. "Just to make sure, we should wait to see
when she leaves. Maybe she forgot her phone or something at my
mom's place and she's going to grab it and leave quickly."

No such luck. Jessica was at the hotel for a full forty-five minutes
before the cameras caught her leaving. Plenty of time to stab an old lady
to death. I leaned in closer, squinting to see if I could catch any dark
splotches on her that might be blood, but no such luck there either.
"Can we clip that part of the footage, including the time stamp, and
email it to ourselves or something?"

"I assume we can." Gabe and I clicked around for a bit and, sure
enough, managed to download that piece of footage. We couldn't figure out how to email it, but luckily he always kept a USB stick on him
for school, so we were able to download the file and tuck it away in
Gabe's pocket. "What are we going to do with this?" he asked. "Go to
the police?"

He sounded almost hopeful, a hope that deflated as I shook my head. "I can't just go to the police on my brother."

"Technically it's not your brother, it's your brother's girlfriend."

"Same thing." My heart squeezed. "I have to talk to them first. We can do the same thing we did with my mom. Have our phones recording the whole time just in case."

"All right."

We shut the computers down, logging out of everything, though we'd left fingerprints all over. If the police came after us for breaking in, there would be no denying it.

Back out in the apartment, the dust was settled thick over the furniture, the air still and silent and heavy. With no sign that anyone was about to storm in here and drag us out, I wondered aloud, "Should we take a look around?"

"Do you think there would be anything useful left?" Gabe asked. "Wouldn't the police have taken anything that could be evidence?"

I shrugged. "Maybe we'll see something they didn't know was evidence."

"Then how will *we* know it's evidence?"

I hadn't wanted to say it out loud, but I had to. "If it might have something to do with Jessica."

Sure enough, the apartment seemed mostly to have been picked over of anything that might be useful; the file cabinets in my grandma's office were mostly empty, their contents presumably taken by the new caretakers of the business, and her safe was open and empty, presumably raided by my parents. There was nothing else of note in the main rooms or the guest wing, which left only Grandma's personal rooms.

Including the room where I'd found her dead.

I didn't realize my breathing had gone all fast and shallow until Gabe said, "Maybe you should sit down. I can do a quick look around down there."

Not going to lie, it was tempting. Definitely something the old Pom would have done. But I forced myself to hold my breath for a moment, then inhale and exhale deeply. Once. Twice. Again. "I can do it."

The hardest part, unsurprisingly, was entering Grandma's room. As I walked down that hall, I couldn't help but flash back to the day I found her. The eerie stillness of the hallway, so like it was now. The tinny sound of her phone ringing and no one picking up. That moment when I rounded the corner into the room and smelled that metallic saturation of blood, saw the limpness of her body.

Though I knew they'd removed her body and presumably sent in a crime scene cleanup team, I still half expected to round that corner and see the same thing. Of course I didn't: a whole patch of the carpet where the blood had soaked in was gone, leaving a window to the shiny wooden planks beneath, and the bed had been stripped down to the frame. You could almost imagine someone hadn't been brutally murdered in the space.

I had to take a moment to reel in the doorway, which gave Gabe a head start. "What's this?"

I followed him to Grandma's vanity, which was still cluttered with all of her various makeups and perfumes and lotions. "It's her banking stuff," I said. "Look, there's her checkbook."

We regarded the stack of papers in silence. I finally reached out and ruffled through them: file folders of bank statements; canceled checks; old receipts. "These payment records are to your mom," I said, holding them up. "Andrea Morales."

Beside me, Gabe tensed. "Why was my mom still getting paid by your grandma? She hasn't worked for the family in years."

I flipped through them again. "I don't know, but they're from last year." All of the checks were. Grandma had never been one for online banking or apps like Venmo—too confusing, not enough paper records. It seemed Grandma wrote a ton of checks: to various people at the hotels; to Rosa and Lori and her other staff; to Opal's mother for help with gala planning; to—weird—Farrah and Jordan. "Do you think . . ."

"My mom is definitely *not* a killer," Gabe said adamantly. How nice to be able to feel that conviction.

"I didn't say she was," I said. "I certainly can't see her killing anyone either. I love Andrea. But you have to admit it's weird she was still being paid by my family despite not working for us anymore. Could be worth a call."

Gabe didn't respond, just went back to the pile of records. "What about this Lori? I haven't heard you mention her."

I should actually probably give Lori a call, make sure she was okay. She'd probably found a new job by now. Hopefully someone who was better to her than I'd been. "Lori was the person who helped me out. Those payments are legit."

Gabe set the papers back on the vanity. "Was it usual for your grandma to keep all this stuff here? On her makeup thing?"

"It's called a vanity," I said. "And no. She didn't keep that stuff in here; it was kept in her office." I examined them all again, as if something I hadn't seen before would jump out at me. It did not.

Gabe mused, "I wonder if it was in here because of the killer. Like, the killer was asking about her bank records, or asking her to write a check."

"Could be. Though it would be kind of anticlimactic for this whole thing to be about money."

"Everything's either about money or sex. Isn't that the saying?" Gabe set down the papers he was holding. "Should we take this all with us?"

"Probably safer not to," I said. "If it really is evidence, we don't want to be accused of tampering. Let's take pictures of it all, though, so we have it."

"Smart."

That wasn't a compliment I was used to receiving. I preened for a moment before reaching for my phone.

Once the pictures were taken and backed up, I gave one last look around the room. This might be my last time ever being in here. Hell, it might be my last time ever being in the Afton.

Should I say something? Give it a salute?

In the end I just walked away, Gabe by my side, back to my home.

CHAPTER

Twenty-Two

A s soon as we got back to the apartment, we backed up the video clip in multiple places, on both the cloud and on two hard drives. Just to make sure we couldn't lose it.

Then I approached my task with grim determination. I texted Nicholas and Jessica, asked if they would be up for dinner with me and Gabe. I hoped that introducing a date for me into the equation would be enticing enough to bypass the weirdness our relationship had going on lately, and I was right. Jessica responded immediately with a bunch of peeping-eye emojis and a time for us to come by. *I'll make pasta*, she said.

Old Pom would've just shown up, maybe with a bottle of wine or something if she passed by the store on the way over. New Pom replied, *I'll bring dessert*.

My dessert had a dual purpose: one, to be a good guest, and two, to keep my hands and my mind busy until it came time to confront my brother and his girlfriend. The mere thought was unsettling, unnerving; Nicholas had a temper, and was definitely a harder nut to crack than my mom was. I doubted I'd be able to manipulate him so easily into a confession. "Are you sure you don't want to call your mom and ask about those payments?" I called to Gabe, who was attending a virtual class in his bedroom.

"How are we supposed to tell her we know about them?" he called back. Which, fair point. "Besides, Jessica is our leading suspect right now. If for some reason things don't work out tonight the way I think they will, I promise we can give her a call next."

My lips thinned. "Are you sure about that?"

"What do you mean?"

This was probably not the best conversation to be shouting back and forth to each other from separate rooms, so I took my cake pan out of the oven, putting it on the counter to cool, and popped over to Gabe's room. The door was open, so it was basically an invitation. "I mean that so far I've pretty much had to interrogate all of my family members for murder," I said. He looked up from where he was sprawled on his navy blue bedspread. My heart twisted a little at the disarray of his pillows. "So why can't you call your mom and ask? It's not like either of us thinks she killed my grandma. But maybe she has some information that could help us going forward."

Now Gabe set his laptop aside, giving me his full attention. "Like you said, neither of us thinks my mom's a killer. We both know and love her. So I don't see the need to call her and ask right now."

"It doesn't seem fair," I said, and honestly, I wasn't sure what exactly I was talking about. It was true that I didn't think Andrea was a killer, but it wasn't like Jessica's face screamed I'M A MURDERER either. And we did both love her, but Andrea would never—could never—love me the way she loved Gabe. She'd taken care of me for money, not love.

But both of those things seemed too hard to speak aloud, so I went with the last one. "That I've had to go through all of this emotional turmoil and you haven't had to go through any. This can just be entertainment for you, and this is my real life that's tearing apart."

Kind of like listening to my true-crime podcast. My stomach flipped unpleasantly. I'd listened to Doe's tale of Danica's disappearance for entertainment. I mean, I was going to keep listening, since I only had one episode left and I had to know this big twist Doe had been teasing all season, but was I really all that different?

Gabe blinked with what looked like surprise. "Pom, what's brought all this on?"

"I'm telling you exactly what brought all this on," I said, but then my heart twisted again, this time hard. Andrea had taken care of me for money. And wasn't that why Gabe had teamed up with me to investigate? For money? He'd wanted to make sure his mother got the money left to her in my grandma's will. If Andrea hadn't been owed anything, would Gabe be helping at all? Or would he have turned his back on me and left, the same way Andrea did when my family stopped paying her to take care of me?

Was that all I was to everybody in my life? Just a check?

And what if Andrea actually was the guilty party, or if she'd had something to do with the murder? If Gabe was only in this for the money owed her, I couldn't trust him to be objective when it came to this next stage. Maybe he'd even sabotage the investigation.

"Pom, what is it?" he asked, his eyebrows now a little scrunched in a way that, if I weren't having a semi-existential crisis, I'd likely find adorable.

I let out a deep breath. "You probably shouldn't come tonight."

"What?" He closed his laptop and hopped to his feet. "Can we talk about this?"

"I think I should finish this alone. I don't need you."

"I know you don't need me," he said, sounding wounded. "But I want to be there. I want to see this through. For justice."

"Do you?" I asked. "I'm nothing more than a paycheck to your family. You just want to collect on the will."

"Well, yeah, of course I do," he said, confirming what I'd thought. "That's not true, what you're saying about you just being a paycheck, though. Maybe it started that way, but it's not true anymore. You're my friend, Pom."

He'd say that if it weren't true, though. Because he couldn't do this without me.

That was a weird thought. Being needed like that.

Gabe kept talking before I could respond, and the wounded tone in his voice morphed into defensiveness. "Aren't you doing this for the money too? Would you really be investigating if it didn't mean getting your trust fund back? Would you really ever team up with me? For anything?"

"That's different. Totally different," I said, because it was. Wasn't it?

He snorted. "Yeah. Sure. Okay." He was quiet for a moment, as if weighing what to say next. Sure enough, what came out hung heavy in the air. "I should've known you'd feel this way. Everything I read about you growing up. It's always all about the money, isn't it? You wouldn't be here with me if you had the choice. Opal's right, you'd never give me a second glance. Not with my current account balance. You'd have acted just like she did in Queens, like I was beneath you."

I wasn't going to lie: he was probably right. If my grandmother hadn't been murdered and all my assets seized, I wouldn't even know his name. I'd still be swanning around at galas with Millicent and Coriander, snickering behind Opal's back at her reduced state, focusing on what club we were going to and what labels we were wearing. I never would have spared him a second glance.

Just because it was true didn't mean it didn't hurt to hear it, though.

My phone buzzed. Nicholas asking when I was coming over. With one hand, I texted him back. Heading over soon. Maybe for longer than a dinner, I didn't know. I didn't know how much longer I could stand being here with Gabe, knowing what I knew, feeling how I felt, knowing how *he* felt. "Sorry. I have to go."

"Pom, wait—"

I fled. Well, as much as you can flee while carefully carrying a cake down the street. I focused all of my attention off my wounded heart and onto transporting my cake safely, shooting eyes full of murder at every bicyclist who dared ride on the sidewalk and risk bumping me. Considering how shitty I was feeling, I might actually have murdered someone who knocked my cake to the ground.

Luckily for them, I made it unscathed to Jessica's building. She buzzed me in and met me at her door, a wide, bright smile on her face, one that faltered a bit when she realized I was there alone. "Welcome! I'm so glad you could come by, Pom!" She made moves toward leaning in for a hug, but I stepped out of the way, afraid for my cake. "I thought you were bringing your . . . friend?" she said.

I faked a hard smile. "He couldn't make it, unfortunately." I held up my bag. "I made a carrot cake."

Jessica recovered quickly from any surprise or disappointment. "Oh, Nicholas's favorite!" Which was both true and calculated on my part. Though it was probably too much to hope that he'd be placated by his favorite cake after I had his girlfriend carted away for murder, it didn't mean I wouldn't try. "Come in, let me find a nice platter for it."

As I followed her inside, Nicholas came out of the bedroom to greet us. He'd shaved for the occasion, so he looked a little more like himself, though I still wasn't used to seeing him in jeans instead of his usual slacks. At least he wasn't in sweatpants again. "Hey, Pom."

"Hey, Nicholas." I leaned in to brush his cheek with mine, then preempted the question I was sure I was about to get. "My friend couldn't make it after all, so it's just me."

"No worries," he said, but he looked like he had plenty of them. Not specifically about me and Gabe, but the bags under his eyes could hold a bathtub full of worries. "I think Jessica's getting everything ready still. Why don't you come sit down?"

Jessica's apartment wasn't big enough for a separate dining room, but the living area had the space for a small table and some chairs, two normal wooden dining ones and two folding chairs they'd clearly pulled out of the closet. I was graceful enough to take a folding chair, avoiding the sight of its empty mate. Nicholas sank into one of the wooden chairs like he'd been on his feet all day. Which he hadn't. (He was so full of crap when he called working at the coffee shop easy. He wouldn't last a *day*.)

"You'll be happy to know I've started my own business," I said, and shared how Gabe and I had started selling my baked goods at the coffee shop. "People have been going crazy over them online, especially all my different sweet-roll flavors. I made one the other day that had a honey-pistachio filling and a lime glaze and you would've thought it was a new Birkin color."

"That's great, Pom," Nicholas said. "I'm proud of you."

But his heart wasn't in it. The brother I knew would've immediately peppered me with questions: if I had expansion plans; what my profits versus expenses looked like; if I'd thought about proper scaling. He was clearly miserable. It almost made me relieved to be presumably putting him out of his misery.

We waited until Jessica entered with the food, and then the food—fresh pasta carbonara with roasted broccoli on the side—smelled so good I waited until we'd eaten half our plates, filling the room with friendly chatter about Jessica's annoying coworker who wouldn't stop calling her Jennifer and the new dog their neighbors got, which was fluffier than a cloud. Jessica was excited about my new business, offering to advise on marketing for free, which meant I felt like absolute garbage about what I had to do next.

Not garbagey enough to skip it, however. I drew in a deep breath. "Hey. Look. I'm really sorry. There's something we have to talk about, though," I said.

Nicholas's fork clattered to his plate. Jessica lowered hers slowly, deliberately, her eyes fixed on her pasta. "Nicholas?" she said.

Nicholas had his eyes on me. "Pom."

They knew. They knew what I was going to say.

So I didn't say it. I pulled the video up on my phone and propped it up against my water glass so that everyone at the table but me could see it. I wanted to close my eyes so that I didn't have to see the pain on Nicholas's face, but I would've known no matter what when they reached the telltale moment from the sharp gasps both he and Jessica let out.

"Well?" I asked, once the video was over.

Nicholas's jaw was clenched so tight he might as well have had tetanus. "Where did you get that?"

I folded my hands on the table. "Does it matter?"

Nicholas glanced at Jessica. Jessica glanced at Nicholas.

Jessica burst into tears.

"It's okay. It's okay," Nicholas said, pulling her into his shoulder.

"She doesn't know anything. She can't prove anything. I told you, you have the protection of the best lawyers in the country."

A coldness flooded through me at the venomous look he flashed in my direction. I felt kind of like a snake had bit me.

Jessica pushed him away, wiping her eyes and sniffling. A streak of carbonara decorated her cheek, though this seemed like the wrong time to point that out. "No. Nicholas, I'm sick of living like this. Of constantly worrying it's going to come down on my head." She shook her head. "Honestly, it's kind of a relief to be able to talk about it."

I had to be careful, keep Nicholas from putting his foot down. But I didn't know how to dance around the question: "Was it you? Did you kill her?"

The entire room held its breath. The plants on the windowsill turned their flowers in our direction. The sirens outside stopped mid-shriek.

Nicholas turned to her. "You don't have to answer that."

But Jessica didn't turn to him. She turned to me. "No. I do. Pom, it's like this."

The world held itself in suspended animation as she continued to speak. "My feelings were hurt that night when your mom didn't invite me to her gala. Did you know she didn't invite me, Pom?"

I hadn't even thought about it, used to Jessica not being invited to things, but I felt bad saying as much. So I just shook my head.

"I never got invited to things like that, even though Nicholas and I have been dating for over a year and a half. That's longer than your parents dated before getting married, did you know that?" She let out a bitter laugh. How un-Jessica. Or maybe not un-Jessica. Maybe I didn't know Jessica at all.

I certainly hadn't tried very hard.

"Anyway," Jessica continued. "I knew your mother didn't approve of me because she didn't invite me to her events, and it hurt. But what hurt even more?" The hurt filled her eyes as she looked over at Nicholas, set them to overflowing again. "Your grandma didn't approve of me either. One of the few things she and your mother agreed on. And it drove me crazy. It was nothing I did! It was nothing I said! I have a good job. I'm nice to people. I love Nicholas and I treat him well. People have told me I'm pretty. I like to think I'm a catch."

"You are one hundred percent a catch," said Nicholas.

Jessica went on as if he hadn't spoken. "But all that mattered to your grandma was that I didn't come from the 'right' family. The 'right' class. I grew up eating Hamburger Helper and playing softball and vacationing at the local lake instead of eating oysters and playing tennis and 'summering' overseas. My clothes weren't the right brands and I show too many teeth when I laugh and even my name is too common and trendy, apparently. I couldn't possibly be the wife of the heir to the Afton empire. So when Nicholas told her that he was going to ask me to marry him and that he wanted her blessing . . ."

"I hoped she would give me the family ring," Nicholas said quietly. "But she told me that if I wanted to inherit, then I needed the right wife. And she was worried Jessica wasn't the right wife."

I gasped. "She threatened you that you wouldn't be the heir anymore if you married Jessica?"

"Exactly," Nicholas said grimly, but Jessica shook her head.

"Of course she didn't come out and say precisely that. She had to couch it in wordplay and passive-aggression and games. But it was what she meant." Jessica's shoulders went limp. "And Nicholas listened to her. He didn't propose."

"It wasn't forever," Nicholas said hastily as I shook my head, then stopped shaking my head, because it was probably a good thing my brother hadn't gone and gotten hitched to a killer. "I just had to let the storm pass and convince her that you *would* be the right wife. Because you were. You *are*." He swallowed hard. "But I'd also been working my whole life to inherit the Afton empire. And she could take that all away."

"I got it. I get it," Jessica said. "I understood. If you told me that marrying you would make me lose my whole family and everything else I'd ever worked for, I'd hesitate. But that didn't mean I was happy about it."

"Of course not," I murmured.

"So when your mom called us in hysterics to come over because she'd had a massive fight with your grandma, I thought that maybe this was an opportunity to bond with her. Find an ally, since I knew your grandma didn't approve of her either."

She clearly didn't know our mother very well.

"Of course that wasn't the case," Jessica said bitterly. "She was drunk out of her mind and wanted to rant about some stupid game your grandma was playing with her on social media. I asked her if she had any advice for how to get your grandma to like me. She just laughed. 'That old hag is never going to like you. If Nicholas marries you, she'll spend the rest of her life making you miserable,' she told me. 'She's a miserable, miserable person. No wonder her husband couldn't keep it in his pants.'"

My jaw dropped. "Grandpa cheated on Grandma?" It wasn't that shocking, to think about it. So many of the men in that circle had affairs, had mistresses, carried on with high-class escorts.

But this was my *grandpa* we were talking about.

"A lot, it sounded like." Jessica's voice was gleeful. "Your mom clammed up after that. Seemed to realize she'd said too much. Told us to go home, that she was going to bed, that she was going to have a terrible headache in the morning.

"So Nicholas and I went home. That's what you saw the first time, the two of us leaving."

"But then you came back," I said.

Jessica gave me a grim nod. "We went home and got ready for bed. The whole time, I couldn't stop thinking about what your mother had told me. Your grandma wasn't a nice person. Maybe . . . being the right wife meant not being a nice person. So . . . Nicholas went to bed, and I went back to the Afton with his keys.

"To my surprise, she let me right into her suite. Asked me what I was doing there without Nicholas. I sat down from her across that big dining room table over a glass of wine and got straight to the point. 'I know what your husband got up to behind your back,' I told her. 'I'd be shocked if there weren't a bunch of illegitimate Aftons running around out there threatening the inheritance, and it would take me two seconds to find them with all those new ancestry tests popping up out there. All I have to do is get Nicholas to submit a sample. Do you want that? Do you want your money and your company going to all these Aftons who aren't yours?'

"'Or do you want your company going to a good man, a prepared man, a man whose fiancée-to-be would do *anything* for him?'"

Jessica let her breath out in a long, low whoosh. Nicholas looked vaguely queasy at the thought of anyone saying all those words to our grandma. I realized I was holding my breath. "What did she say?"

A slight smile quirked Jessica's lips. "She laughed. She laughed! At first I panicked, thinking that she was laughing at me and how doomed I was, about how she was going to call Nicholas right now and tell him his girlfriend was a dirty rotten blackmailer. But she sobered up, and she eyed me with . . . I don't know what to call it but respect. It was the first time I've seen anyone in your family who wasn't Nicholas look at me that way.

"And you know what she said? She told me, 'You know what, maybe you're the right wife for Nicholas after all.'" Jessica gave us all an outraged look, her eyes bulging. "This was what I wanted to marry into? This family where being right for it meant being mean and sneaky and disrespectful to your elders? I was so ashamed.

"But you know what else? I didn't take it back. Because she finally approved, and it wasn't like she was going to be alive forever. All I had to do was outlive her."

I furrowed my brow. "So that's why you killed her?" It didn't fit with what the story seemed to have been leading up to, a rage-filled spontaneous stabbing due to Grandma's cruelty, but if Jessica was *that* determined to outlive her . . .

"What?" Jessica squawked. "No! I didn't kill her! I thanked her and I left!"

"Wait," I said. "So you *didn't* kill her?"

"That's what I just said!"

The three of us regarded each other over our half-finished, rapidly congealing plates of pasta. Jessica's chest was heaving, as if her elevator was out and she'd climbed forty flights of stairs, and her eyes shone glossy with tears that quickly began to fall. "Do you really think I'm capable of killing someone?"

How dare she try to make *me* feel bad? "You have to admit things were awfully suspicious!" I cried. "You never told anyone you were there that night right before she was killed. Why didn't you?"

Jessica reached out for Nicholas's hand. He took hers instead, rubbing his thumb soothingly over her knuckles. "Because I felt like absolute garbage. I'd blackmailed an old lady. I didn't want your family to know. And what if they decided to accuse me too? I don't have the resources you guys have. I couldn't afford to fight back the way you could." A single tear slipped dramatically down her cheek. "I didn't even tell Nicholas for a while. Not until after you moved out of here, Pom. I wanted to make sure he at least knew in case the police brought me in based on the security footage or someone reported seeing me back at the hotel that late."

So that's why Nicholas had been so brusque and standoffish when I'd called him for job-hunting help after I'd moved in with Gabe. "And why you've been so weird about us investigating," I finished the thought out loud. "Because you knew Jessica looked suspicious, and you didn't want us dredging it up. Maybe they wouldn't ultimately have been able to prove anything, but they would have dragged her through the mud and made her life really hard. And who knows? Maybe they would have tried to pin it on her anyway. Mom and Dad certainly wouldn't have been opposed to that."

Nicholas confirmed what I said with a tight nod. "She's telling the truth, Pom. She didn't kill Grandma."

"Especially not after I *finally* got her approval," Jessica said, and her earnest tone actually made me laugh.

"You know," I said, "if we ever find out who did it and get everything back that we lost, I'll make sure you're on the gala invite list. I won't go to any galas my mom throws unless you're invited too. I promise."

With the shine in her eyes and the red roses of emotion in her cheeks, Jessica's sudden smile was extra luminous. "Thanks, Pom."

We stared at each other for a moment; I could feel the bonding in the air, an electrical current. Nicholas snapped us out of it by clapping his hands together, never one for awkward emotional moments. "I hear there's carrot cake?"

As weird as it felt to be eating carrot cake and chatting about what other desserts I'd made only minutes after confessing that I'd thought them capable of covering up a murder, that was what we did. The cake was delicious, by the way. The cream cheese frosting was a little lumpy—I didn't think I'd let the cream cheese warm enough before whipping it with the powdered sugar and butter—but the taste was there. As it should be, considering how my biceps had ached after grating all those carrots.

In a conversational lull, Jessica raised an eyebrow. "So, you and Gabe? Are you dating? I'm disappointed he couldn't make it tonight. I wanted to meet him."

Usually I might have demurred and changed the subject, but after I'd literally interrogated her for murder, I figured it was only fair that she got to interrogate me for something too (I was glad it wasn't murder, though). I let out an awkward laugh. "We're definitely not dating."

"No?" Nicholas said. "That's not the vibe I got from your text."

How much of a vibe could you really get from a text? I hadn't even used any emojis or exclamation points. "We're roommates and . . ." I trailed off before I could finish with *friends*. Because friends didn't use each other for money. Or bring up the behavior of a past self you maybe weren't super proud of.

"Ah, so there is more going on," Jessica said wisely. "Tell me about it."

I didn't want to tell her about it, to be honest. Except . . . if my goal was to do better with Jessica, maybe that involved bringing her in more. Not like I ever would've talked about this stuff with Nicholas, but maybe I would have with a sister. So I took a deep breath and I spilled.

Jessica listened intently the whole time, her chin propped on her hand. Nicholas alternated between looking at me and checking his phone. (Like, why even? It wasn't like he had a work email to check anymore.) I finished with "So it turns out he was just using me. For money."

"I don't know about that," she said slowly. "Don't take this the wrong way, but it sounds like you might have jumped the gun a little."

"What do you mean?"

"It sounds like he's worried about his mom and he doesn't want to disappoint her," Jessica said. "Didn't it take you a while to call *your* mom, even though he wanted you to do it sooner?"

Well, I didn't like having to remember that. "Maybe."

Nicholas slung his arm over Jessica's shoulders, and a twist of envy hit me right then. Not because I wanted my brother to put his arm around me—he could keep his armpits far away from me, thanks—but at their easy intimacy. I wanted *that*.

With Gabe.

The realization struck me, unraveling the twist. I liked Gabe. Really liked him. And maybe that had made me lash out. Because it didn't feel like anybody, whether family or friend, had ever just liked me for me. For my personality and my heart rather than my wallet. So wasn't it easier to push someone away before they betrayed you?

And yeah, maybe he'd been right about how I never would've looked at him twice if I hadn't lost everything. But I *had* lost everything, and that *had* changed me. I was a different Pomona now than I was before. And that made it real, didn't it?

"You look like you're having an epiphany," said Jessica. "I love a good epiphany."

Maybe I *had* jumped the gun. My breath quickened in my throat. What had I done? What if I'd driven him away for good?

I had to make sure I hadn't. But before then, I had to make sure things were okay here. As much as it was the Afton way to plaster over negative emotions with superficial things (not usually dessert, though—typically alcohol or passive-aggressive small talk), I didn't want that to be our way anymore.

So, even though Nicholas and Jessica seemed content enough to interrogate me about my love life (or lack thereof), I brought the topic of the murder back up again. "Look," I said. "I just want to make sure we're okay. I didn't really think you'd killed our grandma. I didn't want you to be the one. But the footage was super suspicious, and it would've been irresponsible not to check out all angles."

Jessica waved a hand in the air. "Don't worry, I understand. Honestly, I'm glad it's all out in the open. Keeping it inside was making me sick." She did seem calmer already: her shoulders more relaxed, her always-on smile less manic, fewer fake-enthusiastic exclamation points bursting out in her speech. "I'm surprised you didn't come to me sooner, though. Your friend didn't say anything?"

Another siren wailed distantly outside. "What do you mean, my friend?"

"What's her name? Opal? The one who had come back from the gala with you?" Jessica shrugged. "I ran into her in the private family hallway when I was leaving the hotel for the second time. She was on her way out, too, she was just running back up to grab something she forgot."

Dread was unspooling coldly through my insides. Opal had stayed the night with me. She hadn't headed home. And she would've needed me to let her back into my apartment if she had actually forgotten something. Then again, I was so drunk I'd blacked out—it was entirely possible I'd gotten up and let her back in without remembering any of it.

But I didn't think so. Because then why wouldn't Opal have mentioned running into Jessica late at night in a family hallway where she shouldn't have been? When she knew we were investigating?

To give my friend the benefit of the doubt, maybe it was the alcohol again. Maybe she'd drunkenly wandered out thinking vaguely that she'd go home, only to get turned around; maybe she forgot all of it the next morning after I'd let her in and forgot about it myself.

Maybe.

Maybe not. Because I remembered seeing Opal and me walking together into the hotel on the security footage. I'd clearly been drunk, weaving and leaning on her to stay upright. But Opal? She'd looked as if she was walking normally. Like she wasn't as drunk as I was. And in order for her to get back in without my help, she would've needed enough foresight to grab my keys off the hook, and a super-drunk person wouldn't have that.

A touch on my shoulder. I jumped. It was Jessica. "Pom, are you okay?"

I blinked. I couldn't say anything. Not until I was sure. "Okay. Yeah."

Nicholas leaned in. "I was just saying that I don't blame you for investigating us, especially considering how weird I've been with you lately. I would've done the same thing. I've actually been looking into that night a little bit myself, though I haven't turned up much. Not nearly as much as you have." Suddenly I understood what Jessica had been saying about how my grandma had looked at her with respect. Because I was pretty sure that was what Nicholas was doing to me now.

I wasn't sure, though. I'd never really seen him look that way at me before.

I would've leaned in for a hug, except we weren't exactly a hugging family. "I've had a lot of help," I said. "From Gabe."

"I hope we get to meet him at some point," Jessica said. "Not going to lie, I looked him up online, and you two would be way cute together."

"To be fair, I'd be cute with anyone," I said.

That made them laugh. Nicholas said, "You know, this might be the best carrot cake I've ever had. I like how you put in dates instead of raisins. No wonder people are going crazy for your baked goods. If I regularly ate dessert, I'd make a habit of stopping by that café too."

"They're not all desserts. I've been making some savory things too. I'm actually working on this babka recipe that uses leeks, garlic, and cheese in the filling. It's a little too wet right now, but I think the next batch will be perfect."

Nicholas actually clapped his hands. "Sign me up."

"Of course," I said, feeling light with pride. If Nicholas wasn't careful with all the compliments and respect and kindness he was throwing at me today, I might start to believe them.

CHAPTER

Twenty-Three

That glorious lightness in my chest lingered only as long as I insisted Nicholas and Jessica keep the leftovers of my cake, as I waited impatiently for Jessica's slow elevator and exited her building to a cloud of smoke from some guy lounging on a bench outside.

I hurried home, one foot in front of the other, staring down at my chunky heels to keep them from getting stuck in a sidewalk grate. As I was hiking up the stairs to my apartment, I noticed that my calves hardly burned at all anymore. What did burn was the excitement I had about seeing Gabe, about petting Squeaky, about getting back to my tiny, dilapidated kitchen and working magic with my hands.

Had I ruined all of that?

Inside, Gabe was sitting on the couch in sweatpants and a T-shirt. He stood as soon as I entered, spilling Squeaky from his lap with a meow of protest. "Pom. I was waiting for you to call my mom."

"You don't have to," I said back. "Listen, I was being unfair. I was . . ." I trailed off, because I didn't know how much to say. I might have been able to admit how much I liked Gabe to myself, but to *him*?

That was scary. So I just finished. "I freaked out a little bit and made assumptions based on how people had treated me in the past. I don't really think you're using me for money." I laughed a little. "There are much easier ways to get money."

He shook his head. "No, I was being unfair too. You were right, you've gone after all your family members and I freaked out at the thought of asking mine questions. I need to know why she was getting those payments. Maybe you're right and it does have something to do with the murder."

"You don't think she had anything to do with it, though, do you? Because I don't." My parents would be aghast to hear me say this. *You feel more loyalty to that woman than to your own flesh and blood?*

Family wasn't only flesh and blood, though. Family was about who loved you and who built you up, not tore you down.

"No, of course I don't," said Gabe. "But we should cover all our bases, right?" He was quiet for a moment. "And I'm sorry about what I said, about you—"

I stopped him with a shake of my head. "No, you were right. But I've changed. Just because it was how I'd feel before doesn't mean it's how I feel now."

I wasn't sure he'd be able to pull the correct meaning out of my word salad, but his face softened. He got me. He *got* me.

Still. Even though I'd convinced myself otherwise, there was still that little lingering doubt I had to get rid of. "Your whole reason for taking part in this investigation was to get your mom what she deserved from my grandma's will. You realize that if there's even the slightest, tiniest chance she had something to do with it, then . . ."

"Then she gets nothing," he finished. "Yeah. I know. I thought about it. And it is still a major reason why I want this solved. But . . . I also want it solved for you. And for justice."

For justice. What did justice mean, anyway? For anyone? Was it justice for me to get all that money and my old life back when I hadn't done anything to earn it or deserve it? It didn't feel like it, especially now that I'd seen all that people like Gabe and Ellie and Sage went through for a tiny fraction of what I had.

But warmth bloomed within me. He wanted to help me solve this for me. Not for money. "Okay," I said. "Let me change quickly into something more comfortable, and then let's call your mom."

I came back out in my yoga pants and one of Gabe's T-shirts that had somehow ended up in my drawer after I'd persuaded him to throw my laundry in with his own so I didn't have to try and work the machine. He eyed me in his shirt, but didn't say anything. "Okay, you ready?"

I nodded. He clicked her name, putting the phone on speaker so that the ringing filled the room.

She picked up after only two of them. "Hello?"

Why did parents always do that? It wasn't like his name hadn't popped up on the screen. "Hey, Mom," said Gabe. "Is this a good time?"

"It's always a good time for you, *mi amor*," she said warmly. Jealousy tickled my chest, and I had to look away. She'd always spoken to me in that tone of voice, but had never called me "my love." I knew she cared about me, but did she love me? Did money changing hands prevent her from being considered my family?

Andrea continued, "What's going on? How are you?"

Gabe hesitated. I got it: I'd have a hard time broaching a difficult subject after hearing all that love in her voice too. "Nothing too much. Just hanging out with Pom," he said. "How about you?"

The warmth didn't leave her voice, but wariness did enter it. "Everything still going well with that arrangement?"

"Yes, everything's going well," Gabe said. His voice had jumped up half an octave. Maybe that was the actual reason why he'd let me take point on our interrogations so far: not because we were speaking to my friends and family, but because he was an absolutely terrible liar. "Like I said, we're just hanging out."

"Just hanging out, huh? Be careful, Gabriel." The wariness in her tone felt like a paper cut. I knew she wouldn't speak that way if she had any idea I was listening, and the apology in Gabe's eyes said he knew it too. "That family has a way of ruining everything they touch."

That hit so hard I had to sit down and fold into myself, elbows on my knees.

"Not Pom, though," Gabe said loyally. "Pom makes everything she touches better."

"Not Pom," Andrea agreed, which was enough to get me to sit up straight. "Pom is a good girl, but you should still be careful around her. She means well, but she's oblivious. And sometimes oblivious people can hurt you without realizing what they're doing."

"Maybe that was true once, but I don't think it's true anymore. She's changed."

I knew Andrea so well I could practically see her shaking her head in bemusement, full lips quirked, as she said, "What's up with you? You got a crush?"

"Mom, stop!" Gabe's face had gone brick red. "That's not what I called to talk about. Though it actually does have something to do with the Aftons."

"What is it?"

Gabe took a deep breath, some of the color draining out of his face. "This is kind of awkward. But I have to ask you why you've been getting payments from Mrs. Afton for at least the past few years." He read off the check amounts and dates that we'd seen. "You hadn't worked for them in years, so what are they for?"

Silence rang on the other end of the line. I held my breath, convinced she'd be able to hear the air moving in and out.

Finally, she said, "How do you know about that?"

"It doesn't matter," Gabe said. "What are they?"

"It's none of your business." I'd never heard Andrea sound this way before, all cold and abrupt.

Which made me even more certain that we had to find out what those payments were. I shifted closer to Gabe on the couch, leaning in to the phone. "Hi, Andrea. It's me. Pom."

"Oh, Pom!" There was a slight pause, probably her trying to figure out how long I'd been listening. "How are you?"

I chewed on my lower lip. "Listen, I'm the one who told Gabe about those payments, so blame me," I said. "I saw them in my grandma's records when we were going through her things, and I was curious about them, so I asked him what they were. I didn't know you'd still been doing work for my grandma."

Maybe we should've waited for this conversation until we could have seen her in person, because I was regretting not knowing her expression or her body language right now. Was she picking at herself, eyes wide with panic? Was she irritated to have something pedestrian and boring questioned?

"I haven't been working for your grandmother or your family. Not in many years," Andrea said. "But I'm afraid I can't tell you more than that."

"You can trust me," I said. Maybe I shouldn't have shared that I was here. "I swear."

Andrea sighed. "No. What I mean is that I legally cannot tell you any more than that. I had to sign an airtight NDA in exchange for those monthly payments. They ceased when your grandmother died, by the way."

Did that mean the NDA was no longer valid? Probably not—my grandma had been shrewd. She—or my grandpa, if it had been created when he was still alive—would have made sure of it.

"Wait," Gabe said. His eyebrows had pinched together. "Does this mean you were blackmailing them?"

"I wasn't blackmailing anyone," Andrea said. "It was a mutually agreed-upon decision. I overheard a conversation between your grandparents through which I learned some information during the course of working for the Aftons that they desperately did not want spread outside the family. I wouldn't have spread it anyway, but they wanted to make absolutely sure. And honestly? I worked hard for your family, Pom, and they didn't pay me enough for it. I didn't feel bad about accepting extra money from them."

From the defensive way that torrent of words poured out, I'd be willing to bet that wasn't entirely true. "Did you talk to the police about this?"

"No," Andrea said. "When I say the NDA is airtight, I mean it. I'll take that secret to my grave."

Grave or not, I wasn't ready to give up. "Did it have something to do with my cousins? Farrah and Jordan? Or their parents?" Maybe there was more to do with the story of their estrangement, even if they had alibis the night Grandma died.

"No," Andrea said. "But Pom, I really can't talk more about—"

"How about my friend Opal? Opal Sterling?"

Gabe looked at me questioningly. Right. I still had to share with him what Jessica had told me.

"I can't, Pom," Andrea said. "You have to understand."

"Even if it might mean letting a murderer go free?"

Andrea's silence spoke for itself. "Look," she finally said. "I don't want to get sued. But maybe . . . maybe go talk to your friend Opal."

So Jessica had been on to something after all. But Andrea wouldn't say anything more after that, not even when I begged. "I'm going to go now," she said. "Gabriel, give me a call tomorrow if you want to talk. Take care. I love you."

I chose to believe she was talking to both of us, not just her son.

As soon as we hung up, Gabe turned back to me. "Okay, what's going on with Opal?"

I filled him in, his eyebrows pinching more and more as I went on. I would say that we sat in silence after I got everything out, but that wouldn't be entirely true, because Squeaky had jumped up between the two of us and was purring his whiskers off. Read the room, dude. "So your mom basically confirmed that she got paid off by my grandparents for something to do with Opal, right?" I said.

"That's what I gathered."

That was another finger pointing at my friend. I wanted to close my eyes before any of those fingers could try to poke them. "Tomorrow. We worry about this tomorrow."

"Right." Gabe shifted in his seat, and I suddenly became aware of how close we were sitting. Squeaky had jumped down at some point to go scrape around his food bowl. The hairs on the arm next to him stood up at the proximity. "Then what do we worry about tonight?"

I'd spent my life breathing with no difficulty—in and out, in and out—but just then my lungs seemed to forget what to do. "How about the question your mom asked you? The one you didn't answer?"

"What are you talking about?"

I shifted in my seat too. Closer to him, an inch. We weren't touching, but the heat radiating off his body warmed me. "She asked if you had a crush on me. You didn't answer."

Gabe laughed. His Adam's apple bobbed up and down in his throat. Nervous. But he didn't shift away. "It was an awkward question."

Sometimes awkward things are also true things, was what I wanted to say, all smooth and suave, and then, in this cool scenario in my head, I'd lean in and kiss him.

In real life, all my nerve fled. I folded my hands in my lap and stared at them. "Yeah, I guess. Sorry."

"Don't be sorry." He paused. "You know, I had a crush on you when I was younger."

"Really? But you didn't even know me. And I thought you didn't like me."

"Yeah, but I saw pictures of you everywhere," he said. "And I didn't like you because you were taking my mom away from me, not because of who you were as a person. I maybe didn't tell you that reason behind why I kept looking you up as a kid. But you can't crush on someone based just on looks. I liked you based on the stories my mom would tell me. There was that time you rallied your neighborhood in the Hamptons around protecting these sea turtles out on the beach or something?"

A smile tugged at my lips. "I was nine. I kept the whole neighborhood from holding barbecues and bonfires there until they hatched."

He shifted on the couch again. His knee bumped into mine. I stopped breathing for a moment when he didn't move it away. The spot where they touched sparked, caught fire. "And there was this other time where you went to this fancy party in some penthouse lounge filled with flowers. My mom was telling me all about the decorations and the food, but the part of the story that stuck with me was you pulling the awkward new kid into the group and making sure she felt included."

"I was twelve," I remembered. "And that was Coriander. She became one of my best friends."

He shifted closer again. I could feel the tips of his fingers graze the bare back of my neck. His whole thigh shifted flush against mine, hard and tense. "And there was this other time when, even though you had zero practical life skills, you didn't just rally and make the best of what you had, you decided to solve a murder and do a damn good job of it. You started your own business based on spit and vinegar and a little flour. You showed that you were brave and funny and smart and damn hot even in a T-shirt and old yoga pants."

I couldn't help but look down at myself. "That's me now," I said, surprised, and then Gabe's mouth was on mine.

Our lips fit together like . . . two things made to fit together—I don't know, I was having kind of a hard time focusing. It felt like we were melting together: the way he caught my bottom lip gently between his teeth and tugged; the way my tongue slipped into the heat of his mouth and tangled with his; the way the smallest guttural moan from his throat made want surge through my entire body. I swung myself on top of him, straddling him with my knees and settling flush against his chest. Here I could weave my fingers into his black curls, feel the shifting beneath me as other parts of him awoke.

He pulled back slightly, eyes glazed. "I was saying that I have a crush on you now."

"I have a crush on you now, too," I said. Both of our mouths curled at how juvenile we sounded. "You took me in and helped me out when you didn't have to. I don't think I ever would've shown any of those qualities you talked about if you weren't here to bring them out."

"Nah, I don't believe that," he said, and pulled me in for another kiss, one that left me dizzy and warm and drowning in his coffee and soap smell.

When I pulled back this time, I was panting. If we kissed any longer, and his fingertips kept on tracing that slice of bare skin be-

tween the bottom of my shirt and the top of my pants, I was going to
go feral. "Wait. Should we talk about this? We live together."

"Right." His dark eyes were half-hooded, but he made an effort to
open them all the way up. "We live together."

If we were going to talk about this for real, I had to get off him. I
rolled off and took my spot beside him on the couch, though not
far—I kept my thigh tight against his, my chin propped on his shoulder. I didn't know how I'd survive without touching him again. "I really like you."

"I really like you, too," he said, taking a deep breath and running
his fingers through his hair.

"I think we could be something," I said. "Do you feel that way?"

"Yeah," he said, his voice a rumble against my chin. "I do."

Moving away from him was as difficult as passing up an invite to
the Met Gala, but I forced myself to do it. "Then I think we should
take it slow. Really see how this goes."

He nodded as if his head had suddenly grown very heavy. "Does
that mean I can take you out on a real date?"

I held out my hand as if expecting it to be kissed. He took it and,
sure enough, pressed his lips to its back. "Please. Take me out on a
real date."

He lifted his head, but didn't let go of my hand. "Have you been
to Jackson Heights before?"

I didn't even know where that was. I shook my head.

"It's in Queens. Don't say anything," he said as I opened my
mouth to protest that I never wanted to go to Queens again. "It's got
the best food out of any neighborhood in New York City. We're
going to go there and spend the entire day eating. Thai food so hot
it'll make you cry. Nepalese dumplings. Colombian bakeries and
Mexican juices."

"I could go for that," I mused. "It's just too bad it's out in Queens."
I mean, I should've known Opal would be guilty when I found out she
lived in Queens now. It was obvious. "Once the murder investigation is

over, I'm all in. I don't think I'll be able to relax and enjoy it until then."

"It's a date," he said, and pulled me in for a hug. I closed my eyes, cheek against his chest. I could fall asleep like this, feeling the throb of his heartbeat on my skin and feeling his breath on my forehead.

As a matter of fact, that's exactly what I did.

CHAPTER

Twenty-Four

As it turned out, we couldn't focus on Opal the next day after all, and not due to some glorious excuse I came up with overnight. I'd forgotten that the next day was Saturday, when I'd planned to meet up with Farrah and Jordan before they returned to the swampy hell-hole from whence they'd sprung. "Isn't it more important to catch a murderer than hang out with your cousins?" Gabe asked when we woke up, still tangled together on the couch (my back ached and my neck was stiff, but I'd still slept better than when I'd tried out one of those floating tents on the Aegean Sea that were supposed to be more relaxing than your mother's womb).

I shook my head. Or at least tried to. My neck didn't want to budge. "In general, probably yes. In this specific case, no. My relationship with Farrah and Jordan is tenuous as it is. I can't cancel on them."

"Not even if they knew it was about bringing your shared grandmother's murderer to justice?"

I snorted. "I'm lucky Farrah and Jordan suggested gallery-hopping instead of having a party on Grandma's grave."

Chelsea, the neighborhood where we were going to skip from gallery to gallery, was a short subway ride away. I was almost at the point where taking the subway alone didn't make me nervous, though I made sure to keep my big sunglasses on to hopefully prevent anyone from recognizing me. (No hat, though. I could commit a fashion faux pas like that when I was sneaking into a hotel and not going to see anyone important, but on an occasion like this, looking good was of the utmost importance. Hence my baggy cropped jeans, graphic tee, and metallic blazer. I just told myself that anyone staring was admiring how artsy I looked.)

Farrah and Jordan were waiting for me outside one of the big galleries housed in an old industrial brick building. When I'd graduated from college, I'd made a bunch of hints to my parents that they should buy me an apartment in one of these former warehouses, but the thought of her daughter living somewhere like that had made my mom's lip curl. Jordan greeted me with an enthusiastic hug; Farrah gave me a limp handshake. "Thanks for meeting with me," I said, mostly to Farrah, who rolled her eyes. Jordan actually rolled her eyes too.

"You make it sound like we're having a business meeting or something."

I mean, for them, it *was* kind of a business thing. While they were up here, they'd been tasked with picking out a few pieces of art for their family collection. I'd done the same thing many times and had never thought about the price, but my eyes nearly popped out of my head now as we browsed the sculptures inside (flowers and trees made out of garbage, meaningful but done many times before) and I saw on their listings how many thousands of dollars they cost. I could work for years at the café and not be able to afford one coffee-ground and crumpled-filter rosebush.

That reminded me: I made a mental note to check in with Gabe after the lunch rush to see how my newest offerings were selling. My baked goods took up the whole pastry case by this point, the old wet-paper ones discarded, and so I'd taken to doing experiments to fill it. Today's was a savory puff pastry concoction designed to mimic a samosa. I'd made the potato-and-pea filling myself, basing it on the one I got from my favorite Indian place.

"What are you thinking about, Pom?" Jordan asked, linking her arm through mine. I'd been gratified to find her in metallic sneakers; my instincts clearly hadn't been off about metallics being super in right now. "The artists? Was this one of the galleries you used to patronize?"

I couldn't tell her the truth, I automatically thought. She might think it was stupid, how into my little business I was. It wasn't like she didn't know about it—the drops had been featured all over my socials—but in our community those things tended to be branded, not something we actually cared about.

Although why not? If she was a true friend, wouldn't she be excited to hear something I felt passionate about, even if she thought it was kind of dumb?

Then again, it didn't seem like I knew what true friendship really meant. Not after Vienna.

And Opal. She couldn't be the murderer. She *couldn't*! Not because her behavior wasn't super suspicious—it was.

Because I couldn't handle another betrayal from someone I thought was my best friend.

"Pom?" Jordan prompted.

Well, now I definitely couldn't tell her the truth about what I'd been thinking just now. "Yeah, a little bit about the art. I miss being involved in this world. But mostly I was thinking about how my business is doing today," I said. "You know, I've been baking everything I've featured from scratch. I tried a few new things out today and I'm hoping people like them."

Jordan's eyes lit up. "Pom, that's so cool! I've been meaning to get up there and try some of your pastries. They always make me so hungry when they pop up on my feed."

I leaned in and gave her an impromptu hug. "Thanks."

"For what?" she asked, baffled.

"Ready?" Farrah said in my ear. I jumped. Jordan backed away.

"Did you pick something?"

"Yup," Farrah said with very little enthusiasm. Even less enthusiasm than she'd greeted me with, which was impressive. "I thought the growing-things-out-of-garbage thing was passé five years ago, but Dad insisted we get at least one because he owns other things by this artist. So I picked the soda-can-ring daffodils. Is that okay with you?"

Jordan shrugged. "Honestly, I don't really care."

Farrah took a deep breath and, as if having to force herself to move, turned to me. "Pom, what do you think?"

I literally touched a hand to my chest, figuratively touched that she'd asked for my opinion. I hadn't even seen the soda-can-ring daffodils, but I said, "I agree that a lot of this collection felt passé, but in my opinion the daffodil was the most interesting one in the lot."

For a brief moment, I thought a smile flitted over her lips. "Okay. Thanks."

We moved on to the next gallery, and the next, and the next. Sculptures of insect-people blended together with abstract paintings that all looked like vaginas. We moved from the biggest, most prestigious galleries to some of the smaller, scrawnier ones (though they couldn't be *that* small or scrawny to afford rent in Chelsea), where you might find a hidden gem who'd blow up in the next few years.

At one of the latter, the three of us browsed through a group show featuring depictions of confinement from recently released prisoners. I'd known a few people who had gone to prison—who *didn't* know somebody guilty of embezzlement or bank fraud? The few who'd gone to prison were only the few unlucky enough to get caught—and the depictions of prison here looked way different than what I'd heard from them, which had put me in the mind of a budget hotel. "You guys," I said, thinking of the way the world was different for the people who'd made this art versus the people we knew. "How do you think we'd be different if we hadn't been born into this world?"

Farrah said, in a tone that suggested I'd asked her how she thought we'd be different in the event we breathed water instead of air, "I don't think things would be that different. I feel like we'd probably be doing the same things. Appreciating art. Fashion."

"Yeah," Jordan said.

I wasn't sure why I was determined to press, but I was. "You literally couldn't be living a life like this if you were born into a regular family, though. You'd have to have a job. You couldn't just fly around and hang out wherever and whenever you felt like it. Even these galleries. You wouldn't be able to afford any of this."

Both their faces creased uncomfortably, shirts folded in the wrong place. "I don't know. Maybe we'd work in galleries," Jordan said. "I always thought it might be fun."

"I don't really want to think about it, anyway," Farrah said. "Come on, let's check out the next place. It's another group show of young and emerging artists of color. Exactly the kind of art I want to support."

I trailed after them on the sidewalk, nose twitching at the salty air blowing off the Hudson River. They didn't want to think about it because it was too close to home—it had happened to me. If they'd asked me the same thing a few months ago, I probably would've echoed what they said for a simple reason: I'd literally never thought about it. I'd taken everything I had, my entire life, for granted, and I didn't think about what things might be like otherwise.

Now I wondered. Maybe I would've discovered how much I love baking earlier. Maybe I would've gone to culinary school or worked in a bakery. Or maybe I would've been forced into trying something else I didn't know I liked until I tried it. I mean, I hadn't thought I'd like baking until I'd decided spur-of-the-moment to make something for Gabe. What if it turned out I was also really good at, I don't know, archery or writing or architecture? Maybe I was a secret architecture prodigy and I'd never know, just because I spent most of my life being complacent with what had been handed to me.

I was so deeply immersed in those thoughts that I bumped into someone at the entrance of the gallery. "Oh my God, I'm so sorry," I said, pulling back, and it was only then I realized I'd bumped into Vienna.

"It's okay," she said automatically, but then she jumped, her eyes sharpening, as if she'd only then realized who she'd bumped into too. "Oh. It's you."

All the words I wanted to say stuck in my throat. The only thing I could force out was "It's me."

We stared at each other for a moment. She'd cut her hair, I realized with a twist in my chest. It was no longer long enough for her to twist in her usual elegant French bun; it was now a choppy bob angled toward her chin. The only makeup she wore was a bright red lipstick that cut like a slash across her face.

I wondered if she was thinking the same thing about me. I'd changed too.

"Excuse me," someone piped up from behind me, because, duh, we were blocking the door. I couldn't step back into the people waiting to come in, so Vienna was the one to do so, moving back into the gallery. I followed her, letting the people behind me stream past.

She couldn't leave until they'd finished, which meant we were stuck there in the corner, staring at each other in front of a painting of a woman relaxing in a hot tub encrusted with plastic jewels. "So, how've you been?" I asked, then immediately cringed at myself. I'd thought that continuing to stare at each other in silence would be more awkward than anything, but, well . . . not more awkward than that.

Sure enough, she gaped at me for a moment. But she recovered quickly, her mouth snapping shut. "Good. My foundation's been working with some of the artists in the show, so I wanted to come by and show my support."

"That's so great," I said. She hadn't asked, but I chimed in anyway. "I've been good too. I'm here today with Farrah and Jordan. They're thinking about buying some of the artists' work."

Vienna's eyebrows popped up, and interest flared in her dark eyes. "Farrah and Jordan? You're talking again?"

"Yeah!" For a moment I almost forgot that Vienna and I were enemies now. "I reached out after my grandma's death and apologized. We're not quite where we were, but we're working on it."

"That's great." Vienna's lips curled up in a smile, and it was almost like we were friends again, like she might reach out and companionably lean her head against my shoulder the way she used to, her hair smelling of roses.

But then the smile flickered out. "I was sorry to hear about your grandma, by the way. I know she was never the . . . nicest person, but no one deserves to go like that."

"Thanks." Jordan's laugh floated over from somewhere behind me. It was so nice to hear her laughing again, to be in a place where I was allowed to hear her laugh, even make her laugh. I'd really missed her.

Like I really missed Vienna.

Impulsively, I leaned in. "Look. Can we talk? Maybe in private?"

She cast me a cautious look. If she said no, or made up some excuse and left, it might actually crush me.

But she didn't. "Okay. We can use the back room."

I tapped Jordan on the shoulder to let her know where I was going, then followed Vienna past a giant painting of a coyote eating a roadrunner and a hanging rainbow weaving that, upon closer inspection, turned out to be made out of rubber bands. She murmured something quietly to the chic woman at the desk, then beckoned me into a small office and closed the door behind me.

The office only had one chair before a desk, so Vienna and I played chicken and both stood. I took a deep breath, a little amused by the bare gray walls in here. Not very artsy. She faced me and crossed her arms. "What did you want to talk about?"

"Us," I said.

Her face didn't crack at all. "You make it sound like we had a breakup."

"We did," I said. "Like, a friend breakup. Honestly, I feel like friend breakups are worse than romantic breakups. And way less people are out there writing songs about them."

That did make her crack a smile. "Maybe they should."

"Maybe they should," I agreed. Then took another deep breath. "Anyway."

My and Vienna's relationship-ending fight was etched in my head more finely than any of the romantic breakups I'd gone through. To be fair, she'd been in my life way longer than any of the guys I'd dated, and had probably seen me naked more often too (the effects of being on the field hockey team together).

It had been nearly eight months ago. Less time than it takes to gestate a baby. Crazy how that short amount of time could take down a teenager-size friendship.

Vienna had been over at my place. Both of us sat on the couch while Lori made us summery mocktails: me lounging over one arm, a leg dangling over the side so that my polished green toenails brushed the rug (I still remembered those green toenails and how they looked as I stared down at them that day); Vienna sitting up straight at the other end on her phone. Out the window shone a stunning summer day over Central Park, though of course the hotel's vigorous air-conditioning kept us from sweating in it.

"So we've got lots of options for tonight," I'd told her as I scrolled through my phone. The crackle of smashing ice sounded in the kitchen. I hoped Lori was making something with lots of lemon. Maybe some cucumber. "I RSVPed yes to that music charity gala, but we could always no-show. They're small enough where they can't afford to take me off the guest list for the future. Millicent is DJing that loft party in Bushwick—it's kind of far out, but I can have the car wait for us so we don't have to walk anywhere—and it would probably be good for our image to be photographed at the library thing, though we don't have to stay very long for—"

"Do you ever get bored of all this?" Vienna burst out, as if the words had been bubbling up inside her a long time.

I wrinkled my brow, not even glancing up at her from my phone. I hadn't even gotten to finish telling her our options, and I'd saved the best one for last: Coriander's terrible boyfriend was debuting his new fashion line down in SoHo, and I couldn't wait to go make fun of it (low-key, of course, so that Coriander couldn't call me out for it). "Um, what are you talking about?"

"All this."

I looked up this time in case she was pointing at the view or something, having become suddenly sick of our favorite park, but she was waving her hand aimlessly in the air. "That didn't help."

"This life," she said. Still didn't help. I hoped she wasn't going to start talking about becoming a monk or something. Or, wait, monks were men, right? "I finished my master's degree almost two years ago, and I haven't done anything since then but go to parties and pose at galas. You didn't get a master's, so you've been doing this for four years. Aren't you tired of it?"

I blinked. I had no idea what she was talking about. My life was great. I could never get tired of it. Literally, considering I got to sleep as late as I wanted every morning. "No. What do you mean?"

"Shouldn't there be more?" She gestured emphatically at me, eyes wide. "We have pretty much every privilege afforded to man. And what are we doing with it? Partying? Shouldn't we be doing more?"

I goggled at her too. At this point it was a contest of whose eyes would pop out of her head first. "Are you still high from last night?"

"No, I'm not high!" She hit the arm of my couch with her fist, which, uncool. "I'm just frustrated and bored and feeling kind of shitty. I went into my tags last night—"

"Oh, there's your mistake," I said. "You should never go into the tags. Or read the comments."

"They just vocalized what I've been thinking a long time."

"Vocalized what?" Something was simmering inside me. It wasn't that I was mad, not yet. "That I'm what, some useless, vapid bimbo?" (Because even though I always said I never read the comments, I always did.) "That you're too good for me?"

A storm cloud passed over her face. "That's not fair, Pom. That's not what I was saying."

But it *was* what she was saying, wasn't it? I'd seen the same lines of inquiry in those nasty comments and hashtags. I'd gotten the same condescending questions from Nicholas, and he'd all but looked down his nose at me. "What *were* you saying then?"

Her mouth opened, then closed. Her lips were chapped, the corners especially so. I could suggest a spa day with a lip mask, I thought, then remembered we were fighting.

She said, eventually, "I was saying that I want to do something more with my life. I want to take my trust fund and my reputation and try to do some good. I don't want to spend my whole life partying and being called a spoiled brat."

So now she was calling me a spoiled brat. I didn't need this from anyone, much less my best friend. My temper flared. "So go do it, then. You don't need me for that. Go be a goody-goody do-gooder on your own. Look down your nose on the rest of us from your high horse."

Her nostrils flared back at me. "You don't have to be an asshole about this, Pom. You could say it's not your thing and you want to keep doing nothing with your life. That you just want to keep squandering everything you've been given."

Seriously, what was her *problem*? We'd been having a really nice day up until now, when she'd decided to *ruin* it. "Maybe you should go. You probably don't want to waste a single moment with your loser best friend."

She shot to her feet. "Fine. I will. Give me a call when you're ready to grow up." She swiped her bag off the table and sailed out the door, slamming it behind her. Paintings shuddered on the wall, then rocked themselves into silence.

I sat there in that silence, which somehow seemed louder than any silence I'd sat in before. This would be a quick fight, I told myself. Soon enough Vienna would come to her senses. She'd come back to me and tell me how much she missed me.

Lori poked her head out of the kitchen. "Uh, do you still want a drink?"

Vienna wouldn't come back, of course. I went to her town house and she slammed the door in my face, which, thank God, nobody caught on video. The schism between us would continue to grow, becoming wider and more jagged with each month that passed. And once the media figured out that we were no longer being seen out in public together, forget it. The fangs came out.

There were no fangs out right now, though. Just me and my ex-best friend standing across from each other in a muggy little room, with me ready to throw the rope. I could only hope that she was ready to catch it so that we could start building that bridge.

"Anyway," I said again. Vienna's black eyes were opaque. "Congratulations. You've really done what you wanted to do." She'd started up her foundation soon after that fateful fight. "It's amazing."

"Are you being sarcastic?"

"No!" I said hastily. "No, I was being serious." We just stared at each other. Panic fluttered in my chest. This was already going wrong. "You're doing really good things. I'm so proud of you." The panic flared—had I come off as condescending?—but her face softened. Not quite into a smile, but something leaning that way.

"Thanks, Pom," she said. "I'm proud too. I'm excited to work with these artists doing such cool things every day. And you know . . ." Now her smile looked a little more like a smirk. "I still get to go to parties and galas and all that too."

"I know. I see the pictures. You always look stunning," I said sincerely. I took a deep breath. Now for the hard part. Well, lots of this was hard. The *hardest* part. "Look. I'm sorry for what happened between us. I took the things you said to me that day as a personal attack, and I shouldn't have. I think I was already really sensitive to that kind of thing because of what people were saying about me. I should've known you didn't mean it the way they did."

"Of course I didn't mean it the way they did," Vienna said, letting out a frustrated puff of air that fluffed up her jagged bangs. "You were my best friend, Pom. I care about—I cared about you." I chose to believe that slip of the tongue was a slip of what was truly in her heart. My own heart hovered a little higher with hope. "But you're allowed to do what you want with your life. If you're happy, you're happy. And it wasn't fair of me to be all judgy. Especially considering I'd done basically all the same things as you. It wasn't fair of me to act like I was better than you because I had a thought I might want to do things differently."

"I've had that thought recently, too," I told her, then went on to share about my baking, and also the feeling that it wasn't fair people like Gabe and my coworkers at the coffee shop were working so hard for so little. "I mean, I don't know how much it means, considering I don't have what I used to have anymore." I blinked, thinking back. "You know, I haven't been clubbing since . . . the night everything happened. I haven't drunk anything since then either."

"I imagine clubbing is a lot less fun when you have to wait in line outside and dance in the sweaty pit with the general population."

"No, it's not that." It wasn't that I didn't still like partying. I loved to dance, and there was nothing wrong with a drink every so often to make me feel a little less self-conscious about how I looked doing it. But maybe I'd been right that I'd been going out so much and drinking so much to cover up the feeling that I didn't have anything else going on. Now I did. "It feels a little bit like I've . . . grown up?"

Vienna's arms were around me before I could blink. The familiar smell of her perfume made tears prick in my eyes. "You're going to do good, I know it. You're going to lead a fulfilling and interesting and good life." She backed away, blinking very fast, as if she was warding away tears too. "You can ask me questions about what I do, if that would help. If you want."

"Thank you," I said. When we both smiled at each other, it felt a little bit like we'd rewound time. No, it felt better than that. Like we'd taken our first steps onto that bridge and nobody had fallen into an abyss. "I'd really like that."

"Of course. And you know, it's not like you don't have anything anymore. You still have a huge platform. And I'm sure you won't be down-and-out for long, even if you don't get everything back that you used to have."

If I was correct about Opal and was able to prove it, I *would* get everything back. But the thought of losing another best friend made the warm, fuzzy feelings fizz into the air and vanish. "Vienna, do you think I'm cursed when it comes to friendship?"

She gave me a baffled look. Right. She wasn't privy to my internal monologue or to any of the facts about the case. "No? But also I don't totally understand the question?"

I changed tack. "What do you think friendship is? Were we friends? Was I a good friend?"

Her laugh came out just as baffled as her first look. "Of course we were friends. And we can be friends again, maybe, if you're up for it." I met her soft face with a vigorous nod, to make sure she didn't miss any of my meaning. "And yes, you were a good friend. You always had my back when I needed you. I like to think I did the same.

"I don't know, I think friendship can mean a bunch of different things," she went on. "Sometimes it's about having fun with each other, but they're not necessarily someone you can depend on. Sometimes it's someone you don't talk to often, but when you do talk to them, it's like all the years fall away and you can count on them for anything. You know? I don't think there's one single definition."

Except probably not murdering each other's relatives. But that might be too oddly specific to bring up right now. "Hey," I said. "Remember Opal?"

"Of course I remember Opal," Vienna said. "She was my friend too."

Guilt struck me again at the past tense. Maybe if I hadn't been so quick to believe the worst, been so quick to tell our whole social circle that Vienna thought they were silly and shallow and stupid, Vienna and I would be confronting Opal together.

Except then I wouldn't be confronting Opal with Gabe. I might not even have met Gabe, because I probably would've been staying with Vienna. I wasn't sure how to feel about that.

I pushed the uncertainty aside for now. "Do you think she's capable of terrible things?"

"I think everybody is capable of terrible things," Vienna said. "That's what makes us human beings."

I filed that remark mentally for the next time I was asked for my feelings on a piece of art I didn't understand. It sounded super smart and also appropriately cynical. "But I mean, Opal specifically." I swallowed hard. "Do you think she could be capable of murder? And not, like, maybe slipping some poison into a drink, I mean, like, a bloody, brutal murder."

"Opal?" Vienna raised one bladed black eyebrow. "Personally I can't imagine it, but I always thought she had a savage side. Did you know that she'd tag me in photos of the two of you out together after our fight? Like she wanted to make extra sure I saw that she was your new number one."

"I didn't know that." That was both petty and mean . . . but not murderous.

"Yeah," Vienna said. "Why are you asking?" A pause while I could see the gears turning in her head. "Wait, does this have to do with your grandma? They still haven't caught the murderer, have they?"

I shook my head. "They haven't. And I don't know. I'm just wondering if there's something I missed the whole time."

"Some people do a really good job at hiding who they really are," Vienna said. "But don't forget that you didn't do something wrong if you didn't see it. Even if they try to make you feel that way." She cocked her head. "Opal, specifically? She hated people thinking she was dumb. It was like she always had to do things to remind people of what she was capable of. Like she always had to remind herself of that too."

A knock came at the door. Before either of us could answer it, a devastatingly stylish brunette poked her head in. "Vienna? There's a buyer here who wants some face time with you."

Vienna gave an exaggerated eye roll. "Anything for the buyers." But there was affection in her voice. She clearly loved what she did.

I hoped I'd get to feel that joy someday too.

Gabe was waiting for me at home. Well, that makes it sound like he was sitting on the couch, ears perking up every time he heard something in the hallway. Actually he was hard at work on some grad school project, but as soon as I walked in, he closed his laptop and stood up to come greet me. "Pom," he said, stopping a few feet away.

I got it. What was this new thing we had? Did we kiss when we walked through the door like a real couple, even though we hadn't even been on a date yet? Were we supposed to hug? Or just say hey, like we were regular roommates?

Gabe probably regretted getting up.

I solved the conundrum by stepping forward and kissing him gently on the lips, then pulling back. No getting lost in a kiss again. Not just because we had a murderer-confronting strategy to figure out, but because Squeaky was winding his way around my feet, either trying super hard to trip me or desperately wanting my attention. I leaned down to scoop him up. "Hey there, handsome."

"He's more handsome than me?" Gabe joked.

I shrugged. "Hey, I wasn't the one to say it." I nuzzled my face in Squeaky's soft head. He purred, nuzzling me back. I'd read once that rubbing their heads on each other was how cats showed love. I hoped it was true. This thing with Gabe had to work out, not just because he was great and everything—which he was—but because there was no way I was losing my cat again. "So on the way back, I listened to the finale of *Here to Slay*."

"Don't tell me," Gabe said immediately. He'd started listening to it during his workouts. "No, wait, tell me. It's about the journey, not the destination."

"Do you read the endings of your books first?" I asked. But I was happy to oblige. "You'll probably see it somewhere online anyway before you make it to the end. So it turns out that Doe? She's actually Danica."

Honestly, it was a move I was surprised someone hadn't made earlier: faking your own disappearance or death, then using the format of a true-crime podcast to interrogate all the people around you who hated you to see what they really thought of you, whether they were seething with secret glee that you were gone or genuinely sad.

More importantly, Danica/Doe had immediately become the subject of a thousand viral posts and think pieces. Her face—both the perfectly made-up, slightly bored model version and the version she'd used as Doe, glasses and no makeup and sharp eyes, or so she said—was everywhere. People were dying to hear her words, her thoughts, her reasonings.

I got it.

Gabe did not. "That's insane," he said. "You have to be a totally insane person to do that."

"I'm not so sure," I said. "I don't think it's so rare for somebody to hide who they are, especially when they're used to everybody's eyes on them." We were both quiet for a second. "Anyway, speaking of Opal."

"Right. Opal," Gabe said. "So we think it was her, but we also thought we had it right two times before. How do we go about this? We don't have any proof except for what Jessica said, and that won't mean anything without more concrete evidence."

"I think I know what we have to do," I said. "But it's going to mean first doing something I really, really hate."

"Dredging up the murder of a family member?" Gabe asked. "Accusing someone else you love of murder? What?"

I shook my head and said, grimly, "Going to Queens."

CHAPTER

Twenty-Five

It took everything I had, but I did it: endured that long, interminable subway ride to the least cool outer borough (only because I didn't count Staten Island as a borough; New Jersey could have it). I inhaled deeply as we trooped down the subway stairs onto the sidewalk. It still smelled better than I would've expected. "Okay, so let's question our suspected murderer," I said. "Third time's the charm and all that. You ready?" I'd checked Opal's location before leaving, then a few times on the subway, to make sure she was still at home and also that her home hadn't magically transplanted itself somewhere more fashionable.

Gabe nodded. "Ready."

We set off down those side streets, my jaw clenched with determination and my phone ready to record. It wouldn't be recording anything now except street noise and the rattling of the elevated subway tracks, but I didn't want to take the chance of making Opal suspicious by fiddling around with it once I was there with her.

Outside Opal's house, I paused for a moment and took a deep breath. While of course I wanted to be right, because who didn't love being right, I also kind of wanted to be wrong. A sick feeling flopped around in my stomach like a dead fish.

As if he could read my mind or see through my skin, Gabe reached out for my hand. Gave it a squeeze. Communicated that he knew I was strong, but that he was right here beside me to hold me up if I felt like I was going to fall over.

Truly amazing how all of that could be said through a hand

squeeze. My ex-boyfriends had never been fluent in hand (neither hand-in-hand nor hand-in-elsewhere).

Well. *Here goes.* Another deep breath of surprisingly floral Queens air, and I was marching up those steps, rapping hard on the screen door. The one variable here—well, the main variable of many—was whether her parents were living here too. Opal had one older sister who lived in LA with her husband and kids, so I was fairly certain I didn't have to worry about her, but her mom and dad might be—

Opal opened the door, her thin, overly plucked brows (she must not have been able to get them done professionally since moving out here) arching even more in surprise. "Pom?" Her eyes found Gabe over my shoulder. "And him?"

"Okay, you've met him twice; I know you remember his name," I said, then shouldered my way in. She shied away against my aggressive movement, wrapped up in that same large sweatshirt and yoga pants combo she'd worn the first time we came out here. Maybe that was fashionable in Queens. "It's Gabe. And hey! Surprise! We're here!"

"This *is* a surprise," she said. "What are you doing here?"

Gabe entered, too, allowing the door to swing shut behind him. The hallway we found ourselves in was narrow and shadowy, the ceiling low, the walls bare, as if Opal—or her parents—hadn't bothered taking the time to decorate. "We wanted to thank you for . . ." I trailed off, then leaned in to whisper. "Not sure how loud I should be. Do your parents live here too?"

Opal gave me a look like I'd asked if her new bag was a fake. "Of course not! They're also in Queens, but I had to have *some* independence." I mean, as much independence as you could have when they were paying for everything, but okay. "I live on my own."

Good. That was one potential issue taken care of. "Okay, cool. Anyway, we wanted to thank you for all your help with sneaking into the hotel!"

I had a pretty good idea as to why she'd helped—she must have known that she wasn't going to feature prominently in the footage in a suspicious way, but that Jessica would, and that anything that deflected attention away from herself was good. Also, by helping, she'd know what we knew, and it probably made her feel better to know we suspected somebody else.

"I didn't end up helping very much," she said. "I mean, you guys didn't even get into the security room, right?"

Time to lull her into complacency. I fixed my face into a somber frown. "Unfortunately not. We had to book it out of there before I got caught. But we'll find another way in. I still think Jessica is the one to watch."

Did her shoulders relax the tiniest bit? It was hard to tell with all that material cloaking them. "I'm really sorry. I wish I could've done better."

"Don't worry about it," I said, smiling toothily. "Anyway, we brought you your favorite: tiramisu." Gabe held up the plastic bag he carried as if to testify. "I actually made it. I've never made tiramisu before, so I hope it's good."

"Oh, wow, thanks," Opal said. She didn't smile back. "Why don't we take it out to the park and eat it there?"

"Oh, I'm worried it might rain," I said. "Besides, I'm dying to see your new place. How about a tour?"

Opal wrinkled her nose. "A tour would take, like, two minutes. There's that park around the corner that's pretty—"

"Two minutes, great!" I said, laughing as if she'd been making a joke. Usually I'd feel bad about railroading someone like this, but we had a greater purpose here. "Maybe we can set Gabe up in the kitchen to plate the tiramisu, and you can show me around."

I knew Opal well enough to know that she might push back at first, but she wouldn't give me a firm no if I kept pushing. "Okay, sure, fine," she finally said, words dragging with reluctance. "The kitchen's over here."

By "over here" she meant literally three steps away. It was a separate room, lit by harsh fluorescent lighting and floored in sickly yellow linoleum. One of the cabinets was missing its door, and the counter had a brown tinge to it I didn't think was natural. "Plates are in there, utensils are in there," Opal said, pointing. Gabe set the bag on the counter with a crinkle. "Okay, we'll be back really soon."

Really soon both because the house was tiny and because Opal was giving me this tour on fast-forward. "This is the living room"— she barely paused in the doorway of a room with dusty green couches and a fireplace topped by an empty mantel—"and down here is the basement"—a door that opened into a dark hole—"and now upstairs . . ."

The upstairs was equally small and cramped. Opal showed me a tiny bathroom with grime everywhere the walls met the floor, then an empty bedroom, then her bedroom. The latter was the only room with any bit of Opal's personality in this house: I recognized her bed and its silky coverlet, the full-length mirror covered with her collection of scarves, the mod wooden bureau surely stuffed with whatever clothes she'd managed to bring with her. Before I could register much else, she closed the door. "And that's it," she said in a rush. "Tiramisu time?"

I didn't move. "There's no rooftop or anything?"

"This is it." Her face had been stone, but now it softened a bit, her lower lip giving the slightest quiver. She was clearly expecting me to judge her for her reduced circumstances.

Despite myself and the situation we were in, I found myself actually feeling sorry for her. "It's not as bad as I was thinking," I lied. Her lip stopped quivering. "It's kind of nice, actually. Lots of room, especially for one person."

Not sorry enough to change my plans, though. "Let's head down and try that tiramisu. You'll have to give me all your thoughts. If it's good enough, I can add it to one of my drops."

In the kitchen, Gabe had set the tiramisu on a chipped porcelain plate. I took a moment to admire it. It had slumped a little on the journey to Queens (or maybe it had just slumped at the thought of ending its life in Queens), and the espresso powder that made the top such a pretty even brown had shed a bit down the sides, but the various layers of cakes and creams were still intact. "Pretty, isn't it?"

"Beautiful," Opal said absently. She didn't have a table or chairs. I guess we were supposed to eat standing up at the counter? Hopefully she at least had utensils.

"I'm just going to pee," I said. "Be right back."

I did indeed have to pee, but I didn't have the time to waste on such a basic bodily function right now. While Gabe was downstairs making awkward conversation with Opal and making sure she stayed there and ate her tiramisu, I pushed open her bedroom door and slipped inside.

The upside to her new home being so tiny was that there weren't many places to search. If I were Opal and I was going to hide a murder shoe, where would I put it?

It wasn't under the bed, where the dust made me barely stifle a sneeze. There didn't seem to be any hidey-holes cut in the mattress, and it wasn't under her pillow or stuffed in the crack between the mattress and the wall. Into the drawers—I grimaced as I rifled through underwear and bras, sorted through T-shirts and pajama pants, grimaced even harder as I handled creased silk blouses that should really be hung up but probably couldn't fit in the tiny closet.

The tiny closet was the only place left to search. A seed of doubt wriggled through me. Maybe I was wrong. Maybe Gabe was right, and anyone would have disposed of the murder weapon. Despite what Vienna had said about Opal needing to prove things to herself.

I opened the closet and stuck my head in. It smelled musty, and something small and creepily cockroach-size darted out of sight as I let the light in. Clothes hung packed from the railing, bowing it toward the center, and her shoes were indecorously piled beneath, so high they almost reached my knees.

I jumped at the sound of the bedroom door opening behind me. "Pom?" Opal said, sounding confused. I swallowed hard, my heart beginning to hammer. "What are you doing? You only pee in closets when you're wasted."

I took a deep breath, then immediately sneezed on the dust. So much for having a moment to prepare myself. "Sorry, I wanted to see if you had a sweatshirt I could borrow. I was kind of chilly," I said, backing out to face her.

Only to find that she was staring at me flatly. As we locked eyes, she kicked the bedroom door shut behind her. "You're a terrible liar."

I girded myself, squaring my shoulders as if putting on armor. "I guess you would know, considering you're an excellent liar yourself."

Cheesy line or not, it hit its mark. Her eyes narrowed. "What are you talking about." Her statement didn't end in a question mark. She knew I knew.

My heart thumped so hard I thought it might burst out through my chest. The jig was up. Vienna's words floated through my mind: *Opal hated people thinking she was dumb. It was like she always had to do things to remind people of what she was capable of.*

If I played this right . . . "I want the shoe."

Her face scrunched together so dramatically I almost applauded. "Shoe? What shoe?"

"Maybe you aren't as excellent a liar as I thought."

Opal shrugged. "Whatever you say. Why don't you come downstairs and have some tiramisu? It's not bad."

"Not bad?" If I snorted, I'd probably puff steam right now. "Not *bad*? My tiramisu is *delicious*." And with that, I dove into the shoe pile.

Expectedly, it hurt. Shoes were sharp and spiky and hard and painful. But I persisted, my fingers scrabbling among the heels and flats and puffy sneakers, searching by feel for that familiar stiletto.

I knew I was on to something when Opal shrieked. "Get out of there!"

OOF. She landed on my back, and she might have been a tiny person, but even a tiny person jumping on you can really knock the wind right out your throat. Her fingers found their way into my hair and yanked hard. I screeched.

As I'd hoped, Gabe didn't come running. He had something else to do. I just had to hope I could hold Opal off long enough for—

DOUBLE OOF. My arms were occupied with the shoes, which meant they were not occupied with protecting my vulnerable front from Opal's assault. And she made good use of that, pushing me over so that my backside hit the pile. A heel—not *the* heel—came very close to going somewhere no shoe heel should ever go (unless you were into that kind of thing, which, no judgment). She straddled my chest, holding me down. "Stop it," she puffed. "You don't know what you're doing."

"I do know what I'm doing," I wheezed back. We sounded like a pair of eighty-year-old chain-smokers. I bucked my legs, but I wasn't flexible enough to kick her in the back of the head. I really should have stuck out those gymnastics lessons. "Where. Is. The. Shoe?"

Opal's arm moved in a flash, whacking me in the head. Thank goodness my skull had been resting atop one of those big puffy sneakers that had been popular a few years ago or else she might have knocked me out. "Shut up!"

"No! I want the shoe!"

Opal's eyes gleamed. "You want the shoe?" Her arm flashed to the side again.

As she turned to me, the only way I could describe the look on her face is that it went dead. Her eyes flattened out, sharpened like they might stab me. The planes of her cheeks lengthened. Her lips parted slightly, as if she were a snake preparing to bite.

I wondered, with a sudden chill, if this was what my grandma had seen right before she died.

"I'll give you the shoe." Something sharp—very sharp—pressed against the throbbing pulse in my throat. My eyes widened in panic. I wanted to turn my head away, but couldn't risk a cut. "Isn't it beautiful?"

I couldn't see it without crossing my eyes and blurring my vision, but it wasn't like she was asking me an actual question. What I said in response wasn't an actual question either. "It was you, wasn't it?" And for the benefit of the recording: "You killed my grandma."

Her eyes gleamed again. That was the only answer I needed.

Twenty-Six

The confirmation in Opal's eyes might be all that *I* needed, but it wouldn't be enough for the authorities. I needed to get her talking. Ideally without doing too much of it myself, considering the lack of air I was managing to suck in and the fact that a deadly sharp stiletto heel was balanced precariously against one of my major arteries. Or veins. I hadn't gone to medical school; all I knew was that stabbing it would drain way too much of my blood. "You killed her," I wheezed. Little black spots were starting to dance in my vision, but I pushed through. "Why? You barely even knew each other."

Opal sneered down at me. Her face was half in shadow from the lack of light here in the closet. "Maybe that was the problem."

"What are you talking about?" I could barely get the words out; I could tell my face was turning purple. "Opal, you're going to kill me."

"I'm not going to kill you. Just as long as you behave."

"No, I mean, you're literally going to kill me. Do you want me to bleed all over the only shoes you can afford?"

Maybe not the best tactic to antagonize the person holding a deadly shoe to your throat, but threatening the remnants of her old life did work. She backed off a tiny bit down my chest so that she wasn't crushing my diaphragm, and she moved the point of the shoe the tiniest bit away so that I could no longer feel it every time my throat pulsed. Feeling started flooding in pins and needles back into my shoulders and arms. "Thank you."

"You're welcome," Opal said, sounding almost like her old self before reverting to Sneering Killer Opal. "Where's your friend? Why isn't he running to your rescue?"

"I told you my tiramisu was really good," I said.

"Is he going to come storming in here to save you?"

I shook my head. "He doesn't know there's anything to save me from. He thinks we cleared you back at the beginning." I gave her pleading doe eyes, which always worked on men, but they didn't seem to move her one bit. "He's probably just happy to give us some time to hang out together. Like the old days."

That made her hand with the shoe tremble, but otherwise she didn't move. "We could've always been that way. Always. Maybe we could've become something even better." She shook her head, banishing the possibility. "If only your grandparents had told the truth."

"What are you talking about? Is this why you killed her?"

Opal's eyes narrowed again. "You seem pretty adamant on getting me to say those words. Why? What's your plan?" She raised her hips from me for a moment and patted my own down. "Aha. I knew there had to be a reason you'd worn pants with pockets. You always used to say they made your ass look big."

"Maybe I want my ass to look big," I said weakly, but it was too late. She'd already pulled my phone out of my pocket and, before I could turn my head away, used my face to unlock it.

"Ah. You've been recording me. Smart." She had my phone facing away from her, so I couldn't see exactly the buttons she was pressing, but I imagined she was stopping the recording and deleting everything. With that done, she tossed it over her shoulder into the room, where it landed somewhere I couldn't see with a thump. "Anyway. Now we can talk."

I shut my eyes for a moment, the wince of defeat written clearly all over my face. When I opened them again, they found her staring down at me, her face almost soft. "Did you ever think we looked alike?"

"What?"

She repeated her words as if the problem was that I hadn't heard them, not that I didn't understand them. Then said, "I'd never thought about it before. But after I found out, I could see it. We both have those big wide eyes. That heart-shaped face. The big natural boobs, unless you've been lying to me about those."

I guess if I really thought about it, I could see it. "What are you getting at?"

"And to think people always said I was the thick one," Opal said with a scornful laugh. "We're related, Pom. I found out a few months ago. The guy I was dating did one of those ancestry DNA tests—you know, the one where you send in a swab of your cheek and they tell you what areas of the world you're from and match you with other relatives who have taken the same test."

Farrah and Jordan had taken a DNA test like that before Grandma summoned them up here, I realized with an electric jolt. That couldn't be a coincidence.

"I figured I'd do one too. I thought it would be fun. That maybe I'd get matched with some third cousins in the city I could hang out with or that I'd find out I was two percent Japanese or Lebanese or something else unexpected way back in the family line." She let out a bitter laugh. "I never expected to find out that my father wasn't my biological father."

I tried to hold my surprise in check, but Opal could probably feel my heart thumping through her powerful thighs (that we'd honed together through so many Pilates classes). I'd met Opal's parents many times at galas and other events that hosted our usual crowd and never thought anything seemed amiss. Had they seemed super in love? No. But whose parents did?

"To my even bigger surprise, the test connected me with your cousins. Farrah and Jordan." They must not have been notified of this, or they definitely would have told me. This had to be why Grandma summoned them here, though: to keep them from finding out, or to threaten them into silence if they did. "The test said that my DNA results were consistent with me being their half aunt. Their half aunt! I was going to message them, but I went to my mom first, hoping she would tell me that the test had made a mistake. I mean, it's happened before.

"But my mom just started crying and begging me not to tell my dad. Apparently she'd had an affair with your grandfather. And what came out of that affair?" Opal pointed to herself. "Me. Blood-wise I'm not a Sterling at all, I'm an Afton."

I opened my mouth, ready for an *oh my God* or *holy shit* or something along those lines to emerge, but nothing came out but a puff of air.

"I didn't let it affect things at first," Opal continued. "I didn't need to blow up our families. I was happy. My dad had no idea, and honestly, I don't think it would've changed much if he had. I'm sure he would've been upset and horrified with my mom, but he wouldn't abandon me. He loves me and I love him. Biology doesn't make a parent and all that. Everything was fine, for a bit."

Her eyes turned hard again. "And then I found out the truth: we were losing all our money. It happened so fast. And, Pom, you had no idea. Do you know how long I've been living out here?"

I tried to calculate the last time I'd been to Opal's apartment, but couldn't. "I would shake my head, but you'd probably stab me."

"A long time," she replied, not moving the stiletto at all. "Too long. So I went to your grandma. At first I was nice about it. Why shouldn't I be? I didn't know if she knew about me, and I figured that she'd welcome a new family member. Even if not publicly, surely she'd want to provide for her own flesh and blood. Well, her husband's flesh and blood."

I could guess how that turned out, and not even because Grandma had ended up dead. She would've laughed in Opal's face, told her to get out of her office because she had no time for some illegitimate bastard.

Opal basically confirmed as much, then went on. "So then I had to get mean. I had to tell her I'd tell everybody what happened, that I'd go public, if she didn't pay me off. You would've done the same, wouldn't you, Pom? I mean, if you could go blackmail my grandmother right now to get your life back, wouldn't you do it?"

Maybe the old Pom would have. The old Pom, who was terrified of being on her own, who didn't think she was worth anything without her family money and reputation. But this Pom? This me? I wouldn't. I'd be okay.

Obviously I wasn't going to say that to the girl with the blade at my throat. "Mmmm," I said noncommittally.

She took that as a yes. "So you get it. You understand, at least a little." The shoe moved maybe a centimeter farther from my throat. "I had to threaten her. It didn't make me feel good, you know. But I had to do it."

This must have been when Grandma started complaining to Fred about that "young woman threatening her." When she had her will changed. It wasn't like she could be any more specific with us without outing the secret and tarnishing the family honor. Opal must have been more threatening than she was making it sound now if my grandma was worried enough to change her will to add the "unnatural death" provision to ensure that Opal wouldn't get any inheritance, even if that meant the rest of us wouldn't either.

"She told me she never wanted to see me again, but I couldn't let it rest. So that night, when I slept over your place, I snuck out to give it one more try. I'd decided on it earlier, before we ever got to the club, so I made sure not to drink too much." That must have been when my grandma started calling me, or continued calling me, if in fact she'd started when my mom called Nicholas and Jessica. She wanted me to come collect my friend. I wondered if she would've told me the truth. Maybe she knew the jig was up. Or maybe she thought that, if she brought me in on the secret, I'd be able to make Opal shut up. I guess I'd never know.

Opal shook her head. "If anything, she was even nastier. She told me that she'd been paying my mom off for years, and she'd be damned if she'd give me anything else." I remembered the check records on Grandma's vanity that had gone to Opal's mother for help "gala planning." My grandma was terrible in many ways, but excellent in planning galas—how could I have missed that? "She sneered at me. Told me I'd never be an Afton, that I'd always be trash. That if I ever spoke to her or to you again, she'd ruin me."

Opal's eyes shimmered with tears. My grandma must have been in an extra-cruel mood after her fights with my mom and then with Jessica. No wonder she'd lashed out at someone she saw as having less power.

"I swear I didn't mean it," Opal said. "I didn't mean to kill her. But I just . . . I just got so *mad* with the way she was talking to me. And the shoe was lying right there. I didn't really think it would be sharp enough to . . . to . . ."

To kill. But it was. And then, once she'd stabbed the old lady once, what could she do but stab her again? And again, until she was dead? It was either that or have Grandma call the cops on her and go to prison.

Opal's empty hand was flexing open and shut, open and shut, her eyes distant, as if she were reliving stabbing my grandmother time and time again. "The heel was small and shallow, and it took such a long time. So much longer than you'd think," she said, her voice choked. "I panicked. It was like I wasn't myself. And then I came to, and I ran back down to your apartment, and I threw up all over your pillow. Then took a long, hot shower and got rid of my bloody clothes." My tracksuit. She hadn't stolen it to be fashionable after all. "And, well . . . you know the rest."

Silence rang out in the room. I wasn't sure what to say back to that. I knew what I wanted to say—basically, *you monster*—but I knew that if I did say something, it had to be what Opal would want to hear if I didn't want that stiletto stabbing me through the throat. And I had no idea what that might be. *You were totally justified in stabbing an old lady to death with a shoe? You deserved that money because of your blood? You're a good person?*

Honestly, it wasn't like I had time to think about any of this in-depth yet—that could wait for when I didn't have an angry murderer on top of me and a deadly blade at my throat—but Opal's entitlement in demanding that money made me feel some kind of way. Like, the only reason *I* had that money and that life was because of who *my* father was. It wasn't like I'd done anything to deserve it. Why shouldn't she think she should get some of it too? Was the entitlement all that different?

"Are you going to say anything? Or just lie there?" Opal said, a dangerous glint in her eye.

It wasn't like I had a choice about lying here, considering she was sitting on top of me and holding me down. "I wish you'd told me first," I said. "I could've talked to her with you. Gotten her to see things our way."

That was clearly the right thing to say. Opal's arm that was holding the shoe relaxed a little bit more, the tip of the blade falling even farther away. "Maybe I should've. But I was so ashamed. I thought you might drop me if you knew we'd lost everything."

"I would never have dropped you," I said earnestly, and just as quickly as I'd known the last thing I said was right, I knew this thing was wrong. Opal's eyes narrowed. Her thighs clenched around me.

"Who are you kidding? Of course you would have."

Her arm tensed. I had only a split second before she'd strike. I had to act.

And I did. Hoping that the shoe was as far away from my throat as I thought, I flung my no-longer-numb arm up toward her, my hand tightly clutching a stiletto. It wasn't as sharp as hers, but the toe was pointy, and it did the trick as it swung into the side of her skull. Opal shrieked, her hands flying up to protect her head, which gave me the chance to buck my hips and send her flying. She didn't quite fly, but she did fall enough for me to scramble out from under her and shove her back out of the closet as we both leaped to our feet, her arms windmilling the whole time.

I blasted out after her. "Did you think I'd be as easy to stab as a frail old lady?" I panted. She answered me with a glare scorching enough to bore two smoking holes in my forehead. "Well, I'm not. And you can't blackmail me either. Gabe!"

Opal's bedroom door smashed against the wall as Gabe rushed in. "You have no idea how hard it was not coming in earlier."

Faced with the two of us, Opal lowered her stabbing arm, her face scrunching up like she might cry. "I don't know what you thought you heard, but you can't prove anything."

I held up a finger. "Oh, but actually, I can." I tapped my cleavage, not only to show it off (I do have stupendous cleavage) but to indicate the tiny recorder I'd taped down there, just in case Opal was smart enough to figure out my phone. "I have it all on tape. Did you know that Gabe's brother, Caleb, is a cop? He helped us out."

"He's also waiting downstairs with some of his friends," Gabe said. "In case you were thinking you might want to lunge at us."

Opal's face was still all screwed up, like she thought she could still cry her way out of this. "It's over," I said, as gently as I could. "Save your tears for the trial."

The sound of boots tromping upstairs sounded behind us. Opal spit on the floor in front of us. "Screw you, Pom."

I didn't say anything back. To be fair, it was comparatively easy to take the high road when the other person was being escorted out in handcuffs.

We left with the cops after giving our statements, considering the house was an active crime scene. As we walked outside, I was shaking a bit from the theatrics. The dialogue had been so dramatic—almost too dramatic. I couldn't help but imagine how well it might play in podcast form. Maybe that was my future: podcast host. I could always ask Doe/Danica for help.

No, I was made for the screen, not for audio. Obviously. We chatted with Gabe's brother for a bit on the sidewalk until he headed out, too, leaving us standing there alone in Queens.

Gabe turned to me. "Well? Now what?"

I tapped my chin with a finger. "You know what? I'm starving. It turns out catching a murderer really makes you hungry." Yes, it sounded blasé. Yes, I was still a little shaky—okay, very shaky—after being attacked, even if Gabe had been only a door away the whole time. But I would wrestle with all of that later. "Conveniently, I hear we're already pretty close to what I've heard called the best food neighborhood in the whole city. And we've solved the murder, which takes care of that condition."

His smile was like the rising of the sun. "You want to go to Jackson Heights with me?"

I linked my elbow with his. "I'd go anywhere with you."

Even Queens. Maybe even New Jersey.

CHAPTER

Twenty-Seven

One Year Later

I t was a beautiful, bright, sunny day over Central Park, and for once the day actually deserved it.

"Good morning!" I bounced awake, ripping open the curtains to let the sun pour in. The park stretched out green and glorious below, and I took a moment to appreciate the view. I tried to do that every morning.

Gabe groaned behind me, the antique wooden bed creaking as he rolled over and yanked the covers over his head. "Five more minutes."

"Go back to sleep if you want, but you'll miss opening day!" I couldn't stop chirping in exclamation points. If I was already like this first thing in the morning, I'd be positively manic later on.

That got him up in about ten minutes. I was already sitting at the kitchen table in my Afton robe, sipping the coffee I'd made. I'd made some for him, too, which was quite nice of me. "There's more in the machine." I still wasn't quite at Gabe's level, but I had to say I'd gotten pretty good over the past year. My brief coffee shop education had been worth something.

The whole experience had been worth something, whether I wanted to see it at the time or not.

He poured himself a brew, adding some milk and sugar, then joined me at the table. Squeaky blinked lazily at him from where he was curled up, purring, on my lap. Gabe scratched his chin. Squeaky purred even harder. "So, you ready for the day?"

I was staring into space, or not really space, but the bright red cabinets I'd had installed in the kitchen the other week. They absolutely popped against the white floor and sleek white fixtures. When Mom had stopped by the other day, she'd told me they were garish. I'd only nodded and told her I was thinking about adding an even more garish neon yellow backsplash. She hadn't known what to say back to that.

"Pom?" Gabe prompted. I turned back to him, blinking.

"Sorry. Thought you were talking to the cat."

"Oh. Right. Maybe I was." He leaned into Squeaky. "Are you ready for the day, good sir? You've got a big one ahead of you—lots of snoozing in the sun and batting around feathers." Squeaky twisted himself upside down, paws in the air, belly on display. "Yeah, I know better than to fall into that trap." Gabe pulled his hand away from the fluff, which, if he'd touched it, would've earned him claws in his hand. "And how about you, my brilliant girlfriend? Do *you* feel ready?"

"I wish I could spend the day snoozing in the sun and batting at feathers."

"No, you don't."

"You're right. I don't." I surveyed my domain proudly. After Opal had been officially arrested for Grandma's death and the appointed committee had listened in good faith to her recorded confession, the lawyers overseeing the estate had released everything back to the family, trust funds and hotel apartments and all. Just like that, I was The Pomona Afton again, free and able to resume my old life.

If I'd wanted to.

The first thing I did was move out of the Afton. Getting out from below my parents—literally—was totally worth the chunk of my trust fund it took to buy this two-bedroom apartment overlooking the park. I'd thought about fulfilling the dreams of Younger Pom and getting a loft downtown, but honestly, I'd grown to like living uptown, where it was a little quieter and I didn't have to push my way through drunk artists or NYU students whenever I was trying to go home. Maybe my new place was a little farther north than I was used to, but I could put up with that in order not to have my mom commenting on every move I made. (I did steal a bunch of Afton robes, though.)

The second thing I did was schedule a meeting with the lawyer with the crooked nose, his team, and Vienna. I sat down at the head of the polished wood table, wondering if this was what it felt like to be a CEO. "I want to start a foundation," I said, glancing over at Vienna. She gave me an encouraging nod. "I'm thinking I want my main issues to be around food and education. Feeding people and granting scholarships to needy students. Can we do that?"

When you have as much money as I do—as I did—it turns out you can do pretty much whatever you want.

Don't take that past tense as me saying I've given everything away. I most definitely haven't. There's a big chunk of it invested in the foundation, where it's consistently generating more money, but if I never wanted to work again, I'd still be fine. More than fine. And owning a foundation is an excellent excuse to throw galas and parties. I was gearing up to throw my first one very soon. So far it was more fun than showing up to them.

I do want to do more, though. Which brings us to today.

I'd picked my outfit with care and much analysis the night before, but even with all that, I still surveyed it where it hung on the back of my closet door with pursed lips. White casual spring sundress with sleek lines and a low neck from an up-and-coming Queens designer (I'd come around to Queens) and glittery sneakers. The plan had been for a white dress that my patterned logo'd apron would really pop against, and sneakers since I would be on my feet all day, but would I regret it? Maybe I should go with black. No, black was worse—flour spills didn't show up on white, but on black they made you look like a ghost. Tan?

"I can hear you second-guessing yourself," Gabe called from the kitchen. "You talked me through this outfit three times last night. It's perfect."

He was right, I thought after I put it on and regarded myself with satisfaction in the mirror. It was perfect.

We both made sure to kiss Squeaky goodbye before heading out. It was only a five-minute walk to my new storefront, a location I'd chosen specifically so that I would never have to take the subway again. As we stopped in front, I regarded it with as much satisfaction as I had myself in the mirror. The sign was bright pink, but classy at the same time: POMONA'S TREATS. Empty Lucite shelves filled the front picture window; through it I could see my first employees—Sage and Ellie, who had jumped at the chance to leave the coffee shop for jobs that paid twice as much and gave them health insurance for part-time work—hustling to set up.

I went in and helped, finishing the bakes on the treats that had been rising overnight and writing the daily specials on the board as Gabe helped stock the displays. As 9 a.m. approached, a buzz filtered in from outside: a line beginning to form. I dusted the flour off my hands, relieved that I hadn't gone with the black dress. "Okay, guys," I said, clapping them together and sending a puff of flour right into my face. I heroically managed not to sneeze. "We ready?"

"Ready," they chorused. My heart floating high in my chest, I flipped the sign on the front door to OPEN.

"Welcome!" I sang as the first people bustled in, taking deep breaths and murmuring that it all smelled amazing. "Welcome to my bakery and coffee shop!"

Pretty much everyone had learned about the shop from my feed, so of course they all wanted selfies. I wasn't sure if I'd ever get tired of people clamoring to take pictures with me. Especially now that it involved me accomplishing something good instead of doing something stupid.

I mean, I still did plenty of stupid things. I just tried to do them in private now.

Vienna showed up in the first wave of customers, her hair in a low ponytail. She'd grown out the bob—it didn't feel like her, she'd said.

"This is so cute. I love it," she said, pulling down her sunglasses to survey the room. "Congrats."

"Thank you!" I said with a smile. Over the past year, I had no idea how I would've run my foundation without Vienna's invaluable assistance and advice. She'd even let me poach one of her employees to help. We were actually planning on teaming up to fund some scholarships for promising art students and budding chefs (don't try to tell me that cooking isn't an art). It was going to be great. "Here. I made lavender-rose sweet rolls just for you." Which I actually meant, because that flavor combination made me and what I'd assume to be most of my customers think of soap, but Vienna took a bite and moaned in pleasure. The noise delighted me. I'd never let her go again.

Other VIPs trickled in over the next couple of hours. Millicent and Coriander, who'd both sworn to me that they'd always known Opal was nefarious—complete bullshit, but whatever—showed up for selfies and free cupcakes. I was starting to find them exhausting, but hey, they both had a ton of followers, so free publicity.

I was thrilled to have Andrea come in too. She was one of the first people not to ask for a selfie, but I made sure to get one with her anyway. I owed her so much, not to mention that maybe (I hoped? Didn't want to jinx it) she might be my mother-in-law someday. She couldn't get rid of me even if she wanted to. Farrah and Jordan were back in Florida, but they both—yes, both—texted me congratulations and told me they couldn't wait to come by when they were in the city next.

Naturally, I couldn't avoid the press. I was delighted to host the people from Eater and Grub Street, but I was immediately on guard when the *Times* reporter showed up. "Pomona, congratulations on your bakery! Everything looks delicious!" said the reporter, flashing me a mouthful of wide white teeth. "I was wondering if I could get your comment on Opal Sterling's ongoing trial? Are you planning to attend before closing arguments?"

I flashed her a smile back. The family lawyers had told me to say "no comment" to any questions about Opal or the trial or Grandma's murder—I got them every week—but that wasn't really my style. "I look forward to seeing our justice system take its course."

When the reporter realized I wouldn't give her anything more than that, she bought a sticky bun and left. I couldn't help but hope that would be the last of them, though I knew that it wouldn't be.

Oh well. So be it. I would persevere.

My parents dropped in around eleven, after the opening rush but before the lunch crowd. "Pom, this all looks great," Dad said as soon as he walked through the door, before he'd even had a chance to glance around. It was fine. He was making an effort. He'd been really trying ever since I told him I was moving out of the Afton, like that woke him up to the fact that he might lose me if he didn't step up.

In contrast, my mom was still dreaming. She peered down her nose at all the treats behind the counter, her upper lip curling the slightest bit. "Is there anything gluten-free?"

"There is," I said. I'd wanted to be inclusive of as many dietary restrictions as I could. "We've got these flourless chocolate cakelets, these coconut macaroons, these berry meringues . . ." I went through the list, pointing them all out, only to have Mom heave a sigh at the end.

"Too much sugar. I'll just have a small coffee. Black."

To be honest, her disapproval still stung a little. I thought it might always sting, but that was how it would have to be. I couldn't change her. All I could do was change things on my end: how much time I spent with her, how much credence I put in the things she said to me.

As soon as my parents left, my mom having taken one sip of her black coffee ("it's bitter") and my dad chowing down on what he proclaimed to be "the best sticky bun I've ever had," Nicholas and Jessica popped in. The proximity was such that I suspected they'd been waiting around the corner for my parents to leave. Couldn't blame them there!

"Welcome!" I called out, arms spread wide. Jessica immediately ran into them for a hug. She backed off wearing perhaps the biggest smile I'd ever seen.

"Congratulations! I'm speechless!"

Jessica had been maybe the most important figure in opening this bakery, having been my official marketing and publicity person (she'd offered to do it for free, but I'd insisted on paying her usual rate). So her speechlessness meant a lot. "I'm speechless at your speechlessness."

As Jessica went off to ooh and aah over the goods on display, insisting out loud that there was no way she could possibly decide on only one, Nicholas sidled up to murmur in my ear. "Is the cheesecake ready for later?"

"Ready and chilling in the fridge," I whispered back. Lemon-blueberry cheesecake was Jessica's favorite dessert. I suspected she'd love it even more when it came out that night scattered with edible flowers and Grandma's heirloom diamond ring.

Nicholas and Jessica left arm in arm, both carrying boxes of treats. I leaned my head on Gabe's shoulder as we watched them go. "I think we'll get a little breather here before the lunch rush," I said. "How do you think it's going so far?"

"I don't think it could be going any better," he said, pressing a kiss to my forehead. Even though he didn't work at a coffee shop anymore— he'd be graduating with his master's in a few weeks and had already landed a job teaching English and history at a school in East Harlem— he still smelled like coffee and soap. The coziest smell. "Pom, you should be so proud of yourself."

"I am," I said. Pride in myself had never been an issue. "I can't wait for Nicholas to propose already. Do you think they'll let me make the wedding cake? Do you think alternating layers of carrot cake and blueberry-lemon cheesecake would be too much?"

"It might be," Gabe said. He was right. As he so often was. It was fine. I could make two separate wedding cakes. A groom's cake and a bride's cake, the way weddings often had a groom's cocktail and a bride's cocktail. Or maybe I could mash them together somehow in a more cohesive way, like a carrot cake cheesecake. I'd have plenty of time. An Afton wedding took at least a year to plan. As a for-sure member of the wedding party—obviously they'd ask me to be either a bridesmaid or a groomswoman, if not the maid of honor or best woman—I was ready to start. "But no matter how you do it, it'll be delicious."

"Unless they order an outside cake."

"Which will surely be terrible," Gabe said loyally.

"I'm sure the wedding will be beautiful. And I'm excited to get to call Jessica my sister and take her shopping for some real gowns." All of a sudden, I was seized by a thought too absurd not to laugh. "Watch somebody get murdered at the wedding and us have to solve it again."

Gabe laughed too. "God, I hope not. Though we were good at it, weren't we?"

"The best." Maybe . . . I'd made a mistake opening this bakery. Maybe instead of POMONA'S TREATS, the sign should say INVESTIGATIONS BY POMONA. OH, AND GABE TOO.

No. No way. One murder was enough.

Right?

The bell over the door tinkled. I spun to greet my newest customers with a wide, sparkling smile, welcoming them in.

ACKNOWLEDGMENTS

Writing a book might be a solitary process, but publishing one is a team effort. Lara Jones, thank you so much for being the absolute perfect editor for this book and loving Pom as much as I do. Many, many thanks to the rest of the incredible team at Emily Bestler Books/Atria, including Libby McGuire, Emily Bestler, Dana Trocker, Megan Rudloff, Zakiya Jamal, James Iacobelli, Paige Lytle, and Shelby Pumphrey. Jonathan Bush, thank you for creating this gorgeous cover.

To my agent, Merrilee Heifetz, what can I say after ten books together except thank you, you're the best? Rebecca Eskildsen, I appreciate enormously all that you do. Thank you to the Writers House foreign rights team for sending Pom around the world (even if it's not by private jet): Maja Nikolic, Kate Boggs, and Sofia Bolido. So many thank-yous to the rest of the team at Writers House as well. Ali Lefkowitz, thank you for taking Pom to Hollywood.

Many thanks and much appreciation to the author friends who get me through the day. You know who you are.

Apologies again to my wonderful family for seeming to exclusively write about terrible families. My parents, my siblings, my in-laws: you guys are all great and none of these terrible people are based on you. Extra thank-you to Sam for his critique on the proposal for this book. Special shout-out to Grandma Roz, who was the absolute opposite of Pom's terrible grandmother. You were the best at discussing character names and story arcs when I was a kid and I so wish you could've seen my career.

Jeremy and Miriam: I love you so much. Thank you for everything.